Throwing Heat

Also by Jennifer Seasons

Playing the Field
Stealing Home

Throwing Heat

A DIAMONDS AND DUGOUTS NOVEL

JENNIFER SEASONS

AVONIMPULSE
An Imprint of HarperCollinsPublishers

Excerpt from *Stealing Home* copyright © 2013 by Candice Wakoff.

Excerpt from *Playing the Field* copyright © 2013 by Candice Wakoff.

Excerpt from *The Governess Club: Claire* copyright © 2013 by Heather Johnson.

Excerpt from *Ashes, Ashes, They All Fall Dead* copyright © 2013 by Lena Diaz.

Excerpt from *The Governess Club: Bonnie* copyright © 2013 by Heather Johnson.

EPub Edition OCTOBER 2013 ISBN: 9780062271488

Print Edition ISBN: 9780062271495

JV 10 9 8 7 6 5 4 3 2 1

Prologue

That Night
Three years ago
Miami

SHE SHOULD BE in jail.

Leslie Cutter signaled the bartender behind the hotel lobby bar for another round and dabbed at the corner of her eye with a fingertip. No way was she going to cry in public. He didn't deserve that kind of satisfaction.

Nobody would see her cry.

Not even tonight, of all nights. Just the opposite. She should be celebrating her victory. She should be rejoicing in the fact that her fancy-pants attorney had saved her ass from lockup. And she would, too, right after she drowned her sorrows in the bottom of a shot glass.

Fraud.

The word echoed in her mind, taunting her. That's

what they'd called it—the legal terminology. But she felt like it was a personal attack against her character. That the word was meant as a label for her, not some charge leveled against her in the courts.

The dark-haired bartender refilled her glass, and Leslie murmured her thanks, her eyes feeling as watery as the amber liquid she held. She should have known it would come down to this. It always did. No matter how hard she tried, somehow or some way she inevitably screwed up.

She tossed back the shot and sat the snifter down on the mahogany counter with a sharp rap. "Way to screw up yet again, Leslie," she muttered with a truckload of self-loathing.

Why was it that when it came to men she had absolutely no sense of judgment? The bigger the piece of shit he was, the blinder she became and the harder she fell. Especially when they dressed themselves up in respectable Armani and spouted sweet nothings in her ear.

Which was exactly what Tom had done while pretending to be her honest, reliable accountant. She'd bought it—hook, line and sinker. And he wasn't the first one. At least this one hadn't knocked her up before leaving her. Instead, he'd just embezzled hundreds of thousands of dollars from her public relations firm in Miami and stored it in an offshore account in the Caymans. All the while he'd been sleeping in her bed and telling her how much she was adored.

When the cops had shown up at her door to arrest her for tax fraud, he'd already been on his way out of the country, leaving her brokenhearted to take the blame.

Boy had she.

Leslie blew out a breath, ruffling a strand of pale blonde hair that had fallen in her face. If it weren't for her brother Mark and his very deep pockets, she'd be wearing a bright orange jumpsuit and stamping license plates at the state penitentiary right now.

She shuddered. God, she looked horrible in orange.

Fortunately for her, Mark's career as a professional baseball player for the Denver Rush lent him a pretty hefty salary, and he hadn't hesitated to throw it around, hiring a top-notch defense team for her. It had paid off too. Her life was in ruins; she was beyond broke and had no future.

But she wasn't in jail.

"Thank God for that," she said as movement in the mirror behind the long bar caught her attention. It was after eleven and the swanky art deco lounge was almost empty except for a few late-night drinkers like herself. The middle-aged man in a business suit who'd caught her eye was sitting at the baby grand piano in the corner plucking a tune, his tie loosened and disheveled. Every so often he took a long sip of the cocktail he'd set on the glossy black instrument before resuming his stumbling rendition of the *Moonlight* Sonata with his head down. The expression on his face made her stomach squeeze in sympathy.

He looked like she felt.

Shifting on her bar stool, Leslie uncrossed her long legs, the expensive fabric of her slacks whispering over her recently waxed skin. As she crossed them again the other way she thought about all the perks she'd enjoyed the last five years, like professional waxing, and how those were now officially luxuries of the past.

Frowning, Leslie unbuttoned her suit jacket and shook back her hair. Damn it, but she liked her luxuries. It wasn't fair that she had to give it all up because of what someone else had done.

Then again, she'd been stupid enough to let it happen, so maybe she did deserve it.

More than already a little in her cups, she tapped her glass and said, "Fill 'er up, bartender."

Drowning her heartache in Patrón seemed like the appropriate thing to do. And why not? Her life was over.

Everything she'd worked so hard for—gone. She snapped her fingers and wobbled on her stool a little, her balance iffy. Just like that. All of it gone.

Hoo-fucking-ray.

As soon as her glass was full again she snatched it up. About to take a drink, she was stopped by the sound of a deep voice coming from right behind her left shoulder. "What're you doing there, Leslie?"

Sliding her unsteady gaze to the left, Leslie snorted at the man who swung a heavy, muscle-bound leg over the bar stool next to her and sat down, the worn denim of his jeans stretching taut across his thighs.

"I'm celebrating, Peter." She raised her glass and gave a grand wave. "Can't you tell?"

Her brother's teammate, Peter Kowalskin, surveyed her through impossibly pale blue eyes, his expression both amused and concerned. "I heard. Tough break, kid."

"You don't know anything about tough." How could he? He was the Rush's ace pitcher, and at the height of his career. Money, sex, cars, fame. She was sure he had it all. He certainly acted like it.

She, now, *she* had nothing.

"You might be surprised by what I know, princess." Peter leaned forward and placed his elbows on the bar, the thin cotton of his white T-shirt pulling snug across his sculpted biceps. "How many drinks have you had?" His gaze was on the once-again empty snifter.

Bitterness washed over her. "Not nearly enough." Was there even enough booze in the world to make her numb? Because that's what she was going for. Numb. Then she wouldn't have to feel anything.

Peter's lips twitched a tiny little smile and her gaze zeroed in on his mouth. It looked hard and unforgiving. Squinting through the liquor, she raised a hand and tapped his lips with a finger. The unexpected heat and softness of them had her yanking it right back. "Why are you here? Mark was s'posed to be meeting me right in this bar after your game." She made a big sweeping gesture. "Was it too much for him to take the elevator down here to the lounge?"

The ballplayer shrugged his shoulders, looking uncomfortable, and Leslie was mesmerized by the way the muscles rolled and flexed. Normally she wouldn't consider him her type. He was too cocky, too crass. But her life as she knew it had gone up in a puff of smoke and she was feeling reckless.

Tomorrow she'd gather the shattered pieces and try to

glue them back together along with her dignity. But for now she was just going to sit right there on the red leather stool in her good-girl navy blue suit and ogle his muscles. Every last one of them.

Why? Because she could, damn it. And because this morning as she'd walked into that courtroom she'd been absolutely sure she was never going to see the light of day again.

The sound of Peter clearing his throat drew her attention. "Your brother sent me instead. He's been, um, detained."

Leslie snorted again. She knew exactly what—or rather *who*—had detained him. No doubt she had legs up to her chin and breasts like over-full water balloons. "So I'm s'posed to thank you in his place?"

The only reason she was in the expensive hotel with its glittering chandeliers and pink fresco walls in the first place—instead of curled up at home with a box of macaroons and a whole lot of tissue—was to give her brother a giant hug for helping her out in her time of crisis.

Looked like she'd wasted her time.

The ballplayer chuckled. "You can thank me anytime you want." The way he said it made giving thanks sound dirty.

Her gaze roamed over his body once again. Maybe she would thank him. Because dirty was good. It was distracting.

She just bet that Pete, with his badass looks and rock-hard body, could be one hell of a distraction.

Why not let him?

Spinning suddenly on her barstool, Leslie reached out and grabbed a handful of his white T-shirt, thoroughly enjoying the surprised look on his rugged face. Before he could open his mouth to speak she leaned off her stool and planted her lips full on his.

The zing of connection shocked her.

Sliding from the stool like water from a glass, Leslie let go of his shirt and wrapped both arms around his neck as she landed in his lap. She kissed him hard and deep, feeling the pain melt away with every passing second her lips were on his.

This was so much better than getting drunk.

Yanking back, Leslie took in his heated, intense expression. "You'll do."

His eyes narrowed. "Care to elaborate on that?"

Did she?

Nope. She was going to show him instead. That way she could ignore the hollow ache in the center of her chest for a few hours and pretend it didn't exist. She could pretend she wasn't on the verge of breaking down. "This is your one chance, Peter. Make it count."

PETER FLICKED ON the lights and shut the door to his hotel room quietly behind him.

"Are you sure you want to do this, princess?"

Leslie was pretty wasted, and her day hadn't exactly been stellar. Not that he was opposed to sweaty, raunchy sex with the smokin' blonde. No, not at all. He'd fantasized about it on more than one occasion already.

It just didn't seem fair to have sex with her when she probably wouldn't even remember it the next day.

Without waiting for her response, he slipped into the bathroom to take a quick leak and called out, "We can just talk if you want to." She was the first woman he'd ever said that to and meant it.

"That's sweet," she called back with her sugary Southern drawl all slurred and lazy.

Yeah, that was him all right. Sweet as honey. All the ladies said so.

Peter washed his hands and scoffed to himself. What ladies? There hadn't been any since he'd first set sight on the blonde bombshell currently sprawled across his hotel mattress like a bed sheet. One look at her luscious curves and intelligent, gorgeous eyes and no other woman would do.

For more than a year he'd wondered what it would be like to have Leslie naked and moaning. He would have found out by now, too, if it wasn't for Mark being her brother. That had put a real crimp on things.

But now here she was in his bed wanting to have no-strings sex. It was like a cosmic reward for being such a good boy. He just hoped like hell that if he did go through with it, Mark never ever found out. No doubt it would piss him way off, because as much as the catcher tried to hide it, he had a huge heart and was a protective bear about his sister.

If Peter was any sort of morally upstanding guy he'd do nothing more with Leslie than take off her shoes and tuck her under the covers. He thought about it briefly. Considered just leaving.

Yeah, maybe he should do that.

Opening the bathroom door, Peter stepped into the room and stopped dead. Leslie was standing in the middle of the floor without a stitch of clothing on, a sultry smile full of invitation on her lips. Her deliciously voluptuous curves nearly dropped him to his knees. His stomach tightened with need.

"See anything you like?" she purred, and tossed back her sleek blonde hair, putting her hands on her lush hips.

Everything.

Yeah, if he was any sort of moral guy he'd walk away right now. Just leave and let her sleep it off. That's what an upstanding guy would do.

But the hell of it was that they had something. A chemistry that crackled like fireworks when they were in the same room together. And knowing that made it so hard to be the good guy and just walk away. Especially when he knew that she wanted him every bit as much as he did her.

He took a step back. Swore. Fought an internal battle of conscience—and lost.

He couldn't do it. He couldn't walk away.

Peter crossed to her and scooped her up in a kiss hot enough to set the room on fire. Her full breasts pushed into his chest and his hands cupped her firm round ass, pulling her flush against him. She moaned and flung her arms around his neck, urging him on.

His conscience yelled at him and he shoved her away roughly, "I can't." Christ, he wanted to, but he just couldn't. It wasn't right.

And that's when she reached out and grabbed his hard-on, began stroking it through his jeans, making him hiss between his teeth, and gave him a smile that was absolutely devastating. "I can."

Then she dropped to her knees before him and yanked open his fly, freeing him, and he forgot how to think. Forgot his integrity.

Forgot everything entirely when her hot mouth wrapped around his cock. He groaned and his head fell back. Jesus, the woman knew how to please.

Somehow they made it onto the bed and Peter took control, sheer lust dictating his actions. He had her on her stomach with her ass in the air before she could gasp, his hand slipping between her legs. When she cried out and bucked against him it only served to fuel him on further.

Peter ripped off his clothing and came up behind her, breathing heavy. "Is this what you want?" he growled against her ear as he slid a finger into her, making her cry out softly and push back against him.

"Yes!" she panted into a pillow and gripped a fistful of cream comforter in both hands.

It wasn't enough. Shifting positions, Peter grabbed her hips and raised her up further onto her knees before replacing his hand with his mouth. He almost couldn't believe what was happening. It was way better than any fantasy.

When his tongue caressed her tender flesh, she came unraveled. Arching and moaning, Leslie came almost instantly. And it spurred him on. Without giving her a break he brought her to another screaming peak.

Pulling back, Peter sat up, and pure male ego flooded him at the sight of Leslie panting, her eyes closed and hair a mess, and smacked her on the ass, smiling. "Had enough, princess?"

She made a sound that he interpreted to mean she hadn't. Good. He wasn't done. Now that he had her where he'd dreamt of pretty much every night since they'd met, he was going to make it as memorable as possible for them both.

Coming up behind her, Peter covered her back with his body and wrapped an arm around her shoulders, making her sit up on her knees, and pulled her tight to him. He growled into her ear. "Ready for another one?" Making Leslie come over and over was all he wanted.

And he did. He moved his hand down her gently rounded belly, loving every inch of her womanly curves, and brought her to shuddering climax twice more, smiling darkly when she sunk her teeth into his arm. Once her tremors subsided he flipped her over, intent on watching her get off one more time before he buried himself in her and found his own release.

Her eyes fluttered open and she whispered dazedly, "You're amazing."

Then she focused her beautiful, almond-shaped eyes on him, and some overwhelming force slammed him in the gut like a one-ton Chevy. He gasped, unable to breathe. Fuck, why couldn't he breathe?

Half-panicked, Peter shook his head roughly and tried to suck in air. But Leslie just kept looking at him, her eyes swimming with emotions he didn't want to feel, and he swore when he felt the echo of them inside his own head anyway.

"In me, Peter," she breathed. "I need to feel you inside me." Her legs curled around his waist and pulled him to her, the head of his cock rubbing against her slick fold.

"Christ, Leslie," he groaned and looked down into her stunningly beautiful face. Her eyes were shimmering with wetness, and as he watched one lone tear slipped down her cheek.

It gutted him.

And he went instantly limp. Pushing away from her violently, Peter leapt off the bed, panic and other feelings he couldn't name pummeling him. He was so overwhelmed by the onslaught that he couldn't tell one from the other. They came rushing at him so fast. All he knew was that he had to get out of there, *now*.

"What is it, Peter?" she asked as she sat up on her elbows, her incredible breasts on full display. Concern cut through her arousal and softened her voice.

But he couldn't see, couldn't think.

Ignoring her, he frantically searched for his clothes scattered across the floor. "Nothing."

Confusion clouded her eyes. "Where are you going? What happened?" And then the words that killed him, "Don't you want me?"

His throat squeezed shut and he couldn't speak. So he just stood there like a jackass, staring at her until understanding dawned and her face crumpled.

"You don't want me." It was a statement, not a question. Denial swirled inside him, and though he wanted to say something to reassure her that it wasn't her, it was him, he couldn't. So he just shrugged, not knowing what else to do.

She looked him right in the eyes and burst into tears. The hot, raging tears of a person who had reached the brink of what she could handle emotionally. She fell apart in front of him, sobs wracking her chest like they were being torn out of her from some very deep place, and Peter couldn't handle it. Watching Leslie Cutter lose it was the hardest thing he'd ever done.

"Leslie," he said hoarsely, desperately.

But she wasn't listening. She was curled up in the center of his bed crying harder than any person should ever have to. And seeing her like that made his heart squeeze tight, made him want to go to her and soothe the raging tide of her sorrow.

But he didn't know how. "Leslie," he whispered raggedly again.

Her head whipped up, her hair a tangled mess around her anguished face. Bitter eyes stared him down, unblinking. Then she jumped off the bed, grabbed up her clothes, and rounded on him, shaking.

"Fuck you, Peter."

Without a backward glance she ran from the hotel room.

And she took a part of his heart with her.

Chapter One

Present Day

PETER KOWALSKIN LOOKED through the peephole in his front door and grinned. Leslie Cutter stood on the other side, her ever-cool exterior two steps away from melting. A frown struggled to form between her perfectly groomed brows and almost succeeded.

Almost. "Open up, Kowalskin."

His crappy day had suddenly gotten a whole lot better.

A moment ticked by while he considered whether or not to make her suffer a little and work for it. The urge to give her a hard time was almost irresistible. Few things in life were as much fun as ruffling the woman's feathers.

"I know you're in there. Are you going to make me wait out here all evening, or are you going to open the door and let me in?" she finished, her voice ripe with irritation.

Just because he could, Peter said loudly so she could hear him through the heavy oak door, "What's the magic word?"

Her face tightened and her hazel eyes flashed briefly. "Seriously, Peter? How old are you?"

Old enough to know *exactly* how to have a really good time. "The longer you stall, the longer you stand there."

Through the peephole he watched her roll her eyes and mutter under her breath. Finally she shook her long hair back and tipped her chin, going all haughty. "Fine. At least one of us has the capacity to be mature. *Please* let me in." She added a sugary sweet smile to punctuate her request.

Pete knew she'd rather bite his head off. And it was funny. Damn funny.

Relenting, he opened the door and stepped to the side as he swept an arm wide in invitation, magnanimous as the best of hosts. "Come right on in."

Scooping up the small leather suitcase by her feet, Leslie held her head high and strode over the threshold. "Thank you."

The look she shot him was more like "fuck you" and he laughed heartily. "For a woman who's temporarily homeless and in need of a place to stay, your tone is decidedly ungrateful."

"I am ungrateful. If you were any sort of a decent landlord then I wouldn't have a flooded apartment right now. My grandmother's handmade quilt was destroyed because of your lack of proper plumbing maintenance."

Her lips pressed in a tight line. "Now your butt is stuck with me until everything is fixed."

He did feel bad about that. That old converted warehouse where she lived had been nothing but a money pit since he'd purchased it a few years back. Maybe it was time to cut his losses and sell it.

Not before he made it right for Leslie, though. "The super has assured me that he's on top of it." And he was just going to take Jerry's word for it, since actual property management was about the last thing he wanted to do.

With a hand at the back of his neck, Peter rubbed at the sudden tension and tossed her a lopsided grin meant to disarm. "If you don't have rental insurance I'll cover what's been damaged. I know it won't bring back your grandmother's quilt, but it's the best I can do."

Leslie took two steps down into the sunken living room where his iPod was playing music softly in the background and glanced over her shoulder, her sleek sheet of hair whispering across her back with the movement. The hard glint in her eyes seemed to soften a degree. "Thanks anyway, but I've got it covered."

Peter took a good long look at the woman standing in his living room and felt his palms go sweaty. It's what always happened whenever the two of them were alone and in close proximity. Leslie was the kind of woman who had that effect on people.

"I heard about your breakup with John because of his last-minute trade to the Red Sox. Your little Southern heart couldn't stand the idea of bedding a Northerner?"

Her chin came up. "Just because you're from Philadelphia and you think you're perfect doesn't make the East Coast utopia, Kowalskin." A mischievous glint came into her eyes. "My good Southern manners simply keep me from pointing out your delusion."

Laughter bubbled in his chest and let loose. "Well, thank God for that. I'm not sure my heart could handle the truth."

Her lips twitched and she looked away, but he caught the grin anyway. "I'm glad I could save you the heartache."

Peter took the steps and padded barefoot across the plush carpet toward her. "Here, let me take your bag and show you to your room like a proper host."

Leslie eyed him. "Since when do you give a rip about proper?"

She had a point. Since when did he give a shit? Probably since about the time she walked through his door. "I'm trying on something new."

The woman laughed right in his face. "Good luck with that."

Stopping directly in front of her, he could make out the gold and green flecks in her eyes. He knew that they went dark as a forest when she was aroused. Even now they were beginning to change color.

The woman was a lot of things, but immune to him wasn't one of them.

She'd never admit to it though. Not without a good hard shove, anyway. Lucky for him he didn't mind getting pushy.

The time had come.

Peter pressed closer to her, invading her personal

space until they were eye-to-eye. Hers rounded almost imperceptibly and he grinned. But she stood her ground, squaring her shoulders and trying desperately to look down her nose at him. Given that they were about the same height he imagined it wasn't so easy to do.

Because it was just so tempting and self-control wasn't his strong suit, he leaned in and hovered close.

"What do you think you're doing?" she asked, sounding suspiciously breathy.

Taking a moment to savor the scent of her, he inhaled something creamy and coconut and bent his knees, effectively lowering himself. Tension began to coil inside him when her breasts came into view directly in front of him. Her sharp inhale pushed them out toward him and he fought back the urge to groan.

She had breasts like a goddess.

Her body went taut, but before she could snap at him, he grinned and wrapped his fingers around her suitcase handle. "Just grabbing your luggage." He held it out for her to see. "Don't get your panties in a bunch." Then he stepped back, the charged air dissipating with the distance, and turned toward the stairs. "Your bedroom's upstairs."

Leslie cut in front of him, her ass swaying rhythmically with every step of her long legs, and he couldn't help admiring the way the pocket stitching on her jeans drew attention to her cheeks. They were embellished with tiny sequins that sparkled with every sway of her lush hips. Once she reached the bottom step she tossed him a look. "Shows what you know. I'm not wearing underwear."

Jesus.

Momentarily at a loss for words, he trailed behind her to the landing, his gaze glued to her backside. Damn if he could see a panty line—which meant she wasn't kidding.

Tease.

Shaking his head to clear the building haze, Peter barely managed to rip his gaze away from her incredible ass in time to direct her into the second room down the hall on the right. "Over here," he pointed and took the lead.

He'd known having Leslie stay with him while her apartment was being repaired was asking for trouble. But he was the kind of guy who thrived on it. Bad decisions were his forte, "reckless" his middle name.

And that girl, well, she had trouble in spades.

It trailed after her like a lovelorn stalker. From the moment he'd first met her four years back she'd been entangled in one mess or another. But then she'd moved to Denver, started dating his teammate John Crispin, and her life had seemed to settle down.

Until now.

When she'd called him at two A.M. pissed as a three-legged goose and cursing his name because her bedroom was flooded and she was stranded on her bed, he'd felt guilty. Like, mega guilty. The superintendent had warned him a few weeks back that the building's plumbing was in pretty bad shape, but they were nearing the postseason and all his focus had been on making it to the Division Series, and he'd told Jerry that he would look into it soon. Then he'd forgotten about it.

Leslie calling him all kinds of creative oaths with that pretty mouth of hers had proven to him just how wrong he'd been to assume that plumbing was the sort of inconvenience someone could put off dealing with.

And yeah, he could have comped her hotel stay, but what would have been the fun in that?

Moreover, he was a little surprised she'd actually taken him up on his offer.

Then again, she wasn't the most sociable thing. With Crispin traded to Boston and Mark and his wife Lorelei in the middle of a big move, Leslie had more or less no other options besides him.

Oh, there was that young bartender at the club she managed, but the kid was still so green that if he ever got her alone he'd be a nervous wreck before the front door was even shut. Part of him felt for the guy. Sympathized even.

Leslie Cutter was every man's wet dream.

When he was a kid, while other boys had posters of Cindy Crawford and Claudia Schiffer plastered on their walls, he'd been obsessed with the curves of 1940s pinup girls Ava Gardner and Marilyn Monroe. He'd spent his fair share of nights growing up fantasizing about them.

And now he had the modern-day equivalent standing a few feet behind him in jeans and a pink T-shirt that fit her like second skin.

It was enough to make the horny teen in him weep.

"Your room," he said as he reached the door and pushed it wide.

Stepping to the side as she brushed past, Peter caught a

whiff of creamy coconut again and something stirred low in the pit of his stomach. Ever since that night in Miami the scent of that damn tropical nut did that to him. Got him all kinds of fired up.

"This is a great room." She sounded surprised.

"Did you think I was going to offer you a dungeon or something?"

Leslie walked to the side of the bed and ran her hand over the sleek gray duvet. Glancing at him out of the corner of her eyes, she quipped, "Something like that."

"Were you hoping for whips and chains?" The words were out of his mouth before he could stop them.

Her eyes flashed. "Would you even know what to do with them, if I was?"

Nope. But he was a real fast learner. "Try me, princess."

Leslie flipped her hair back and managed to look as regal as the nickname he called her. "You wish."

Yeah he did. It'd been the bane of his existence for going on three years now.

"There's a bathroom just through that door." He pointed to the door on the far right wall, trying to change the subject before he got himself all worked up over nothing.

He and Leslie were never going to happen.

She'd made that abundantly clear after the night they'd sort-of spent together in Miami. Normally that would've been just fine and dandy with him. Except that night had gone down in history as what he sadly referred to as "The Shame." That blew, and it made it hard to just shrug it off.

That ugly little fact had stuck in his craw since the moment she'd fled his hotel room. Her moving to Denver had only made it that much worse. Every time he laid eyes on her it was salt in the wound. And since she was the sister of his best friend and teammate, he saw her a whole frigging lot.

Somehow they'd come to an unspoken agreement about that night, neither of them wanting to rehash the past. It was their secret. Mostly because of the embarrassment, but also because Mark would no doubt bust his nose if he knew what Peter had almost done with his sister.

"Hey, Peter. Thanks for letting me crash here for a few days." Leslie's voice cut through his musings and pulled him back into reality.

"No worries. We're leaving tomorrow to begin the Division Series in St. Louis anyway. I'll be in and out of here for the next few weeks and it's nice knowing you'll be staying over." He crossed his arms over his chest and added, "Normally I have to hire the neighbor kid to come check on things, and I think he's been stealing, so this is better."

"Oh, well, glad I can be of service." She stood on the far side of the king size bed, trying to hide her stress. But he could see it in the set of her shoulders, the tightness around her mouth. She needed rest.

Relaxing, Peter glanced briefly around the large room, hoping the clean, simple décor would do. He liked things uncluttered. Maybe it was because his personal life could be such a mess. "Let me know if you need anything, okay?"

She tossed him a dismissive glance, already toeing off her shoes. "Will do."

Closing the door, he strode all the way down the hall to his bedroom. When he reached his door he glanced over his shoulder and noticed her suitcase sitting on the floor. Grabbing it, Peter turned the knob and swung her door back open.

"Hey, you left this in the hall."

Leslie swore in surprise, her T-shirt stuck up around her chin. He'd caught her in the middle of taking it off. Her large breasts were on full display in that pitiful excuse for a bra she wore. He could see her dusky areolas through the white lace.

Holy hell.

Heat pooled in his groin and he went achy. The kind of dull throb that made it real clear his dry spell had gone on for way too long. It started in his balls and weaved its way upward.

Muttering around the pink cotton, Leslie pulled it the rest of the way off and threw it on the bed. Her eyes lit defiantly. "What are you looking at?" she demanded, hands on her hips.

Ignoring the heaviness in his balls, Peter leaned nonchalantly against the door frame, crossed his legs, and hooked his thumbs in the front pockets of his jeans, suitcase dangling from his fingers. The woman was staring him down unflinchingly, and all the while her nipples were puckered and almost completely visible behind the delicate lace.

It was killing him.

Letting his eyes go hazy, Peter ratcheted up the Philly in his voice just to annoy her and drawled, "Nothing of yours I haven't kissed before." He held out the suitcase, dropped it.

And left her sputtering.

Chapter Two

LESLIE SIGHED AS the last customer filed out of the club for the night. It was almost two in the morning and she was exhausted. Normally the late nights didn't faze her—she was a night person anyway—but for the past two nights she'd been sleeping in Peter's house. It wasn't exactly a recipe for great night's sleep.

"Hey, Leslie. I'm going to close out the drawers now."

Glancing up from the notebook open on the bar, Leslie flicked her gaze over the young bartender and nodded. "Sure thing, Seth. Just make sure you put the cash in the money bags this time." Cute the kid was, smart he wasn't.

"You betcha, boss."

She flinched. Make that dumb *and* overzealous. It was lucky for him she had a soft spot for stupidity. "I'm going to finish this list and lock up. After you and the girls finish what you're doing you can head home," she added, referring to the servers.

With any luck, Peter wouldn't be back until tomorrow and she could veg out on the couch with the leftover Mexican from last night's dinner and some *Big Bang Theory* before heading to bed.

"Killing the music now," one of the employees called from the far corner of the open club. Silence suddenly permeated the space, a welcome relief to her ears. The acoustics in the restored brick building could be deafening.

Straightening, Leslie stretched her arms over her head and smothered a yawn. Her feet were as exhausted as the rest of her and she kicked out of her black stilettos, wiggling her toes as soon as they were free. A groan escaped at the sheer pleasure of it.

Running a nightclub was serious work. Running a nightclub in sexy heels was even harder. But a woman had to have her priorities, and looking good was one of hers. Plus, the extra inches pushed her to six feet and provided a better vantage point to view the club. And if it also made her a little intimidating, well, she didn't mind.

Looking like an Amazonian man-eater was just fine with her. It kept the dicks at bay.

Placing a hand on her lower back, she rubbed where it ached and surveyed her domain. Seth had his head lowered and was concentrating on the cash drawer. Obviously he'd done one too many beer bongs during his recent college days and couldn't count past the fingers on his right hand because he kept starting over. But he looked just adorable standing there with such a quizzical expression on his face.

He reminded her of Elliot's boyfriend Keith on the TV sitcom *Scrubs*—only Seth was as much dumb as he was pretty. And that's why she kept him around. Leslie wasn't ashamed to admit she liked the eye candy.

And the female clientele loved him.

"Goodnight, Leslie."

Turning her head, she caught sight of Megan, one of the servers, as she headed toward the back door. Waving, Leslie smiled and said, "Night, girl."

Just a few more loose ends and then she could head out too. When she'd taken over management of her brother's nightclub, Hotbox, almost two years ago it had barely been functional. She'd taken the old brick warehouse and turned it into a thriving business. All of which she took pride in. Of course she did. But she missed owning her own business like hell.

It was one of the things that grated so much, even after all this time. Leslie was good at public relations and her firm had made big waves, putting her name right up there alongside elite members of the industry. She had been going places.

One bad lapse in judgment and her life had crumbled like the Berlin Wall.

And here she was, after turning her brother's club into a hot spot for local music. In two years, no less. That wasn't a small feat. She knew that.

But she wanted more. She wanted Hotbox to be *hers*.

Which was why she'd been scrimping and saving every spare penny for a down payment to buy the club out from Mark. It was her new dream, her goal. When

she'd first approached him about selling it to her, he'd offered just to give the business to her. But she couldn't do
that, couldn't simply take it. He'd already done so much
for her.

Besides, she needed to do this on her own.

After finding out that her credit wasn't in good standing and that no bank would offer her a loan without a
huge down payment, she'd had to face the fact that doing
it alone could take a long, *long* time. Still, she'd rather
that than have something given to her that she hadn't
earned.

And if she could finally get Kowalskin to perform
with his guitar at the club like she'd been after him to do
for the past two years, his presence would draw so much
attention that it would put Hotbox on the map for big-
name artists and turn it into a real music destination. But
the jerk kept refusing her offers and saying no. So all she
could do was sit idle while life sorted itself out.

Leslie grabbed a pen and tapped it against her notebook, that restless, searching feeling hitting her again.
It made her feel impatient, edgy. Yet it was undeniably
there. A nagging feeling that there was supposed to be
more to life than what she was doing—this whole waiting
thing.

Puffing out a breath that fanned a few stray strands of
hair from her face, she looked at the second-story balcony
with its tables and carefully arranged couches. Lights
hung suspended on long iron poles from the exposed
brick ceiling. Copper ducts ran along the top, adding an
industrial touch to the overall open, rustic space.

The main floor was wide open and uncluttered, the long bar taking up one wall and the large stage another. An area in front of the stage had become the dance floor and tables dotted the perimeter. In the daylight the warmth of the old red bricks made the place feel almost cozy. Which was good, considering it was her second home.

Seth grabbed her attention. "I think I'm done here, boss."

With a sigh, Leslie set down her pen and went to assist him. It took another fifteen minutes, but they got it sorted out, and in another five she was back in her heels and locking the back door behind her.

The freezing autumn air surprised her as it nipped her cheeks. Just last week it had been almost ninety. Some days she wondered if she would ever get used to the unpredictable weather in Colorado.

Huddling into her thin black jacket, Leslie pulled the zipper up to her chin and fumbled with the keys, her blood still thin even though she'd been in the state for two winters now. Her fingers had gone cold and her dexterity was almost nonexistent. Stamping her feet against the frigid temperature, she finally got the club locked up and turned to the parking lot at her back.

Longing filled her as she glanced down the back alley to her right. Her apartment was just around the corner in another old brick warehouse, a wonderful two-minute stroll away.

She was real big on her conveniences.

Knowing that she couldn't simply go home because

it was one big construction zone right now was a real morale killer. Having her own space, a place that was all hers where she could relax in and let the barriers down, knowing she was safe and surrounded by her things, was priceless. Not having that made her feel adrift and irritable. And staying with Peter didn't help. Just being in the same house as him put her on edge.

Rubbing her palms together to keep them warm, she made her way to the red Mini sitting alone in the parking lot. That little car was her one extravagance in this new beginning of hers. Hell, she thought as she climbed inside, she'd even learned how to cook thanks to Rachael Ray. Before that woman's recipe books, boiling pasta had only been a lesson in frustration.

Now she made a mean clam linguine. For one.

It was always for one.

And she wouldn't have it any other way. Men were the root of all the problems in her life.

Thinking over the past three years of her life kept her occupied as she made her way through late-night Denver traffic. Once she pulled into the driveway to Peter's house she felt the tension of the day melt from her shoulders. Not that she'd ever tell him, but she loved his home. It was big and private, with huge trees and a great swimming pool.

More than that, it was homey. Which was decidedly odd for a guy like Kowalskin.

Speaking of . . . he wasn't back yet.

Noticing the lack of his obnoxious canary yellow FJ Cruiser in the oversized garage, Leslie drove her Mini in and parked. His metallic blue Ducati was there, but he never left it in the long-term parking at the airport. One of these days she was totally going to swipe it and take it for a cruise through the mountains. Yeah, one of these days soon. No doubt the aspens up in the park were stunning now that it was October.

That was one of the things she liked best about living in Colorado. The change of the seasons. In Miami there was only hot and less hot.

Once inside, Leslie changed out of her work clothes and pulled on a simple pale blue cotton cami and a pair of boy-cut printed panties. Briefly she considered throwing on a pair of pants, then dismissed the thought as the call of the refrigerator lured her and her stomach growled. God, when was the last time she'd eaten?

It must have been around eleven that morning, she thought as she padded down the plush carpeted stairs. No wonder she was ravenous.

Entering the large kitchen, Leslie flicked on the light over the center island as she made for the fridge. Inside were the remains of her dinner from the night before, and that shredded beef chimichanga was all hers. With any luck the guacamole hadn't already gone all brown. It just didn't taste the same after it had.

Feeling the urge to sing, Leslie began humming an Amy Winehouse tune and swung the door to the fridge wide. Instead of the typical single guy's fridge with beer and an expired carton of milk, Pete's was super well stocked with fresh produce and fancy cheese. A bottle of expensive chardonnay chilled on the door and a small pile of Honeycrisp apples filled one of the bottom drawers, making her smile. Quality food was so nice.

Mentally tagging a fat Honeycrisp as hers, she leaned into the icebox in search of her to-go box from the restaurant just as she hit the song's chorus. Feeling it, her mouth opened and the words belted out as she shifted celery aside, perusing the middle shelf. "They tried to make me go to rehab. I said, no, no, no."

She was really into it by the time she'd spotted her leftovers way in the back, which always happened with music. It was a part of her, filled her up. She loved singing.

Shoving aside a container of organic Greek yogurt, she grabbed the to-go box. "He's tried to make me go to rehab, but I won't go, go, go."

"Are you trying to kill me, girl?"

Leslie jumped and rapped her head against the fridge hard enough to see stars. "Shit!"

One hand holding the leftover box, the other rubbing the rapidly forming knot on her head, she spun around to find Peter standing behind her with his duffle still on his shoulder. "Damn it, Peter. Why'd you have to go and sneak up on me? I nearly knocked myself out."

Something is his pale eyes flickered to life as he stared at her, a lazy half grin on his lips. "I woulda had you covered, sweets. I know CPR."

Her head stung like a bitch. "Well that's a relief." He'd probably just use it as an excuse to shove his tongue down her throat.

Noticing where his gaze was lingering, Leslie was

about to make a snarky comment when he said, "You seem to be missing your pants."

"Are my panties too much for you to handle?" She sounded tough, but the truth of it was she felt very self-conscious with Peter staring at her bare legs. Not like he hadn't seen them before, but still. That had been an invitation.

This wasn't.

"There's so little of them that it must be a real waste of time to put them on. Really I'm just thinking about the economy of it all. For your sake."

Right. And she only drank wine for the antioxidants.

"You're such a giver, Peter. Always worried about the other person."

He flashed a wide smile at that. "It's my curse."

They fell silent and she wasn't sure what to do. Her whole plan for the next hour had been ruined. "Hey, why are you home now? Aren't you supposed to be back in the morning?"

Peter dumped his duffle on the floor and shrugged out of his leather jacket. The muscles in his shoulders rolled with the movement, but she pretended not to notice. Just like she pretended not to notice that he had some darn good chest muscles, too.

"We got pushed to an earlier flight."

Trying not to feel crestfallen that her plans to veg alone were smashed, she yanked open the silverware drawer and grabbed a fork. Taking a big bite to stop her from saying something she shouldn't, Leslie made a face. Cold chimichanga was really not good.

Peter tipped his dark head to the side, his baby blues dancing. "You know I have a microwave, right?"

Yeah, but it meant she had to walk directly in front of him in her underwear. Wasn't going to happen. She was just going to put up with cold Mexican leftovers. "I'm good." To illustrate her point she shoved another forkful into her mouth.

Creases at the corners of his eyes crinkled as he smiled, making his blue eyes pop. Clearly the location of the microwave hadn't been lost on him. The man loved to see her squirm.

Like the bee sting she'd acquired in his backyard during a barbeque a few months back. While she'd been in extreme agony from the delicate location of the sting on her hoo-ha, he'd spent the entire time laughing like an idiot as he'd worked the stinger free.

It was like he enjoyed seeing her suffer, the jerk.

"The last time you told me that, you were three sheets to the wind and definitely *not* good."

Leslie dismissed the comment. "That was entirely different."

"Was it?" he asked as he began to walk toward her.

She went stiff. "Yes, it was." He had a way of moving that was sleek and stealthy like a panther. It made her nervous and edgy, especially since he was so stinking unpredictable. Just like the Colorado weather.

He stopped directly in front of her, in worn jeans and a white T-shirt. The man loved his white t-shirts. This one had the vintage Rolling Stones logo on it with the big lips and stuck-out tongue from their *Forty Licks* album. Of course he would wear something crude and suggestive like that.

It was always mildly disconcerting being so close to him. For one, he projected himself to be way taller than he really was. She was five-ten and he had maybe an inch on her. That put them eye-to-eye. And the expression in his face was always clever, watchful like a coyote's. It could be *way* unnerving.

For two, his energy was intense. And it wasn't always controlled. There was a whole lot of Peter packed into one very fit, very hard package.

An image of that night back in Miami flashed across her brain. She knew what it felt like to have that hard agile body on top of her. Unbidden, her gaze dropped from his black stubble to the flat planes of his abdomen. Before it could roam lower she yanked it back to his eyes and caught undisguised humor in the crystalline depths.

"See anything you like?" He reached out a hand, scooped up a dollop of sour cream with a finger, and plopped it into his mouth.

She jerked her box away. "Hey, that's mine!"

He sucked the condiment off and said around his finger, "You know, I've been thinking about that night in Miami a lot lately."

Suddenly uncomfortable with the direction of the conversation, Leslie retorted, "Why, are you having problems again?"

Peter took a step forward and she took one in retreat. It effectively pushed her up against the center island. "That was an anomaly, Leslie, and you know it."

His body was so close she could feel the heat coming off his thighs. It reached out and caressed the skin of her bare ones. "I don't know anything of the sort."

He reached out a hand and cupped her chin. His blue eyes were piercing. "You do know that we have chemistry; that there's this thing that's lingering between us. I know you like to pretend it doesn't exist, but facts are facts. It's been amusing, but it's run its course and I'm ready to get it out of my system."

The warmth of his hand was almost scalding. "Just what do you suggest then?" she asked, pretending that she wasn't standing in her underwear holding a box of cold leftovers. With Peter it was best to never back down or show any weakness. He'd exploit it if you did. "Nice hair, by the way." It was extra messy tonight, the short black strands a tangled, wavy mess.

"I fell asleep on the flight, but don't change the subject." He pushed closer into her until his energy washed over her.

Heat flared low in her belly and went straight to her groin. Damn her body for reacting to him. "What do you want?"

Her gut told her she already knew.

Leaning in, Peter nipped the skin just below her ear, making her shiver, and whispered, "I propose a bet."

There's a shocker. The man was full of them. "Why would I agree to one?" She sounded breathless. She wasn't supposed to sound breathless. He'd rejected her. Didn't her body remember? Her pride sure as hell did. Why was it betraying her?

Firm lips nibbled her earlobe and she went wet. Damn it. "Because I have something you want." What could that possibly be?

"What's that?" Now she didn't just sound breathless. Her voice was quivering some too. *Stop it, body.*

The hand on her chin slipped down to caress her shoulder gently before it slid further down to the indentation of her waist. "You get me. Performing with my guitar at your club after the season is over. You can do as much PR about it as you want. And since I know you want to buy the club from Mark but don't have the money—"

"How do you know that?" she interjected, surprised.

"Because he told me." His hand squeezed her waist. "Let me finish. As added incentive since you want Hotbox, not only will I play for you, but I'll pony up the cash you need for a down payment."

Her eyes flew wide. "You would do that?"

He nodded, eyes hot with challenge.

Boo-yah! God, that was exactly the coup she needed to get her feet underneath her again! She could buy the club *and* put it on the map in one fell swoop. It was a dream come true. But she'd been trying for two years to get him to play at the club. No manner of coaxing, prodding, or begging had worked. For a guy who lived out loud like he did, it was surprising just how against it he really was. So why the sudden change of heart?

Wait a minute.

Her eyes narrowed. "What's the whole bet? What's in it for you?"

Peter gently tangled his fingers in her hair and held

her head captive. An unholy gleam came into his eyes, and he grinned wickedly and nipped her chin. "*You*. I bet that I can get you to sleep with me by the end of the last day of the World Series, or I'll play in your club and give you your down payment."

Surprise shook her. "Wait. You want a do-over?"

"You bet your ass I do."

"But it went so badly for you the last time."

He looked her in the eyes, his blazing like blue fire. "Then you have nothing to worry about, princess. C'mon, scratch this itch with me. Do us both a favor."

The man knew how to play her, knew what she wanted most. And he was right—she had nothing to worry about. But she had everything to gain. Peter playing in the club would bring the kind of attention she needed to take the business to the next level. And if she could actually buy it with the money she'd earn by keeping her hands to herself? Well, then life would be perfect.

Sure they had a history. And she'd admit it. Yes, they had chemistry. But it's not like she was in any real trouble of sleeping with him. Right?

Her stomach quivered. "You're on."

Chapter Three

PETER DUG HIS cleat into the pitcher's mound and signaled to Mark Cutter, who crouched behind home plate.
Winding up for a slider, he pulled back his elbow and
zeroed in on the catcher's mitt. Tension coiled inside
him, ready to unwind like an overtightened spring. Blood
coursed through his veins, making him feel alive and
hyper-focused.

Pitching in the Major Leagues was such a rush. Pure
adrenaline all the way.

Peter was all about the rush.

It was his life. From his team's name to the way he
threw himself into everything full throttle, balls blazing.
That was just how he was built. And it had given him a
life of few regrets.

His only one was currently in the process of getting
a do-over.

Leslie had no idea what she was in for. But she would,

starting just as soon as he finished this game. With the little plan he'd put in place about her apartment, the next few weeks were stacked in his favor. A sly smile crept over his face at that. He was so going to win this bet.

No matter what it took. Snapping back to the present moment, Peter took a deep breath, blinked hard as his left eye went temporarily fuzzy, and mentally swore.

He blinked again and his vision cleared enough to continue. Relieved, he inhaled deep and let the ball fly. His arm slung forward like a rocket and the ball flew toward home plate, breaking over and down as it confused the New York Mets batter. The player swung and missed the ball as it slipped under his bat by a good six inches.

Cursing a blue streak, the player slammed his bat into the dirt as the umpire pumped a fist and yelled, "*Strike!*"

Yes.

The batter stomped off, and Peter earned the last out of the inning for his team. The cheering from the crowd only grew with the guy's agitation. It was one of the best aspects of playing at Coors Field. The fans were involved and rowdy. They were his kind of people.

Tossing them a salute and a grin, Peter loped off the field with the rest of his team toward the dugout as the Jumbotron followed his movement. He glanced up to see himself on the big screen in his green and yellow jersey and white pants, feeling the joy of it all. Even after all these years it was still one helluva thrill.

He was damn sure going to miss it when it was all said and done.

For now he had his fans and his team, and his arm was firing like it had twelve cylinders. And Leslie was sitting in the bleachers along the first base line, gorgeous as always, cheering her boys on with her sister-in-law Lorelei.

Today, that was enough.

Entering the dugout, Peter slapped Drake Paulson's ass and said, "Show 'em your stuff, killer," as the first baseman crammed on his batting helmet and grabbed for a bat. He was up in the rotation and ready to slam one home.

"If I hit a homer you got to buy me dinner, brother," the veteran shot over his shoulder with a lopsided grin, the smile making him look a little less ugly. How the dude got laid as much as he did was beyond Peter's comprehension. It simply defied the laws of physics.

"Whatever, Snuffy." The team had taken to calling Drake that lately because the brown afro on his head and thick chest hair made him look like Snuffleupagus from *Sesame Street*.

The player pointed a finger at him and added gruffly, "I don't mean Taco Bell's ninety-nine-cent menu, either. You're taking me out somewhere real nice like a proper girlfriend."

Peter pushed up the bill of his hat with a thumb to get some air on his damp skin. "Any other requests? A corsage maybe?"

Drake made a face and tugged at his batting glove. "Shit. This ain't the prom, Pete. Keep it in context."

Right.

JP Trudeau bumped into him as Paulson strode toward the batter's box. "Hey, man."

The kid looked happier than he'd ever seen him. More relaxed too. Funny how regular sex could do that to a guy. "Things are going well with you and Sonny I take it."

The shortstop plopped down on the bench next to him, looking mildly surprised. "Yeah, it's great. Why do you ask?"

On the far side of the bench, Mark Cutter leaned forward in his catcher's gear and said, "Cuz lately you've been smiling like a dog with two dicks."

JP laughed and rolled his shoulders. "What can I say, man? It's good."

Peter slapped the young player's shoulder. "Why don't you give up the deets? This dry spell I've been on has turned into one long-ass drought."

"Would you stop yapping? We've got a game on, you knuckleheads," barked the team manager, Arthur McMurtry. "Sorry, coach," Peter mumbled.

"Since we're up by five and it's the ninth inning, I want you to rest your arm, Kowalskin. That's why I waved you over here. Caldera's filling in for you. You're done."

Those last few words rung in his ears. The echo lasted for just a moment, but it was enough. It left him feeling hollow, like a foreshadowing of things to come. Which it was, and that scared him. It was hard as shit knowing this was his last season.

Shaking it off, Peter slumped onto the bench and cast a quick glance down the row at his teammates. It was a blast and a privilege playing with them. Of his thirty-four years, he'd spent the last fourteen with the Denver Rush. The players had become his family.

What was he going to do without them?

Feeling his morale dropping, Peter turned his gaze to the game just as Paulson connected with a pitch and sent it flying over the outfield wall into the stands. Crap. Looked like he had himself a date later.

The veteran jogged around the bases, taking his sweet time while Rush fans cheered his home run. When he passed in front of the dugout, he pointed at Peter and hollered, "I want fancy, sissy boy!"

JP turned to him. "You realize taking him out for something fancy is only asking for trouble, right?"

Yeah. The last time Paulson wanted highbrow, he'd wound up tanked on Dom Perignon and screwing their server in the coatroom, making her miss the last hour of her shift. There'd been a lot of ticked-off customers wondering what had happened to their checks.

Peter nodded. "I'm steering him clear of the bar."

Sometimes Drake was like having a toddler around. You took your eyes off him at your own risk.

And that was exactly why Peter loved him.

He owed the veteran and Mark for some really memorable times. The most infamous being the night Peter lost a ten-dollar bet and wound up hungover on cheap beer with a tattoo on his dong.

To this day he didn't know how he'd managed to go through with it. But he knew he must be some epic kind of jackass to have stamped a tattoo on his dick for all eternity.

Alas, such was the story of his life.

Drake entered the dugout, out of breath and sweaty, then plopped down with a *humph* next to Peter. "Where we going, brother?"

"Hell if I know," Peter shrugged. "You're not gonna get all picky on me are you?"

Mark smirked from down the bench. "The guy's got expectations, Pete."

Grinning at that, he pulled off his hat and raked a hand through his damp hair. "Don't I know it."

Paulson took offense. "Just because I have standards, don't make me high maintenance, man."

Something occurred to him as he looked at the first baseman. "How come you aren't hitting the town with some tight-bodied little thing later? It's not like you to be in short supply for company."

Drake leaned his head against the dugout wall and scratched his unshaven chin. "I'm taking a breather."

"Did all those spring chicks finally wear you out, old man?" jabbed JP.

"Look who's suddenly getting big for his britches now that he's got a woman?" Drake said.

"Yeah, I know. But I don't blame him. Sonny is seriously foxy." He looked around Drake to JP. "You lucked out, dude."

The player flashed a grin. "True that." Then he stood up and moved to the dugout entrance. It was his turn in the hole. "You should find something real, hoss," he said behind him to Paulson. "Then maybe you wouldn't feel the need to take a breather."

"*Pssh*," the veteran waved him off. "I'll leave the love crap to you boys. It ain't my thing."

Something in the tone of his voice sounded off and Peter narrowed his eyes. He knew the smell of bullshit. Mostly because he specialized in it. "So you say now, bro. But you aren't immune." His hand waved toward the men sitting on the long dugout bench. "The best of them fall at some point or another." He ended with a nod toward Cutter.

Drake pegged him with a deep brown stare. "What about you? You haven't gone down yet."

An image of Leslie came to mind and he shoved it aside, plastered on a smile. "What can I say? It just isn't in my cards."

"Maybe you should get a new deck."

No thank you. "Yeah, maybe."

What the hell? Where'd that come from? The words had popped right out of his mouth before he'd even known they were there.

He didn't want a new deck. Nope. He was happy with the one he had.

So why had he said that?

Leslie popped into his head again. This time she was topless and splayed out over a cream cotton comforter. Her body was willing and supple, but her eyes were filled with shadows as a tear slipped down her cheek.

What the fuck?

Peter shook his head hard enough to make his brain hurt. Why had that memory come back to him now? He didn't want it there. He wanted new ones to replace the old. That way he wouldn't have to remember anymore what it had been like to see Leslie Cutter fall apart.

More, he wouldn't have to remember how it had felt.

"You thinking about that new deck already, bro?" Drake broke into his thoughts.

Peter shook his head and looked at the field just as JP hit a grounder and made it to first base. "Nah."

Drake laced his fingers behind his head and stared straight ahead. "Yeah, me neither."

"Hey, Leslie. Can you hand me my soda down by your foot?" said her sister-in-law, Lorelei Cutter, as she sat back down in her seat. "Sorry that took forever. The line for the bathroom is outrageous."

Leslie glanced at her sister-in-law from behind her Ray-Bans. "Are you feeling okay, hon? You don't look so hot." Her normally tawny skin was super pale and she looked worked.

The brunette shook back her long hair and sighed. "I'm not sure, actually. I'm afraid I might be fighting something. My stomach has been off for a few days now."

Leslie handed her the soda, all concern. "You think it's the flu?" Seemed to her the wrong time of the season for it, but who knew? Stranger things had happened.

Lorelei shook her head. "I don't think so. I'm not feeling achy and I don't have a headache. It's just my stomach."

Huh. Maybe it was a virus. "How's Mark been feeling?" she asked and scanned the field, looking for her brother.

She found him on deck and about to bat. As she watched he strode up to the plate and prepared for the pitch.

Glancing back at Lorelei, Leslie found her staring at Mark with a silly grin on her face. "He's been fine," she said, her eyes glued on her husband. "Healthy as a horse."

Thinking that her soda looked pretty darn good, Leslie nabbed it from her and stole a sip. "Thanks, love. I was parched," she said as she handed it back.

"If I didn't adore you so much I'd clock you for swiping my sugary caffeinated beverage."

Leslie grinned at her, knowing the woman didn't mean a word of her threat. "Wow. Somebody's feeling a wee bit bitchy today too."

Lorelei blew out a breath and slouched in her stadium seat, propping a foot on the empty one in front of her. "I know it. And I feel terrible about it too, but it just won't stop. It's like I have PMS on steroids."

Leslie could relate. She was a monster every month for about a week. "No worries."

Someone walking behind them whacked her on the back of the head. "I'm sorry!" the person exclaimed.

Whipping around in her seat, Leslie came up against a teenage girl holding a small mountain of hot dogs who was trying to make her way down the aisle. "It's all right, hon."

The girl smiled gratefully. "Thanks."

Turning back around as the scent of ball field dogs hit her nose, Leslie tugged down her faded black Jack Johnson T-shirt and felt her mouth water. She sighed and looked at Lorelei. "Now I need a hot dog, damn it."

Her sister-in-law laughed and said around her soda straw, "Normally I'd join you with a burger, but I believe I'll abstain this time."

Leslie froze. *What?* Since when did Lorelei ever turn down greasy salty goodness?

Spinning in her seat until she was face-to-face with the brunette, she lowered her Ray-Bans and looked her over thoroughly. The early October sun was at an angle in the sky that made her squint against the glare. "You don't want anything to eat?"

Lorelei shook her head, her green eyes confused. "It's weird, isn't it?"

She nodded.

"I don't know what's wrong with me. I mean, I never turn down food. Especially not a cheeseburger."

Leslie looked her dead in the eye. "You've never been pregnant before, either."

Lorelei jolted and bobbled her cup of soda. "I'm not . . . I mean . . . I can't be . . . he's been so busy . . . we aren't even trying yet!" she ended almost desperately, her face white and her eyes huge.

"That's the funny thing about sex. You don't even have to try." She should know. She hadn't been trying at seventeen, either.

Lorelei stared at her, eyes all shimmery. "You think I could be?"

Leslie snagged the soda again and took a good long slurp, staring at her hard. It was written all over her pasty face.

"Yup."

Chapter Four

LESLIE SET THE tray of drinks on the table and laughed at the sight that greeted her. About a dozen Rush players gathered around two tables shoved together, the men in various stages of intoxication. They'd come into Hotbox after the game to celebrate their victory against the Mets.

They did that once in a while. It boosted attendance every time they did, which was just one more reason why Peter playing in the club would be such a big deal. The famous Rush pitcher got attention.

Live music pumped through the state-of-the-art sound system as a local indie band rocked the house with their African-influenced breezy folk music. When they'd first come into the bar looking for a place to play and she'd heard their sound it had been a done deal. They were like Rusted Root and Jack Johnson combined and it was freaking awesome. It made her feel good to give the little guys some exposure too.

"Hey, sis, where's my wife?" Mark had to nearly shout to be heard over the music. "I thought she was with you?"

Leslie handed outfielder Carl Brexler a nitro-tap microbrew and winked at him when he thanked her. "She's passed out on the couch in my office."

Instantly concerned, her brother began shoving away from the table to stand. "Is she okay?"

Leslie put a hand on his shoulder to restrain him and pushed him back down. "She's fine, just tired. All the packing y'all have been doing has tuckered her clean out. Just sit back, enjoy yourself and let her rest."

She left out the teensy bit about how his wife was probably pregnant. No way would she spoil that awesome surprise for him. Knowing Mark, he was going to flip when he found out. Having kids had always been something he'd secretly wanted. It had given her endless material for his torment as kids.

And she had used it. Oh my, how she had.

"Are you sure?" He looked dubious, his gray eyes filled with worry.

Leaning down, she pecked him on the cheek. "I'm sure. Just relax." Pointing at the stage she added, "This band is terrific and they aren't signed by a record label yet. Listen and see if you want to point them to your buddy at Delta Records."

Mark loved music almost as much as she did. Settling back in his seat, her brother snagged a buffalo wing from the basket on the table and smiled. "Will do." He took a bite and said around a mouthful of chicken, "What's with the getup, by the way? You look extra dressed up tonight."

She did?

Leslie looked down her body, taking in her black skinny jeans, snug black top, and bright red heels. Nothing was out of the ordinary. "What do you mean?"

"I mean the earrings and nail polish and other crap."

She gave him a look, frowning. "I'm not wearing anything I don't normally wear, Mark." Maybe she'd taken a little extra care with her appearance today, but that was it.

Oh, there was that bit about a bet and all, but she wouldn't flaunt her body just to drive a certain somebody crazy now, would she? That'd just be mean. And unladylike. Bad manners all around.

Leslie grinned to herself. She *so* would.

"I know that look," Mark stated. "What are you up to now, sis?"

Brushing him aside, she replied, "I have no idea what you're talking about." Before he could probe any further, she slid around the table and deposited the rest of the drinks. When she was done, she crossed her arms, tray in hand, and watched the band on stage.

The hair on the back of her neck stood up and the skin there began to tingle. What the—?

Before she could spin around to look for the source of her ESP, a hot body brushed against her back. Hard hands slipped whisper-quiet over her hips and very briefly cupped her butt cheeks.

She knew exactly who it was. "Get your hands off my ass, Kowalskin."

Breath puffed softly down her neck, scalding her there. "You like my hands on your ass. And my mouth."

Jerk. He would have to go and remind her about that. "I was drunk."

Quiet laughter echoed in her ear. "You still liked it." One hand moved over her butt, making her shiver inside until a thumb was caressing and pushing into the top of her cleft, right where the two cheeks met. "Especially here."

She wanted to arch back into his hand it felt so good. Instead she stepped away and ignored the heat that had flared between her thighs. "Again, I was drunk, Peter. That does nothing for me now."

Liar, liar, big fat liar.

And he knew it. Laughter rumbled in his chest and he smacked her butt hard enough to sting. "You liked that too."

Ugh! "Go away."

Obviously disinclined to acquiesce because he didn't budge, Leslie shot him a glare as she retreated to the safety of the bar. He just hooked his thumbs in the front of his jeans and watched her walk away, not trying at all to hide the fact that he was staring at her backside. He was probably picturing it naked.

Irritation welled in her. Damn the man, but he could be infuriating.

Once behind the bar, Seth stepped up beside her, sweet and eager. It was cute, this case of puppy love he had for her. "How are you doing, boss? Can I get you a drink?"

Taking a deep breath, Leslie calmed her racing heart and said, "I'm good, but thanks."

From her vantage point behind the bar, she scanned the crowd and noted that the place was nearly packed. All the couches on the balcony were in use and the dance floor was crawling with gyrating bodies. Two women were wrapped around each other kissing near the table full of ballplayers, and she glanced at the team's ace pitcher to see if he was watching. Hot lesbians making out made for a pretty good show.

Jealousy sliced through her, totally unexpected and completely unwelcome. What did she care if he got his rocks off watching scantily clad women go at it?

Just to prove she didn't, that she could've seen him staring right at them without feeling a thing, she forced her gaze off the action and looked for his messy black head and white vintage Led Zeppelin T-shirt. She found him at the far end of the table sitting next to Drake, who must have arrived while he was busy harassing her. The big veteran was glued to the scene playing out nearby, but Peter hadn't even seemed to notice.

Nope, he'd snagged somebody's beer and was kicked back in a chair with his ankles crossed, watching the band onstage. A thick black leather bracelet covered his wrist and his jeans were faded and frayed. His leather jacket was tossed over the back of his chair, and he had a five o'clock shadow covering his lean cheeks. When he reached for his glass the tattoo on the inside of his bicep peeked out from under his sleeve. She couldn't see from the distance, but she knew it was a way cool yin-yang dragon.

A little bit humble and a whole lot of cocky, Peter

Kowalskin was totally badass. He looked it and acted it—like nothing was off limits.

But he wasn't into watching chicks.

Relief washed through her, taking the jealousy with it. And the fact that she felt relieved that he wasn't into the girl-on-girl make-out session was seriously frustrating. Why should she care?

She didn't. He could do whatever the hell he wanted.

That's what she told herself as she made up a ton of busywork to keep away from the Rush's table. When she'd run out of excuses, she left the floor and headed down the back hall toward her office, thinking it was time to check on Lorelei. The noise from the club became muffled as she made her way to the back, and the relative quiet began to smooth her frazzled nerves.

Once she reached the end of the hall and came to her office door, she pushed it open silently and slipped inside. Lorelei was sacked out on her plush purple velvet sofa, snoring loud enough to wake the dead. Kicking off her heels so she wouldn't wake her, Leslie bit back a groan and wiggled her cramped toes. As beautiful as the shoes were, and as powerful as they made her feel, they were still hell on her feet.

Casting a quick glance at her sister-in-law, she was reassured to find her still sound asleep. Dark circles smudged beneath her eyes and she was curled up on her side with Leslie's hand-knit blanket over her. The multi-colored chenille throw had been her first attempt at knitting something harder than a scarf, and it looked pretty good if she did say so herself. A few tie-offs had come loose, but the unraveled threads gave it a fringy kind of appearance.

For a woman who was rarely domestic, even she found it odd just how much she enjoyed the craft of knitting. But it had only taken one good Colorado blizzard for her to discover how relaxing it could be—and how well it helped pass the time when thirty-mile-an-hour winds whipped the snow coming down into whiteout conditions and kept everyone indoors.

It was all part of her fresh start, this trying new things. Cooking, knitting—getting all grassroots and stuff. For her anyway. Such a far departure from the life that she'd lived before. Then it had been work and the beach. Those were the only two things that had turned her crank.

Well that and killer shoes.

Glancing down at her only remaining pairs of Jimmy Choos, a sad little sigh escaped before she could stop it. Lorelei stirred at the noise and shuffled on the couch, a hand flopping off the cushions to dangle near the floor. She came dangerously close to taking out a struggling potted bamboo plant without even knowing it.

As quietly as she could, Leslie moved the pot out of harm's reach and noted how many leaves had already turned yellow. She'd bought it just last month. Poor thing.

Just then a knock on the door sounded, startling her. Whirling around as the door opened a crack, she saw her brother's dark blond hair come into view, relieving her. He must have come to retrieve Sleeping Beauty.

"Is she still asleep?" he whispered not so softly.

"Not anymore I'm not," came a grumpy reply from under the throw blanket.

Pushing the door the rest of the way open, Mark strode in and crouched down next to his wife, concern and love filling his voice. "Are you all right, baby?"

Lorelei pushed the blanket aside and sat up, her dark brown hair a tangled mess. "Yeah. What time is it?" she said around a huge yawn.

Leslie watched her brother kiss his woman tenderly on the temple before he replied, "It's time to get you home."

Straightening, he helped her to her feet as she said, "I sat down only for a minute. I swear." She looked confused and embarrassed by her impromptu napping session.

She shouldn't be embarrassed about it. Heck no. The couch had more lure than any Greek siren ever could. Leslie had succumbed to its temptation more than once. She wasn't ashamed to admit it. And she wasn't even pregnant.

That couch sucked you in like a vortex.

Mark wrapped a strong arm around Lorelei and pulled her close into his side. It was so sweet, she thought as she watched the two, the way her brother behaved around his wife. For too many years his warmth had been hidden under an ice sheet of cynicism, a terrible first marriage to one crazy bitch the source and blame. But then Lorelei had come along hell-bent on stealing from him to save her family and his calculated aloofness had melted under the passionate tornado that was her.

Now when Leslie looked at her brother she saw the real Mark. The guy with the big, tender heart and ready smile. She couldn't be happier for him. He deserved that kind of love.

Her sister-in-law snuggled into his side and smiled up at him, her eyes brimming with adoration and affection. And he looked back at her just the same. It was wonderful. Heartwarming even.

The stab of envy took her completely by surprise.

Blowing out a breath, Leslie mentally swore. Why did she have to go and start feeling envious of couples in love all of a sudden? What was that about?

Not since she was a teenager had she been interested in happily ever after with a man. Life had taught her the hard way that it simply didn't happen like that in reality. At least not for her. Which was perfectly fine, since tangling with a man only made things messy. She had the list of damages to prove it. Each one as painful or bad as the rest.

So why—out of the blue—she found herself getting riled over it, she just didn't understand.

"We're going to head out, sis." Mark's voice snapped her back to the moment and she tuned in just as they were stepping through the door.

"Yeah, y'all have a good night." She waved them off, ready to have a moment to herself. It had been a long day and she could really use five minutes of alone time.

Which brought her right back around to the fact that she liked her life just the way it was—complete freedom and independence. Not a snowball's chance in hell would she give that up for all the couple moments in the world—no matter how cutesy they were. It wasn't worth it.

And there wasn't a man alive who could ever make her change her mind.

Chapter Five

PETER WAITED UNTIL Mark and Lorelei had left and then he walked down the long hall until he reached Leslie's office door. He'd seen her disappear to the back earlier and figured she was still there since he hadn't seen her come out. Fighting back a smile and resisting the urge to rub his hands together in anticipation, he turned the doorknob and peered inside. He couldn't wait to see where this interlude would lead.

Leslie was seated behind her desk and her head was leaned back against the chair's headrest. When she heard the door creak she jerked up straight. Realizing who it was, she tilted the chair back on its spring with a smirk and put her bare feet up on her desk. Then she crossed her slender ankles, and his attention was drawn to her coral-painted toenails. Each big toe had a white flower accent on it, and it was sexy as all hell.

He'd never considered himself much of a foot guy, but

he was in danger of acquiring a fetish now. She must have caught the direction of his gaze because she wiggled her toes playfully, a sly grin taking over her gorgeous face. "Is there something you want?"

There was a whole lot of something that he wanted. And it was right in front of him all wrapped up in a sassy attitude. God, he loved that about her. The woman was all kinds of sauce.

For a guy like him who didn't want the responsibility of holding onto anything, Leslie Cutter was the perfect woman. She was as wild at heart as he was and even harder to handle. "I want the same thing that you want."

She cocked her head and eyed him, her pretty hazel eyes assessing. "You mean to permanently erase that night from my memory bank? Because that's what I want—to forget that ever happened."

Peter tossed his jacket on the purple velvet sofa and made a *tsk-tsk* sound. "That mouth of yours is too pretty to be sullying it up with lies, sweetheart. Shame on you."

Her brows slashed low and her eyes narrowed like a feline's, flashing with warning. "You're one to talk about shame."

The way she said it had something hot stirring to life in his gut. It was the first time she'd willingly referred to that night. Not the most flattering thing to hear, but at least she was talking about it.

Pressing his advantage, Peter strode casually over to the bookcase beside her desk and began perusing the shelves. She stiffened at his closeness and his body reacted to her by going hyperaware and focused, just like it did during a game.

And of course, his palms went sweaty.

She was the only woman who had ever made him nervous. Wiping his hands as casually as he could on his jeans, Peter glanced over his shoulder and caught Leslie checking out his ass. He grinned to himself, his ego boosted. Yeah, his ass was a good one.

It ought to be, he thought, with all the work he put into it. Being a professional athlete meant keeping his body in prime shape, and it was nice to know the effort paid off in other places besides the ball field. "Is there something you want?" he shot back with a raised eyebrow, amused at being able to toss her words right back at her.

"You wish," she retorted and tossed him a dismissive glance. Only he caught the gleam of interest in her eyes and knew her for the liar that she was.

Peter took a step toward her, closing the gap by a good foot until only an arm's reach separated them. He leaned forward and caged her in placing a hand on each armrest of her chair. Her eyes widened the tiniest bit, but she held her ground. "I wish many, many things."

"Really?" she questioned and shifted slightly away from him in her chair. "Such as what?"

Peter couldn't help noticing that her breathing had gone shallow. How about that? "I wish to win the World Series this season." It would be a hell of a way to go out.

Her gaze landed on his mouth and flicked away. "Boring."

Humor sparked inside him at that and he chuckled. "You want exciting?"

She shrugged. "Why not? Amuse me."

That worked for him. Hell yeah. If she didn't watch herself he was going to excite the pants right off of her.

Just excitement, arousal, and sexual demands. That's what he was looking for this time around. And it was going to be fun leading her up to it.

But if he wanted her there then he had to start.

Pushing until he'd tipped her chair back and only the balls of her feet were on the desk, her painted toes curling for grip, Peter lowered his head and until his mouth was against her ear. She smelled like coconut again, and his gut went tight.

"I wish I had you bent over this desk right here with your hot bare ass in the air."

She made a small sound in her throat and replied, "Less boring."

Peter grinned. Christ, the woman was tough. "Do you remember what I did to you that night in Miami? The thing that made you come hard twice—one on top of the other?" He sure as hell did. It had involved his tongue, fingers, and Leslie on all fours with her face buried in a pillow, moaning his name like she was begging for deliverance.

She tried to cover it, but he heard her quick intake of breath. "It wasn't that memorable."

Bullshit.

He slid a hand from the armrest and squeezed the top of her right thigh, his thumb rubbing lazily back and forth on the skin of her inner thigh. Her leg tensed, but she didn't pull away.

"Need a reminder?" His tongue slipped out and traced the delicate curve of her ear.

"I might," she whispered, and he could feel her breathing go shallow.

Lust pooled low in his belly. Reminding Leslie what it had felt like was exactly what he wanted to do. "I thought you weren't going to sleep with me. Are you going to fold that easily?" Not that he was complaining, but he'd thought she'd be a tougher nut to crack than that. He'd anticipated it even.

What he hadn't expected was for her to spread her thighs in invitation. But that's exactly what she did, and the lust in his belly shot straight to his groin, making him instantly hard and achy. Pulling back to look in her eyes, Peter was surprised by the wicked gleam he saw there. What was she up to?

"Isn't this what you want? Me, willing and pliant?" She put a hand on top of his and guided it closer to her crotch. He could feel the heat coming off her and it nearly made him whimper. "Here, how's this?" She moved his hand until he was cupping her and could feel her moist heat through the fabric of her pants. "Is this what you want?"

Jesus.

His hand jerked and curled into her, making her gasp. It had been far too long since he'd had his hands anywhere on her body. "It's a start." His cock throbbed and strained against the fly of his jeans.

No problems there.

Enjoying himself immensely, Peter cupped her and began rubbing the seam of her pants with his middle finger, taking his sweet, sweet time stroking up, then back down. And he felt her go from hot to steaming.

Her head fell back against the chair and she closed her eyes, letting out a soft moan. It nearly buckled his knees, made his chest squeeze. "You always were good with your hands," she gasped, arousal making her voice throaty.

He was good with his mouth too. Capturing her lips with his, Peter kissed her soft and slow, his tongue stroking hers in an erotic dance meant to melt any resistance. Sinking further and further into her until all he knew was the feel of her hot little pussy under his palm and the way she tasted.

God, he'd missed her.

The thought entered his head and shocked him, pulled him back from the drugging effect of her kiss. His heart began to jackhammer in his chest, but before he could pull back further Leslie grabbed a handful of his hair and tugged him back down.

"Don't stop," she whispered against his mouth. "You feel so good."

Her hips had started to move in time with his hand, her body searching, yearning for more. Whatever her game was, she was clearly enjoying it. This was either going to be the easiest bet he'd ever won or the woman was playing him like a fiddle.

Either way he was totally on board.

Hunger bit into him with jagged teeth and he pushed

his finger against her, making her cry out. It wasn't his mouth on her like he wanted, but it was enough for now. It was enough to make her come.

And making Leslie Cutter orgasm had just become his singular mission.

Peter took her mouth again, impatience nipping at him, causing him to become rougher, more demanding. Taking the heel of his palm he pushed it into her mound and began rubbing it in a circle, knowing that the friction on her clit would drive her crazy.

"More," she groaned and arched upward, her hands dropping to his shoulders, her nails digging into him there.

It turned him on and he gave her more, kissing her hard and passionately. Whatever she wanted, he wanted to give her. Everything. Anything. Just as long as she rewarded him with a gorgeous, delicious orgasm.

Nothing in the world quite compared to the sight of her in the throes of an intense climax. The memory of the last time had plagued him for years, crept into his dreams, and overrode his fantasies until they starred only Leslie.

It was time to get her out of his head.

And it was definitely time to get her back into his bed. He needed to have her, to purge himself of her. Then he wouldn't be in danger of her taking over his heart anymore. Because she already had a toehold, damn her.

Shoving the chair back on its spring as far is it would go, Peter kissed her passionately. The heel of his palm continued its gentle assault, not letting up even when she drew her legs up until only her toes were on the desk and her knees were bent.

"Tell me how much you want this," he panted after he broke the kiss.

"I want this," she whispered, her head back and eyes closed.

Not good enough. After all the trouble she'd caused him, he wanted her begging for it. "How bad do you want it?" He nipped her bottom lip hard enough to sting and she cried out softly. "How bad do you want to come for me, Leslie?" he demanded, blood pounding in his ears and his cock hard as granite. If it was anywhere close to how badly he wanted to make her come then it was going to be one intense orgasm.

Dropping his head further, he saw her nipples puckered beneath her black top and covered one with a mouth. He wasn't gentle. And she liked it.

Nails dug hard into his shoulders and she bucked against him, crying out, "So bad! Now, Peter. Make me come, now." She ended her demand with a moan and a "please." Then she dropped her hands until they covered his, urging him on.

Feeling the urgency in her, he sucked a nipple through the thin black fabric of her shirt and grinned when her legs began to quiver. Knowing she was on the brink of going over, Peter flicked his tongue over her hard little peak and bit it between his teeth.

She broke.

Her orgasm tore through her and she cried out, "Oh God!"

It was the sexiest fucking sound in the entire world.

Releasing her nipple, Peter drew back until he could see her clearly. Her eyes were still closed and her cheeks were flushed. She was panting and boneless and sated and it made him feel like a goddamn superhero.

And there wasn't a tear in sight.

Not this time.

Peter released the chair and let it drop back down, the abrupt movement jarring her eyes open. When he saw them his stomach tightened. They had gone dark as a pine forest and were completely dazed and unfocused. Damn, but it did his ego good to see her like that. All soft and satisfied and floaty.

Turning his back on her, Peter strode to his jacket on the couch and picked it up, put it on. Then, staring at her slick, kiss-swollen lips, he asked, "How many times did you come that night, Leslie?"

She stared back at him, her eyes a little glassy. "Three or four, I think. Why?"

Because he was keeping count.

Moving to the door, he pulled it open and glanced back over his shoulder at his fantasy woman with the pinup curves and smart mouth, who looked decidedly sex-rumpled and replete.

Damn right.

He had a score to settle. "That's number one."

Chapter Six

A FEW DAYS later Leslie was in her car and on her way to Pole Fitness for her strip dancing class. Outside, the October air was fresh, the sky was blue, and the leaves were parading about in their autumn glory.

Inside, the radio was cranked and The Dirty Heads were in her CD player, making her body sway with their song "Lay Me Down." Her left hand kept time to the beat as she tapped her thumb on the steering wheel and downshifted when the light up ahead turned red.

Reggae music was her weakness.

It made her soul light up. Considering how many things there were in life that could get a person down, she considered island music a godsend. Losing herself in the rhythms of the Caribbean had gotten her through some pretty tough times when all she'd wanted to do was cry.

Pulling to a stop as The Dirty Heads told her to wipe the dirt off or take her shirt off, she put the Mini in first gear just as a text came through on her cell phone. Knowing she shouldn't because texting while driving was illegal in Colorado, Leslie quickly pulled down her Ray-Bans and scanned the message anyway.

It was from Peter, and it was the first she'd heard from him since he'd left for St. Louis.

Home. Had grass, want beer, need ass. Where you at?

Laughter bubbled in her chest and she let it loose. God, that man was funny when he wanted to be, referencing their bet like that. *Sorry pal,* she thought. *My ass is winning this thing.* Hotbox was hers.

After their rendezvous in her office he'd headed out of town, providing them both with an opportunity to assess the current situation and decide how to move forward. Not that she really had anything to think about. There was simply no way she was going to have sex with Kowalskin and lose this bet.

That didn't mean that she wasn't going to drive him bat-shit crazy at every opportunity though.

And have a little fun herself. Besides it being just so much fun to torment Peter all on its own, there was the added benefit of the man's oral abilities and incredibly nimble fingers. It was the rest that had left her unsatisfied, since the night had been cut short. But for now she didn't have any qualms about putting the former to use for her enjoyment.

Leslie knew he didn't mind either.

If ever there was a guy who could corner the market on commitment-phobia it was him. Not in all the years she'd known him had he ever had a girlfriend. Or at least not a steady one.

Certainly there were women. There had to be. It was Peter Kowalskin, for goodness' sake. He didn't just sit around all night playing canasta. Maybe he simply got laid on the road.

The light turned green and Leslie let out the clutch and cruised through the intersection. She was heading west and could see the Rockies in the distance already snowcapped and looking beautiful. It looked like they were going to be in for a brutal winter, if the early snows were any indication. Then again, the high country always got pummeled way more than the Front Range—at least that's what Lorelei told her.

She was deep in thought about which ski pass to buy this winter when her phone went off. She grabbed it out of the front pocket of her purse and answered without checking the caller ID.

"Leslie Cutter."

"You didn't answer my text."

She rolled her eyes. Men. "I'm driving, Kowalskin. You wouldn't want me to wreck my pretty little car by texting and driving now would you?"

"Fine, you're off the hook this time. Where are you going?"

"Somewhere you're not. What's it to you?" Listening to him on the phone started her blood humming in her veins. Aside from the accent that he played up sometimes only to annoy her, he had a sexy voice. It was a little youthful and a lot rough-and-tumble with a hard edge. Just like the rest of him.

"I've got plans for us, princess, and I don't have much

time. So you need to get your butt back here. I have a surprise."

She didn't trust his surprises. Not as far as she could throw them. "I'm not missing my pole class."

"C'mon, Leslie. If you don't come here then I'll come to you." He made it sound like a threat.

The studio came into view and she whipped into the parking lot. "You can try, but there are a lot of pole fitness studios in this city. Good luck trying to find mine."

He snorted. "Girl, please. Do you honestly believe that I couldn't just make a few calls and find out where you shake your ass?"

Since he put it like that . . . "Whatever. Hey, I have to go." She was about to disconnect and then remembered. "Wait! Have you heard anything about my apartment? Has Jerry called you with an update? I was hoping to move back in this weekend."

There was a shuffling and what sounded like a garage door opening. "Not that I know of. I'll double-check my phone when I get a chance, but don't hold your breath. I've been preoccupied."

Leslie did have to give him that. Playing ball for a living kept the guy busy, especially in the postseason. "Thanks, I appreciate it." She reached for her gym bag and retrieved it from the back seat. "I don't want to impose for longer than absolutely necessary." The line went quiet. "Are you still there?" she asked as she climbed out of her car.

Peter sighed softly and finally relented, saying quietly, "You're not an imposition, Leslie."

The breath froze in her chest. How was she supposed to respond to that? Wiping a hand on her cropped black yoga pants, Leslie chose to ignore his comment. "Um, okay, well I'm going now. I'll talk to you later."

Hanging up, Leslie shoved the phone back in her purse and opened the studio door. Once inside she glanced around and noted that she was just in time. About a dozen women milled about in various workout getups, and she particularly liked the mini-shorts and legwarmers look. How very *Footloose*. Somebody remind her again why the eighties were making a comeback?

The music changed and went lusty. Her class was about to start.

Slipping into the room and dropping her stuff, she waved to some of the other regular girls and kicked off her shoes. "Hey, y'all." Unlike most of the other women in her class she wore neither mini-shorts nor stripper heels. She needed the cushion from the fabric on the back of her knees for pole work and the heels, well, just no way. She wanted to keep her ankles unbroken and in good health, thank you very much. It was hard enough just walking in them some nights.

Quickly grabbing an open pole, Leslie caught a glimpse of her reflection in the full-length mirrors on the front wall. Her hair was pulled back in a low bun to keep the strands out of her face when she twirled and she had on a dark pink workout tank top along with her yoga crops. Giving a little shimmy to loosen up, she studied herself and approved.

She looked good. All these pole dancing classes had

paid off and her body was nice and firm. Curvy as a Roman statue, but toned and healthy and strong. Leslie knew she packed a punch and liked it that way.

Skinny was so overrated.

With a slight smile she gave a little booty shake. Some junk in the trunk was where all the fun was at. More cushion for the pushin'.

The Pussycat Dolls began to play on the radio, being uber-sexy and singing about loosening buttons with Snoop Dogg. Following the lead instructor, Leslie went through the warm-up routine and then settled into the fun and vigorous workout. Enjoying herself, she swung her legs up and spun on the pole, lowering backward with every whirl until she was upside-down. She was breathing heavy when her spin and the song came to an end, but she had a huge grin on her face. *Leslie Cutter, stripper at large. Watch your men, ladies.*

Totally amused with herself, she was giggling a little when she came to a complete stop, her upside-down head facing the door. Her eyes focused and the giggle lodged in her chest. A pair of scuffed up black skater shoes and frayed jeans blocked her vision. Shit. She knew those Vans.

Kowalskin.

Annoyance welled up inside her along with a healthy dose of the butterflies. He'd found her. She couldn't believe he'd actually been serious about that.

Still panting, Leslie flipped upright and dislodged from the pole. Her heart was pounding and her blood was racing, but that was from the striptease routine, not the hard-bodied man standing by the door currently staring her down with ice-blue eyes full of bad intentions. The half smirk and cocked hip sent alarm bells ringing in her head.

The man was up to no good.

Suddenly on alert, like a predator had just walked into the room and she was its main course, Leslie crossed her arms over her chest and waited until the furious whispering in the room had dropped to a low enough level to allow her to speak. The whole class had stopped the minute he'd entered. He had that effect. And his face was so recognizable.

Yes, ladies. It's him. And yes, he's every bit as wild as he looks. "What do you want, Kowalskin?" She let him hear the irritation in her voice.

It occurred to her that she wasn't entirely sure if it was him or her thoughts that she was annoyed with, but she shoved the idea aside fast. Of course it was him. It was always him.

He slid a look at her from the corner of his eyes, his spiky black lashes and the mischievous glint in the blue depths making her knees weak. Energy and raw sexuality. That was Peter. And he was turning it loose on her.

"Excuse me, ladies," he said to the room after shooting her a cocky wink. "Is there room for one more?"

Warning bells turned into flashing sirens. What? No, he wasn't crashing her dance class, was he? Would he?

Of course he would.

The question was *why*? While she watched, he put his sunglasses in his hat and tossed it on the floor by the wall.

He was about the only man she knew who could get away with wearing a black fedora and look good. On him the hat was way sexier than it had any right to be.

The room fell silent as all the women stared at Peter in awe. And she couldn't blame them, really. The man looked hot in his clingy black button-up, leather bracelet, jeans, and finger-combed black hair. The lean, rugged face and piercing eyes only added to the total package.

One of the young women behind her muttered under her breath, "Oh my God."

Jealously sunk its teeth into her again.

Mine.

What the—? The *hell* he was. Now the irritation she felt really was aimed at her. Kowalskin belonged to nobody, least of all her.

She didn't want him.

"Go away, Peter."

The man just ignored her and sauntered over to the last remaining open pole. To the petite brunette next to him he flashed his wolfish smile and said, "How about you show me how this thing works?"

She stuttered and blushed profusely. "Okay. Yeah." Then she stopped and stared at him blankly. "Um, what?"

Poor girl. "Leave her alone."

He wrapped an ankle loosely around the pole and gave a little shake, causing a collective murmur to rise above the music. Finally the instructor, Carlie, cleared her throat and said loudly, "Let's continue shall we?" She disappeared into the stock room and started a new CD.

An elbow in Leslie's ribs sent pain and surprise darting through her. She whipped her head around and saw the redhead who'd been next to her leaning in to whisper, "That's the pitcher for the Denver Rush, isn't it?"

Leslie nodded, still annoyed. "Yeah."

"How do you know him?"

She didn't want to explain because she had a feeling if the women learned of her connection to the Rush, her life of relative obscurity there would be over. And she wasn't in the mood to be popular. "I manage a club he frequents." There, hopefully that will shut her up.

Peter caught her attention when he called out to her, "Hey, princess. Go on a date with me."

There went her obscurity. Terrific.

She shook her head. "No."

He ground against the pole, rocking his hips suggestively, and she raised a brow. Even though he was totally joking, the man could move. His body rocked with an innate rhythm that had heat flaring low in her belly.

"I'm not leaving until you say yes." He spun around and used the pole at his back to shimmy against. It made her laugh.

"No." She had to raise her voice to be heard over Christina Aguilera. So this was his game. He was going to embarrass her into agreeing to go on a date with him. She found it odd that he'd want one with her, but before she could think about that any further, he got her attention with his response.

"Okay, fine." He straightened and began rolling up his sleeves. Bracing his feet apart, he grabbed the pole with both hands and said, "Let's dance, ladies."

And he did. For the next fifteen minutes he shimmied, shook, and rolled—one outrageous move after the other. At one point he even jumped up the pole, locked his legs around it and spun around saying, "Pleeease, Leslie?"

At first she'd been annoyed, then embarrassed, and then finally amused as all get-out. Watching Kowalskin striptease was pure entertainment. And by the time the class was over he'd not only won the adoration of a dozen women, but he'd worn her down too. How could she say no to a man who'd tried an upside-down spread eagle—and failed miserably to her great amusement—just to get a date with her?

She couldn't.

It didn't mean she wasn't going to get him back for pulling this little stunt though. "All right, Kowalskin. You win," she said to him as the class wound down.

A little out of breath, he grinned like the devil and raised his hands in the air. "She said yes!"

The women watching in avid fascination cheered enthusiastically. From the back someone called out, "Smart girl!" and Leslie laughed right in his face.

Obviously they didn't know Peter.

Chapter Seven

PETER WAS WAITING outside for her when she exited the studio with her bag over her shoulder. He'd just finished signing an autograph for one of the class regulars—a sweet, plump woman in her late sixties who was gushing and holding the scrap of paper with his name on it to her chest like it was something precious.

"You make sure you tell Bob hi for me, Laverne. And take care of that left hip of yours, okay?" He smiled charmingly like he was a good boy and not the wolf in sheep's clothing that she knew him to be. "Remember to alternate hot and cold pads on it for the next few days and you'll be back to good in no time."

Laverne giggled like she was sixteen and swatted playfully at him, her green eyes sparkling. "Oh hush."

When Peter spotted Leslie his smile took on an edge, and he removed himself from the small crowd of admirers, giving Laverne's arm a gentle parting squeeze.

"Excuse me, ladies. My date has arrived." With an unholy glint in his eyes, Peter strode her way.

Carlie walked past her just then and put a hand briefly on her shoulder, whispering, "Way to go, Leslie." There was a smile on her face that was more than a little good-naturedly envious. "He's a stud."

She didn't need to be told. "Thanks, hon."

Sometimes it was easier to let people assume something than it was to sit them down and explain the truth. And there was no harm in letting them think there was more going on between her and Kowalskin than there really was. It gave them something to talk about.

If there was a tiny part of her that thrilled at the idea of people thinking she and Peter were an item, she tried very hard to ignore it. It was wrong anyway. Wasn't it?

"All right, you got me out here," she said after the crowd had dispersed. "Now what are you going to do with me?"

The man had his hat back on and looked like a whole mess of trouble, an arresting cross between intense athlete and soulful artist. The unexpected blend did funny things to her. And when he looked at her out of the corner of his eyes with an expression that promised her the most erotic time of her life if she were so inclined, her panties went instantly damp.

But when it came right down to it they were completely and utterly incompatible. For whatever reason, when the moment of truth came she just didn't do it for him. The proof of it had been humiliating and deflating.

She gave Peter a tough time because the fact of it was

that she still felt the sting of his rejection every single stinking time she was around him. One moment he'd been all hot and heavy on her and then, *boom!* Nothing. Zilch. Nada.

Wet, limp noodle.

And now the man wanted a date and a do-over. Why? What did it matter to him?

More importantly, what did it matter to her?

She adjusted the strap of the duffle bag slung over her shoulder as he said, "Leave your bag and I'll drop you back here when we're done. I'm taking you places."

Leslie spotted his bright blue Ducati parked next to her Mini Cooper and swallowed a grin. She'd been dying to get the chance to ride on his snazzy crotch rocket. Not that she'd ever let him know that. He'd just get an even bigger head and lord it over her at every opportunity. Like he needed more to be egotistical about anyway.

Although she really wanted to leap on the back of his motorcycle and holler, "Freedom, baby!" with her hands in the air, she rolled her eyes and pretended reluctance. "Really, Peter? I don't have a helmet and you're wearing a hat." She pinned him with a suspicious stare. "*Why* are you wearing a hat, by the way? Did you not wear a helmet?"

The guy was reckless but he wasn't normally stupid.

"I was a good boy. I just shoved it in the front of my jacket after I zipped it up." He took his hat off and held it out to her. "But that wasn't the most ingenious idea so why don't you toss this in your pitiful excuse of a car and we'll get going?"

She took offense and snatched the fedora out of his hands. "My car is *not* a pitiful excuse. Mini Driver is fabulous and you know it." Yes, she'd named her car after the actress. Come on. How could she not?

He smirked. The gall of the man, making fun of her beloved automobile. Now she was back to feeling annoyed.

"Call it whatever you want, but it isn't a real car unless you can put the seats back and screw in it. Can you?" The look he shot her clearly said he doubted it.

And honestly . . . "I don't know." It hadn't been tested.

Peter raised an eyebrow, giving her a Look with a capital L, pitching her stomach off-center. It wasn't fair.

"We're wasting valuable time, girl. Toss it in and let's ride."

Caving because she was curious, Leslie dumped her stuff and grabbed a jacket that had fallen onto the floor. It was a black, fitted jacket that Mark had bought for her to celebrate her first winter snowstorm. The material was lightweight, but high-tech and super warm. Tossing it on, she zipped it up to her chin and shoved a pair of gloves in her pockets just in case. Leslie turned around and found Peter already on the Ducati unstrapping a helmet for her from the bike's seat.

"Are you going to tell me where we're going?" she asked as she took the glossy black helmet from him and put it on.

He grinned and flipped the visor down on his own helmet. "You'll find out soon enough. Hop on."

She did just that, and when she was on the back of

his shiny sports bike, he fired it up. The way the motorcycle was designed she had to raise her legs up high to reach the foot pedals. Her knees cradled his hard body, and when he grabbed one of her hands and pulled her forward, putting it around his waist, Leslie found herself effectively wrapped all around him.

Peter revved the engine and the sleek machine vibrated beneath her with barely leashed power, making her eyebrows shoot up in surprise. *Nice.*

Leslie smiled. Whatever he had up his sleeves was going to be all kinds of fun.

"Punch it, Kowalskin," she demanded, suddenly very eager to get on with the spontaneous adventure.

The pitcher revved the engine again and yelled over the noise, "Hold on tight!"

With that he kicked the Ducati in gear and leapt into the road. Her ass greeted air and she scrambled forward, wrapping her arms tight around Peter like he was her lifeline. His laughter trailed behind him and he shifted gears again, making the motorcycle leap like a stallion, no doubt just to make her squeal.

It totally worked.

She screamed like a frightened schoolgirl and her thighs gripped his hips tightly, her fingers digging into his supple leather jacket at his belly. The man was solid as a rock everywhere. Absolutely everywhere.

She wasn't sure that anything could feel better. Except maybe kittens. But the feel of Kowalskin's sculpted muscles flexed and ready had her thinking that maybe it was a toss-up. In fact, if she had to choose between a soft, fluffy kitten to pet or Peter, she was pretty sure at this moment she'd choose him.

Hot men on hotter motorcycles were a total turn-on.

She'd never been able to resist the combination. It had landed her in some very hot water when she was a rebellious seventeen-year-old. Back then she'd taken one look at Billy Wayne Tucker with his crooked grin and beat-up dirt bike and fallen head over heels for the cocky Southern boy.

For an entire summer she'd ridden around on the back of that old bike in a daze of hormones, convinced that it was true love. And it had been—her first, tender foray into the complex emotion. Everything about the kid had called to her, his wild-child ways an irresistible beacon to her carefree soul.

That summer he took her heart and her virginity and filled her up with romance and sweet promises under the stars. And when she found out she was pregnant her first time out of the gate, he solemnly promised to love her forever with big, sincere eyes and then went straight down to the local recruiting office and signed his life away to the U.S. Navy, bailing town the very next day.

Soon after that she'd miscarried, whether from the broken heart she'd suffered or her physiology she'd never know. But it had been for the best, and no one—not even Mark—knew the whole sordid truth about why he'd left and how hurt she'd been. Or how terrified she'd been to find herself pregnant, and how devastated she'd been to go through the miscarriage alone. But most especially, how she still thought sometimes about the kid that had almost been and felt a little sad.

Regardless, she'd learned a hard lesson about the very real dangers of losing her heart to a man. For more than a decade she avoided those kinds of men, choosing instead dependable types that never quite reached her heart. It kept her safe and in control. Even her ex John had never meant more to her than a reliable warm body. And yeah, she knew how that made her sound. So sue her.

It had worked too.

Right up until her reliable and nonthreatening tax accountant boyfriend defrauded the American government in her name and ruined her life.

Peter shifted in his seat and began leaning to the right as he hit the on-ramp to the interstate headed west toward Golden and the mountains, grabbing her attention. Gripping harder, Leslie leaned with him, her body pressed up against him like she was stuck on Velcro. And it felt good. Really, really good.

They cruised along the Peak to Peak Highway, looking at the autumn leaves and enjoying the mighty Rocky Mountains in their golden glory. The aspens were absolutely stunning this fall, and Leslie ogled the richly colored leaves, taking it all in. So different it all was from where she'd grown up in rural northern Florida. As much as she loved palm trees and giant elephant ears, it was Colorado with its unpredictable climate and gorgeous rugged scenery that had her heart.

Kind of like Kowalskin.

Leslie sighed and relaxed against him as they neared the turn off to Peaceful Valley. Thinking that he was going to take her on a short hike, she was surprised when he ignored the sign and kept on driving. Then they turned off the main road and wandered a maze of dirt roads until they came to a small lane blocked by a NO TRESPASSING sign hung on barbed wire fencing. The lane was really nothing more than two ruts that headed back into a small forest of aspens and stately pines.

They slowed almost to a stop at the entrance and she shouted, "Are we going in there?"

Far off in the distance to her right she thought she could see the horns of a large bull elk. It didn't look like the kind of place for a casual stroll.

Peter shouted back, "Sure we are. It's where the surprise is at," and started down the road, which slowly enveloped them in golden leaves and dappling light.

It was breathtaking.

The slender lane meandered back along the floor of a small valley. About a half mile in they rounded a bend in the road and the view opened up before them. A flat meadow sprawled out, dotted with aspen groves and a slow, wandering creek. Leslie's eyes widened as the stream lead to the valley wall on the far side and she saw a rushing waterfall framed by huge pines. It pooled into a small sub-alpine lake with water the same color as Peter's eyes.

It was paradise.

An elk bugled in the distance just as Peter rolled the Ducati to a stop in the grass by the bank of the small lake. The sound of the rushing waterfall and the calls of wildlife all around made her heart squeeze. How amazing would it be to have a cabin right here and get to experience this every day?

Peter came to a stop and turned the engine off, the sudden silence almost jarring. A gentle breeze picked up as he pulled his helmet off, rustling the aspen leaves in the gorgeous light.

Give her a hammock and a good book and she could stay right here forever.

"What do you think?" Peter asked after he'd straightened and taken his helmet off.

Leslie pulled hers off, too, and brushed a few strands of hair back. "It's stunning."

"Yeah? You think?"

She took a long, slow look around the broad meadow, envisioning it lush and green in the summer and brimming with wildlife. No doubt it was a haven for foxes and deer. It already had elk. "Yes I think, Peter. This place is perfect."

"I'm glad you like it."

Leslie arched her back and began to climb off the motorcycle. She laughed when her legs felt shaky. "Why do you care if I like it or not?" It seemed out of character for him. "By the way, is it okay that we're here? Do you know the owner?"

Peter swung a muscular leg over and stood too. "Yeah, I know the owner."

She waited for him to divulge more information but he didn't. "Well, who is it?" She finally asked, a little exasperated after waiting on him for a few minutes.

He held out his hands and motioned down his body, tossing her a self-satisfied grin. "You're looking at him."

Chapter Eight

"SHUT UP."

"Nope, I own it."

"But it's so beautiful." She gestured loosely at the waterfall behind her.

He smirked. "Yeah, it was almost too beautiful for me." Hanging his helmet on a handlebar, he continued, "But seriously, I found this five-acre gem about four years ago and have big plans for it come next year." He'd wanted to bring her here, show it to her. He thought she'd appreciate it. And yeah, maybe he wanted her opinion. Who cared?

Besides, it was a hella good make-out spot.

Leslie unzipped her coat and briefly turned her face into the gentle autumn sun. She had an almost euphoric look on her face, and he felt something stir low in his belly while he watched her enjoy the fresh air and sunshine. Her hands were on her hips and she breathed deep, smiling. "It's perfection, Peter."

Still smiling, she opened her eyes and focused on him, her guard down and happiness lighting her up. Peter felt the power of it hit him like a freight train and it nearly buckled his knees. Christ, the woman was sexy. Potent as moonshine and with twice as much kick.

Forcing his body to chill, Peter shrugged out of his coat and tossed it over the bike seat. His attention was on her as she made her way toward the lake's edge. "I agree it's fantastic the way it is, but I want to build a cabin over there in the middle of the meadow near that aspen stand," he said, pointing over his shoulder to a large grove behind him, the leaves suddenly a golden yellow blur to his eyes. "It'll have a helluva view of the waterfall from the front porch, and I plan on spending some quality time with my ass in the swing that'll go on it."

He could see it, all of it, down to the tiniest detail. The first time he'd laid eyes on the land he'd seen the vision, and he had the sketches at home to prove it. A huge front porch dominated the cabin in his mind and he saw himself sitting on it while he picked at his guitar, watched the sun go down over the flower-filled meadow, and tried to figure out what the hell to do with his life after baseball.

The need to get it sorted out was barreling down on him fast.

The sudden sharp pain in his chest was his reminder that life was about to make one big paradigm shift, whether he was ready for it or not. His days in the Major Leagues were over. It hadn't been announced to the team yet, but he was retiring after the season was over.

Both he and the Rush's management had quietly done

everything they could medically do to stall his exit from the game when his degenerative eye disease had been discovered. And he'd hung in there for years. But his left eye's health was declining rapidly now, affecting both the center and periphery of his vision. Even with the surgery he had scheduled for next month, his eyesight would never be right again. Certainly not good enough to pitch in professional baseball anymore.

It was just something he was going to have to learn to live with. Hell, it was time for him to find a new hobby anyway. And he planned on doing just that in his cabin in the mountains just as soon as he won the World Series. Some old-fashioned sweat and hard work while building the place would do him good.

Shaking off his thoughts, Peter turned back to Leslie and found her sitting on the bank watching the waterfall.

"Mind if I join you?" he asked as he strode across the ground to her.

She shook her head and patted the dead grass next to her in invitation. "Have a seat."

He lowered himself and had a thought that made him chuckle. "I spent a lot of my youth getting high and telling lies with my friends at this run-down and overgrown little park in the shit part of Philly. It had a pond kinda like this, but without the waterfall, and was probably filled with sewage water."

Leslie smiled. "Shame on you doing naughty things."

There was no shame about it. He'd been a wild kid and had a damn fun time. "You're not fooling me, princess. I know you were a hellion when you were young too." She still was.

It's what he liked about her.

She didn't even try to lie. "I totally was. But I didn't hit my pot days until college. Before that it was general rebellion fueled by a brother who cast a really big shadow and my own desperate need for attention."

Peter settled back on his elbows and glanced at her sideways. "I've wondered about that. It wasn't so easy being Mark's little sister was it?"

She pulled her knees up to her chest and rested her arms on them. "It was a pain in the ass. Don't get me wrong," she rushed, "I love my brother to death, but because of who he was with his talents and his dyslexia, our parents spent most of their energies on him. I was just kind of left hanging." She laughed softly and added, "There was so much that I got away with, though, just because they weren't paying attention. That was pretty sweet."

Still, Peter could tell it had also bummed her out. He leaned toward her and nudged her with his shoulder. "Hey, think of all the hearts that wouldn't have been broken had you been a demure good girl. Where would the fun have been in that?"

The breeze picked up and stirred a few loose strands of her pale blonde hair at her neck. He wanted to give in to the urge and plant a whisper-soft kiss on the exposed skin there, but he didn't. He just sat back and took her in.

"True," she murmured. Then she glanced at him over her shoulder and asked, "Tell me about you. What were you like as a kid? What makes you"—she waved at him lounging there—"*you*?"

It was the first time that Leslie had ever asked about him. Interesting. He wondered briefly what that meant and then shrugged it off. She was probably just making conversation.

He reached out and rubbed a loose strand of her hair between his fingers, playing with it briefly. Her hair was soft as satin. "It was just me and my pop growing up in South Philly, a stone's throw from the projects. He did a lot of drinking. When he was sober he worked at a dog food factory and when he wasn't he liked to rail against the government and all the injustices it had laid upon him, blaming Uncle Sam for the state of his life. He was checked out most of the time."

"You don't talk like a guy who came from the ghetto of Philadelphia."

Amusement filled him and he slid her a look, saying like only a Philly boy, born and raised could, "You mean how I should talk like this, yo?"

She tossed back her head and laughed. "Something like that, yes. How'd you change it?"

"Practice." Along with a very handy online English course on proper grammar. It was the one and only college course he'd ever taken.

A bird flapped its wings in a tree nearby as Leslie tucked a strand of hair behind her ear and asked quietly, "What happened to your mom?"

"She left my dad for another man when I was still in diapers." It happened to all the men in his family. They just couldn't keep their women. It was not-so-affection-ately known as the Kowalskin Curse.

"Bummer."

Peter smirked. "Yeah."

Just then Leslie turned to him, her eyes full of curios-ity. "So then how did you get to be a professional ball-player?"

With a crooked smile full of chagrin he raised a hand and rubbed the back of his neck. "When I was thirteen my pop caught me selling weed in the alley behind our house and beat the shit out of me. Afterward, he enrolled me in some Big Brother–type state-funded program and I met the man who introduced me to baseball and changed my entire world."

She studied him. "Isn't that a little old to be just start-ing into the sport? Mark started playing when he was five."

Peter shrugged. "Yeah, I guess. But I had a gift and ambition. More than that, pitching gave me something to look forward to and feel hopeful about. It was a way out of poverty, and I grabbed onto it with both hands, threw everything I was into it. By the time I got through high school I'd been on some pro scouts' radars for a while and got picked up by the Rush's AAA affiliate in Buffalo." He shrugged casually. "The rest is history. I've been playing ball ever since."

He considered himself one hell of a success story.

And that's why he paid it forward now that he had money. He funded numerous charities and organizations designed to help children in the projects get a chance at life by educating them and opening doors normally un-available to kids of their socioeconomic status. Over the years he'd helped a lot of people.

That familiar panicky feeling began to tighten his chest and he breathed deep, then slowly exhaled. For a guy who thrived on challenge he sure was being a pussy about things. It was just a little life overhaul. Nothing he couldn't handle.

Leslie placed a hand on his knee and he stiffened. Just that one small touch from her felt erotic. "That's an awe-some story, Peter."

"Thanks."

"Did this guy you mentioned teach you to play the guitar too?"

Her finger was making little circles on his bent knee and it was driving him nuts. "Nope. I learned to play by reading about it."

She looked at him like she didn't believe him and stopped circling. "You *read* about playing guitar?"

He nodded and watched some puffy white clouds float on by. Any minute she should start rubbing again. He hoped. Her touch felt good. "Yeah." It was one of his things. He read all the time. Like *all* the time. If he didn't his brain went stir-crazy.

And he was good at utilizing what he read, so now he played guitar.

"What else do I not know about you?" she sort-of-demanded. It wasn't really a question, and he couldn't tell if she was miffed or intrigued. Knowing Leslie, she was probably a little bit of both.

"I have a ridiculously high IQ. Makes me obnoxious."

The woman snorted. "Is that what you blame it on?"

He grinned and pinched her side gently. "I'm Ukrainian and Black Irish."

She rolled her eyes. "I mean something interesting, Peter."

He thought about it for a moment. "I wrote really bad poetry when I was sixteen."

"Get out." That got her attention.

She began rubbing his knee again and he swallowed the urge to groan. "It's true. I played ball, but I was also this sensitive artsy kid searching for an outlet. This was before I discovered the guitar," he added, lest she think he still wrote really bad poetry.

"Better. But, where's the really juicy stuff?" She gave him a look. "I know you have some."

Oh, did she mean like the fact that he'd been with exactly one woman besides her in the past three years and that was only to prove that he could get a hard-on after his disaster with Leslie? Yeah. He was keeping that secret.

He sat back up. It was time to change the subject. "I brought you here so I could get down your pants."

She shoved him in the arm and laughed. "You did not."

He grinned like the devil. "Girl, you know I did."

Leslie shook her head, still smiling. "Then you've failed miserably."

"Have I?" he asked, feeling his muscles bunch as he prepared to pounce. Failure wasn't in his vocabulary.

"I'm not seeing any making out now, am I?" She looked around like she was scouting for it.

If he didn't know better he'd think that Leslie wanted him to kiss her. That maybe she was egging him on. "Maybe I was trying to be a gentleman."

She laughed at that. "In who's dream?" Then she tossed her head back, exposing the graceful line of her throat, taunting him.

He had her flat on her back with her hands pinned over her head before she could even let out a scream. "This is no dream, princess."

Leslie didn't even try to struggle against him. In fact, if he wasn't mistaken, there was a naughty little gleam in her gorgeous eyes. And he was sure he wasn't mistaking the foot seductively rubbing the back of his calf all of a sudden.

What was up with that?

"You want to make out with me, don't you?" he said as the realization hit him. Her breasts pushed against him and she'd spread her legs to cradle him. He could feel the heat of her crotch, and arousal pooled heavy in his groin. When she rubbed suggestively against him the blood went thick in his veins.

"It seemed appropriate, given we're on a date." The flirty, playful teasing almost made him whimper. She knew just how to slay him.

Peter stared down into her hazel eyes and watched as they started to turn dark. God, she was beautiful. "Well, now I'm confused," he said. "It was my understanding that you didn't want to lose this bet." If she did that was fine by him. Getting Leslie naked was on the top of his to-do list, and if she wanted to expedite the process then he was all for it. After he accomplished that he'd think about what came next. Because right now he didn't know. He just knew that Leslie had a hold on him and he had to do something about it before it drove him insane.

"Making out isn't having sex." She pulled a hand free and it began to slide up the back of his thigh. He sucked in air sharply, loving the feel of her under him, all lush and pliant. She definitely knew how to tease.

Then her hand reached his ass and he lowered his head so that he could kiss her neck, wanting her hand to stay there forever. So she wanted to up the stakes and play a little?

Sweet. "Let's not waste such a perfect opportunity, then."

"Mmm, let's don't," she whispered just before he covered her mouth with his.

Coaxing her mouth apart, Peter ran his tongue along the seam of her lips until she opened for him on a soft moan, her hand still gripping his ass. Desire hummed just beneath his skin, urging him to take the kiss deeper, to dive into Leslie.

But he didn't. Instead, he kissed her slowly. He kissed her like a man savoring his favorite meal, exploring the sweet taste of her at his leisure until she began moving impatiently against him. Even then he continued to kiss her like he had all the time in the world. And he didn't stop until she was writhing beneath him and pulling at his hair.

Smiling against her lips, Peter rocked against her

gently, creating a delicious friction until she was panting impatiently.

Leslie wasn't the only one who could tease.

He fed her one last slow, drugging kiss and then pulled away to look at her. She had her eyes closed and her cheeks were flushed.

Until she realized that he was done. Then her eyes fluttered open and filled with pouty sexual frustration. She slapped him hard on the ass just as he was standing. "Dirty pool, Kowalskin. Very dirty pool."

He laughed out loud. Of course it was.

It was his specialty.

Chapter Nine

PETER DROPPED HER off back at Pole Fitness and left with a wink and an engine rev, peeling pavement as he hit the road. After that, Leslie headed back to his place to find it empty. Relieved to be alone, she showered, dressed, and was back at her office shortly thereafter. If she was feeling a little off-balance she was doing a great job of ignoring it. She had a ton of work to attend to, what with the Halloween party that Hotbox was throwing and a promotional package to organize for when Peter played at her club. Which he was going to. He was *so* going to.

Leslie smiled slyly as she unlocked the door to her office. She had Peter right where she wanted him and it was so much fun. This whole bet idea he'd concocted was turning out to be highly enjoyable. And now that she had a reason to really lay it on him and drive him wild, well, that was just awesome.

She shook her hair back and tossed her purse on the

purple couch. If there was a part of her that was using this opportunity to get back at him for rejecting her three years ago, then she was all right with that too. She wasn't above a little passive-aggressive behavior.

That night, Peter had taken her places she'd never seen before and then, just when something inside her had unlocked and flung wide open—*because* of him—making her feel things she'd thought impossible, the jerk went and lost interest right then and there.

And then he made her do the one thing she'd swore she would never do again over a man.

He made her cry.

Somehow, some way, Peter had slipped behind her defenses and gotten to her. He'd touched her and made her feel.

Not before or since had she ever been that exposed and open to another human being. Even though the night had started out being nothing more than a drunken distraction from her wrecked and ravaged life, it had turned into a whole lot more very quickly.

With Peter she'd glimpsed something elusive, something vast and full of wonder. It had rocked her.

And he'd slammed the door on it.

"Which is just fine by me," she muttered to herself, half disgusted at the direction of her thoughts. Romantic musings were all they amounted to anyway. The reality was that she had a chance to grab her life and her future by the horns and rebuild it right now. Peter was her opportunity and she was going to take it, come hell or high water.

Her career, her business—those were the things that were solid. They were what she could count on. Hadn't she learned by now that every single time she put her trust in a man she was involved with she just got tromped?

Peter wasn't any different. He had just seemed like it for a moment. But given time he would do the same.

Sighing, Leslie walked to her desk and flopped down in her chair. There were still tons of decorations to hunt down and orders to double-check. And she still didn't know what she was going to dress up as for the Halloween bash.

Maybe something uber-provocative to flaunt in front of Kowalskin? Like Xena, Warrior Princess or a German barmaid costume. Whatever she chose it had to be good.

Because Halloween night was the end of the bet.

The terms of the bet were through the last night of the World Series, which was scheduled to be played on All Hallows' Eve—her favorite holiday of the year. And this year it was going to be the best one ever.

At midnight on October 31 she would win her life back. As much as she loved running Mark's club it still felt a little like charity. Which she appreciated, really she did. Her brother had given her a fresh start, a place to hide while she licked her wounds. But now she was ready to step out of the shadows and reclaim what was taken from her.

The phone rang, startling her, and she snatched it up. "Leslie Cutter."

"Ms. Cutter, this is Jerry Patowski."

Her spirits lifted. The superintendent from her building was finally returning her twelve or fifteen calls. It was about time. "Hi, Jerry. I've been trying to call all week. Is there any word on my apartment?" She missed it and wanted to go home. Mostly she wanted to soak in her own bathtub and sleep in her own bed.

She heard papers shuffling and a file cabinet squeaking, then a muffled cough, before he said into the speaker, "Nope. Sorry 'bout that, Ms. Cutter. But, more damage than anticipated was found and it's gonna be a while still. Plus the plumbing's so old the brand isn't made anymore."

"Can't you just use a different one?"

He sighed and then said like he was explaining something to a child, "Not unless you gut the whole thing. Old fixtures are part specific. I had to order some special parts from overseas. It could be another week or so before they arrive."

Leslie bit down on the frustration. "Can't you expedite the parts from wherever they're coming from?"

"That *is* expedited."

"How many shipments are you expecting?" She didn't have the patience to wait for several boxes to trickle in from halfway around the world. Not that she really had any choice in the matter, but still.

"Just the one."

Fine. "Well, can I at least come by and grab some more stuff?" She'd been wearing the same bra for over a week. Even though it had been washed already, she appreciated having more to choose from than one lace bra and one sports bra.

"No can do, ma'am. We can't let you inside the construction zone. Ain't safe, and there's the liability. The big boss would toss me out on my ass if he knew I'd let you in."

She'd deal with Peter. "If I can get him to agree, you'll let me in so I can get more stuff?"

The super guffawed into the phone. "You can try, girlie. But he ain't gonna let you in. I promise."

She'd just see about that. "Thanks for getting back to me on this, Jerry." Finally. "We'll be in touch."

Setting the phone back in its cradle, Leslie smirked. She wiggled a heel off and it fell to the floor. Then she tucked her bare foot underneath her. What she wanted was clean underwear and something to wear to work besides her skinny jeans. She'd ask Peter about it.

If she were still in Miami with her old life she would have simply run out and bought more, but this new one of hers didn't include a hefty salary to spend frivolously. This fresh start included budgeting, cooking from scratch, and not tossing a few hundred bucks away on new clothing if it wasn't absolutely necessary.

Leslie sighed again. *Life.*

Turning her mind to other things, she dug into work for the next few hours, making phone calls and checking the status of things. About six months ago she'd started preparing for the big Halloween party, getting the word out and generating interest. Now that the time was drawing near she was touching base with people again.

It was Hotbox's first costume party, and she was going to do it right. The whole place would be turned into a giant haunted house, and the band she'd hired had agreed to dress up like zombies. The night's winner of the costume contest would receive two coveted tickets to see Blues Traveler perform live at Celtic Tavern. The small venue promised a really good time and Leslie wished she could enter. She'd love to watch the band. John Popper played a mean harmonica.

Tucking a stray strand behind her ear, she went back to work making sure that all the gift certificates, tickets, and ad promos were in order. By the time she was ready to go for the night, not only was everything in order, but she had gotten a famous local radio duo to come down to Hotspot and do their coverage live on Halloween night.

Feeling proud of herself, Leslie turned the reigns over to her assistant manager and headed back to Peter's house. His FJ Cruiser was parked in the garage so she knew he was home. As she entered through the side door Leslie wondered how he was going to react when she asked to get some of her things. If he was still awake, that was. For a big time ballplayer he sure hit the sack early.

Entering the house, she saw that the lights were still on and wandered down the wide hall toward the kitchen, her heels clacking on the hardwood as she went. Once she reached the kitchen and crossed to the refrigerator for a drink, a sound came from upstairs. It was muffled, but it sounded like Kowalskin was yelling something at her.

Glancing at the clock, Leslie noted that it was late and frowned. What did he need from her at midnight that wasn't either a booty call or . . . well, a booty call? Popping the lid on a can of coconut water, she took a drink and headed back down the long hallway to the stairs.

Once on the second floor she made her way down the corridor to the last door on the right. Peter's bedroom. It was one of two rooms in his house that she'd never set foot in. Nerves kicked to life in her belly as she pushed the door open and stepped inside.

It wasn't what she expected. "Whoa."

The room was clean and simple and decorated in varying shades or brown, gray, and cream. A thick cocoa-colored rug covered the floor and a huge brick fireplace dominated the far wall. Opposite the bed were a snazzy flat screen TV and a door that was cracked open with the sound of running water spilling through.

An acoustic Gibson guitar was leaning against a window frame by the bed, and on the wall over the head of the bed was a huge black-and-white canvas print of Bob Dylan's face, up close and personal. The picture was way cool, with only half his profile showing.

Overall the room was uncluttered and surprisingly simple and cozy. Leslie shook her head. Would she ever understand Kowalskin?

"Leslie, is that you?" Peter called from behind the cracked door. From the sound of running water she could deduce that he was in the shower. Man, this was too easy.

She was so going to get him back for embarrassing her at her dance class.

Strutting across the plush rug, she swung the bathroom door open and said loud enough to be heard over the noise, "Yeah, it's me. What do you need?" Hopefully it was something she could torment him with, like a towel.

He pushed the shower stall door open and poked his

head out. His hair was wet and dripping and slicked back from his face. It only succeeded in making his eyes even more insanely amazing. "Hey, something's acting up with the plumbing. I noticed it the other day when you started a load of laundry and I tried to rinse some dishes but all the water was ice cold. So don't turn on any faucets or flush until I'm done in here, okay?"

Leslie couldn't believe her good luck. Paybacks usually took longer to construct than this. "Sure thing, Peter," she smiled innocently.

She was going to lure him into complacency first. Leaning against the door, she crossed her arms over her chest and asked, "How was the game today?" She'd missed it with all the work.

Okay, so maybe she'd missed it a little on purpose. Their trip to the mountains had flustered her and she'd needed some space.

The glass door was fogged up, but she could just make out the shape of his body and knew he was just starting to soap. He rubbed the bar across his chest and then moved lower to the flat plane of his belly. When his hand went even lower lust pooled heavy between her legs and she shifted.

The leisurely way he was soaping down there made her wonder if he didn't know she could see him. It would be just like him to put on a dirty show on purpose.

"The game was good. We beat the Padres 6–1, so we're moving on from the Division Series to the League Championships next week."

"You know that if you win the World Series Mark is

going to claim it was all Lorelei's doing, right? He thinks she's his good luck charm." It was sweet really. Wrong, but sweet. The Rush were winning this season because they were a seriously talented team. But if her brother wanted to believe it was because of his wife then so be it. It didn't hurt anything.

"C'mon, Leslie. She *is* his good luck charm." He poked his head back out and leveled a look at her, water dripping from his nose and the black shadow of his beard glistening wet. "You know that better than anybody."

True. Since Lorelei came along her brother was happy. Really, really happy. That did make her good luck, she supposed. Still didn't mean she was the reason the Rush were on a hot streak. Mark was the superstitious one, not her.

"You guys are well on your way to the World Series." She hoped they made it. Really she did. It would be the Rush's first in a long time.

Peter had been listening, but now his gaze was roaming all over her body and going lazy. "Hey, pretty lady. Want to climb in and scrub my back for me?" The smile he gave her was anything but sweet.

She should have known.

Pushing away from the door, Leslie strode to the shower and pasted on a sultry smile. "Well sure, sugar."

His pale eyes narrowed on her. "That was too easy."

She shrugged. "I'm turning over a new leaf."

He raised a brow, giving her *that look*, and her knees went weak. "Oh, really?"

No, not really. "Absolutely. Here, why don't you turn

around and hand me that soap? I can reach your back from outside here."

Though he still looked dubious, she knew he wouldn't be able to pass up the chance to have her hands all over his naked skin. And she was right. He fumbled for the soap and held it out to her, eyes still watchful and shrewd. The sinewy muscles in his outstretched arm made her want to purr. But she ignored the urge because she couldn't believe that he was falling into her trap so easily.

Taking the soap, Leslie motioned for him to turn around, and she had to bite her lip to keep from smiling. He spun around and she caught a glimpse of his hard, incredibly tight ass and heavily muscled thighs. *Wow*. Just. Seriously. *Wow*.

It was *so* much better than she remembered.

Before she was tempted to do something else with Peter entirely, she took a deep breath and said sweetly, "Give me just a minute, darlin'. I have to do something first."

He mumbled a reply that sounded something like, "Hurry," and she dashed to the sink. Once there she cranked open the handles making sure the faucet was turned on all the way and then ran from the room.

"*Goddammit, Leslie!*" His bellow of outrage and curses followed her into the bedroom and she fell on the bed laughing.

She laughed until her stomach hurt, she was crying, and her side ached. It was so worth it though, so completely worth it. Because she'd warned him.

Payback was a bitch.

Chapter Ten

TWO DAYS LATER Peter stepped onto the pitcher's mound at Coors Field to the sound of Smash Mouth's "All Star" pounding through the stadium speakers. It was the first game in the League Championship Series and the Rush were getting ready to take on the Philadelphia Phillies in the bid for that sweet-ass spot in the World Series. He was ready for it. Pumped up and anxious to get the game underway.

He was feeling intense and focused. Seven games— four if they were lucky—were all that separated him from his final blaze of glory. And he wanted it so bad he could taste it. Though his career held a ton of major highlights and he'd had more fun than he'd thought possible, there was still one thing left to do.

Not once in his impressive career had he been to the World Series. The Rush hadn't won the pennant since before his time in 1973. It seemed like he and his team were in some damn long-standing droughts.

Time had come to end it, Peter thought as Smash Mouth told him to *get his game on, go play*. Amen to that. It was definitely time. For a lot of things.

Something flashed on the Jumbotron, catching his attention, and Peter glanced into the stadium seats, glad that his eye was behaving today. The crowd made him smile. Rush fans filled Coors Field to over-flowing, green and yellow becoming almost a blur.

Squinting against the sun, he looked up and saw nothing but clear blue sky in the middle of October. Loving that about Colorado, he wound up and pitched one over home plate, loosening his shoulder. Mark wasn't out yet, so he was throwing to Toby Jackson. The young up-and-coming catcher threw the ball back to him, his grin visible behind his face mask.

After his shoulder was nice and warm, a local celebrity came out and the Rush lined up along the first base line for the National Anthem. Then the state governor trotted out to the applause of the crowd to throw the first pitch. Peter had to hide a smile when the ball went rogue and barely made it over home plate. Pitching was not as easy as it seemed.

Preparing to go throw some strikes, Peter was about to move when a flash of pale blonde hair caught his eye. Turning to find Leslie in the stands sitting next to Lorelei and JP's woman Sonny and her boy, he was surprised by the breath that hitched in his chest. Sometimes the woman caught him off guard and it was hard to breathe.

She was laughing about something and had her head

together with the Charlie's. It looked a lot like they were telling secrets. As he watched she raised her hand and the boy gave her a high-five, both of them grinning like thieves with a full bounty. He wanted to climb right into the bleachers with them to find out what was making her smile like that so that he could do it too.

He shook his head and tried to ease the tightness in his chest. Why did everything with that woman lead to some sort of bodily dysfunction on his part? It was unnerving.

Drake walked by and clapped Peter hard on the back. "Thanks for doing it fancy the other night. I do love me some rib eye. You ready to rock and roll?"

He felt the buzz of anticipation and nodded. "You bet your ass."

Just then JP passed by, his attention in the stands on the strawberry blonde with the sweet smile and big blue eyes. When he came close enough, Peter elbowed him in the rib cage and grinned. "Eyes on the game, dude."

Like he was one to talk.

The shortstop waved to his girlfriend and her son, love and affection for them written all over his beaming smile. "Don't judge. If you had what I had, you'd be grinning like a fool too."

Probably.

Drake shoved him in the shoulder, gaining his attention. "Ignore the pretty boy. We got us a game on."

Knowing that Paulson was right, Peter took one last glance at Leslie in the stands, felt his gut tighten in response, and then forced his mind on to the game, pushing her out. He didn't want her in there anymore. She was taking up way too much space.

To the thrill of the Rush fans they played "Wild Thing" as he made his way back to the mound. Forcing everything else from his mind, Peter focused on his pitching and the game. He was one of the best in the Major Leagues and tonight he was going to prove it. His shoulder was loose enough and his left eye vision was holding as steady as it could. If something didn't feel one hundred percent with his arm he shrugged it off. It was fine.

The first Philly batter stepped up to the plate and Mark signaled a play from his position crouching behind home. Reading it, Peter shook his head. He didn't like that pitch, it played to the batter's strengths. So Mark signaled again, and this time he accepted it.

Winding up, his knee pulled tight to his chest, he zeroed in on Mark's glove and let the ball fly. Like a bullet it shot out toward home plate. A small sting flashed briefly in his shoulder as he completed his follow-through.

The Phillies player connected with the ball and sent a line drive barreling back at Peter. It happened so fast he barely had time to register it before the ball was upon him. Shifting in his cleats, he dodged just as it was about to take out his left knee and snagged the white leather with his glove.

Sucker.

Rolling his shoulder, he tugged the brim of his hat, wiped his hand on the thigh of his pants and prepared for another pitch. Cutter shuffled in his pads after the new batter entered the box, signaling for a ball low and outside. Assessing the new player, Peter nodded, gripped the ball in the horseshoe, and sent it flying.

The Phillies batter swung hard and missed the ninety-six-mile-an-hour fastball by inches.

"*Strike!*" called the umpire with a pump of his fist.

The crowd cheered. Damn right. He owned that plate. Adrenaline pumped through him, his breathing came in rapid bursts.

Peter was high on the game and it felt good. It felt right. It was his life.

Snatching up the bag of resin nearby on the mound, he dusted his hands together and tossed it back down. He tugged his ball cap again and shifted his weight. Then he wound up and fired another fastball straight down the pipe.

"*Strike two!*"

A grin split his face as the Phillies batter cursed, stepped out of the box, and stomped around. Finally he put a toe back in, dug deep into the dirt with his cleat, and did the same with the second one before pulling the bat into hitting position.

This was the way it was supposed to be. Just Peter and a batter and a strike zone that had his name written all over it. It was a mental battle of wits, calculation, and angles. And he loved it with everything he had. Nothing else in life compared or could make him feel the way playing ball did.

His gaze slid from home plate at that thought right on over to Leslie in the stands and his chest went tight again. That's right, he thought as he forced a deep breath, nothing compared. He didn't want it to. Too much commitment.

Peter played. He played ball and he played at life. That was just the way he liked it. No responsibilities. Who wanted them anyway? They were a huge bore.

This thing with Leslie was just physical anyway.

Pushing the thought aside, he wound up and was about to release when his gaze slipped to Leslie once more. Their eyes locked and he felt his body tense. An encouraging smile spread across her gorgeous face, stunning him, and his shoulder seized just as he released the ball.

He heard the pop and searing pain snaked down his arm, making his vision blur. Peter doubled over and grabbed at his shoulder, panic and pain lashing him. *Son of a bitch.*

His arm was jacked.

EVERYTHING INSIDE LESLIE froze and the smile melted from her face. As she watched, Peter crumpled on the pitcher's mound. Play stopped and the Rush's manager came running. She could have sworn the crowd collectively gasped when their beloved ace pitcher tried to move his shoulder and couldn't.

Shit.

Leslie was up and out of her seat before she'd even decided to stand, her heart pounding and fear turning her stomach to a jumble of knots. "Oh my god, Peter!" was all she said, and she began pushing her way through the seats full of spectators to get to him.

Lorelei grabbed her arm and stopped her. "Leslie, you can't go out there."

Swallowing panic, she glanced down at her sister-in-law and replied tersely, "That's a stupid rule. I'm breaking it."

The brunette smiled gently. "I know, honey. But look, the medics are already out there. He's going to be fine."

Bullshit. Peter didn't look fine. In fact he looked like he was in some serious pain. His face was pinched tight and he was scowling hot enough to scare the devil.

Charlie piped up from down the row, "Want me to see if I can get down there for you, Leslie? 'Cause I was a batboy. They'd let me in. I could check on him for you."

His freckled face was full of earnestness and he was swimming in his authentic Rush jersey. It carried JP's name and number on it and she could tell the boy was super proud of it. "That's sweet, Charlie."

She might have let him too, but then the medical team escorted Peter off the field to the sound of the crowd cheering him on. The pitcher was still holding his shoulder, but he let it go briefly to wave and smile to the crowd.

Knowing him, he was only doing it to save face. Because it hurt him like hell, she could see that. And it made her all kinds of upset.

Her mind made up, Leslie plopped back down in her seat with a huff. She'd give him twenty minutes and then she would try to make her way back to him. If she had to she'd use Charlie. Because she had to see him to make sure he was all right.

Kowalskin had had injuries before—many of which she'd witnessed. None of those had ever bothered her like this. For whatever reason this was different. And she really didn't want to think about why. All she wanted to do was get to him.

So even though anxiety had a tight hold around her neck, Leslie forced herself to breathe deeply. He was okay, she told herself. He was Peter Kowalskin, badass professional ballplayer. Of course he was okay.

Sonny turned to Leslie, her eyes the same shade as her son's. "Peter's a tough guy, sweetie. He'll be all right."

Lorelei spoke up, adding, "Yeah. Remember the time he tried to do a back flip off his diving board and slipped and whacked his head? We all thought he was seriously injured because of the blood, but he was totally fine. Not even a concussion. I bet this is the same thing."

Right. Okay, the pep talk was working. The panic was receding. "I'm sure y'all are right. I mean, it's not like he has ever been that careful with his body and he's made it this far."

Lorelei reached over and patted her knee reassuringly. "Absolutely. He's got a reckless streak, hon. I'm sure this isn't his first shoulder injury."

But it was the League Championships. What if his shoulder made him miss the World Series? He'd just told her how much he wanted to win it. If the Rush made it and he couldn't play, he was going to be so angry.

Play resumed on the field, relief pitcher José Caldera filled in for Peter, and the team smoothly earned three outs. It wasn't the same. Looking out there at Coors Field with all the Rush players moving about normally as they headed into their dugout, Leslie felt something missing.

That something was him. Kowalskin was the heart of the team.

What would they do without him?

"Hey Mom, look! JP's up to bat and I bet he hits one hard enough to make it to second." Charlie beamed at his mother. It was plain to anyone that he was happy as a clam to have JP in his life and that he was incredibly proud of the Rush's shortstop.

Leslie rolled her eyes. The boy was in the seat next to her and she leaned over, nudging him in the shoulder. "The guys haven't gotten you involved in their silly bets now, have they?" She'd seen more idiocy caused by their ten-dollar bets than in all the Jackass movies combined.

Charlie giggled and nudged her back. He was such a happy kid. "Nah. I just think JP's gonna hit a grounder to the outfield and he's so fast that he'll make second base before the Phillies can make the relay."

Her eyebrows shot up in surprise. For a ten-year-old he sure knew a lot about baseball. "You and JP been talking shop, kid?"

Sonny caught her eye over his blond head and nodded. "All the time." Then she pulled a face that made Leslie laugh.

Guys and sports. It was hopeless.

The easy chatter had lowered her anxiety level and the knots in her stomach had unwound some while she had talked to Charlie, which was probably for the best. She'd been on the verge of jumping the guardrail and running out onto the field.

Leslie kept up the small talk while anxiety buzzed

inside her, making her jumpy. She kept an eagle eye on the clock and when it hit the twenty-minute mark she stood up and excused herself.

"I've got to hit the restroom, y'all." Why she felt the need to keep her true destination a secret, she wasn't entirely sure. But the thought of admitting that she was going to find Peter because she was worried sick about him made her feel way too vulnerable. It was easier this way.

They all waved her off and she hit the steps, impatience making her hurry. Quickly making her way through the corridors of the clubhouse, she waved to security as they let her pass, the guards long familiar with her relationship to Mark. Soon she came to the training room and stopped short when she saw the door wide open. She could just make out Peter sitting with his back to her on a padded table. Medics surrounded him, asking him questions. When one of them grabbed his shoulder, rotating it gently and he flinched, her stomach went queasy. God, he must be in so much pain.

She was suddenly rooted to the spot. She cried out softly, her hand fisting against her mouth.

His head whipped around and pale blue eyes pegged her with a hard stare. "Why are you here?"

Leslie opened her mouth to speak, but couldn't around the sudden lump in her throat. Instead she swallowed hard, her eyes beginning to sting. He clearly didn't want her there, and it hurt. All she wanted was to offer him comfort. And here he was again, rejecting her.

One of the medics stepped in front of Peter and said,

"We need to get some x-rays on your shoulder to find out the extent of your injury."

He nodded, still staring down Leslie with distant eyes. "Fine."

She finally found her voice and said as she took a step closer bringing her flush with the doorway, "I came to make sure you're okay."

His jaw ticked. "I'm fine."

He didn't look fine. In fact he looked like he was about to pass out. "Can I do anything?" She had no clue what, but she wanted to do something to help him feel better. Why didn't he want her there?

Another medic walked over to the door and grabbed the handle. Peter flicked a glance at him before turning back to Leslie. "Yeah, you can go back down and watch the rest of the game. No reason for you to miss out. I'm good."

He'd mentioned that already. And she wasn't buying it now any more than she had thirty seconds ago. Why was he so insistent on being alone? It wasn't a bad thing to have people care about him, damn it. "Peter—," she started.

He cut her off with an order to the medic holding the door handle. "Shut it," he said flatly. The blasted man didn't even spare her a glance.

The door closed on her, leaving her staring at nothing but green metal, and her heart caught somewhere between worry and outrage.

It was so not a good feeling.

Chapter Eleven

THE HOUSE WAS dark and quiet when Leslie arrived home. It had been a hectic night at the club and her feet were ready to weep. All she wanted were her cushy slippers and to check in on Peter, although if he was still in a mood he wouldn't be happy about it. Though she'd texted him and tried to call after he'd kicked her out; he was either ignoring her or avoiding all calls in general.

Not that she could blame him, really. When she'd called Mark after the fifth time of trying to reach Peter, her brother shared that Peter had dislocated his shoulder. He wasn't going to need surgery and it wasn't that serious, but he was out for the rest of the League Championships. Probably the World Series, too, if they made it that far.

The news had no doubt put him in a sour mood.

Still it stung her to be ignored by him. He mattered to her more than she wanted him to. Whatever. Still, Peter not answering her texts or calls was frustrating. All she had been trying to do was see if he was okay. Just like back at the clubhouse.

Why did men do that? When they got upset, why did they go and hole up like badgers? Talking about feelings was a good thing.

Closing the door behind her, Leslie kicked off her heels and nearly groaned when her feet stretched out in relief. She really needed to find a better footwear alternative. Even if her shoes were damn sexy.

Scooping up the red heels by their ankle straps, she padded upstairs and felt the day's stress leave her body with every single step. It was amazing that his house could do that for her. Even her apartment—which she adored—didn't have the same energy. But Peter's house was almost as good for her as reggae.

Go figure.

During the drive home an early-season snow had started to fall gently, causing the temperatures to plummet. With that in mind she changed out of her work clothes and put on a pair of yoga pants and the Rush hoodie from earlier that day. Then she slid into her fuzzy slippers and headed back into the hall.

A light at the bottom of one of the doors drew her attention. At first she thought it was Peter's room, and then she realized that his was at the very end of the hall. She realized she'd never actually been inside it before. Maybe it was a bathroom?

Thinking that he must have left a light on, Leslie moved down the hall and quietly pushed the door open. Inside she found a library with music on softly and Peter in a chair with his back to her, sitting silently. He made no movement when she stepped inside, and she thought that maybe he'd fallen asleep there by accident.

Books lined built-in bookcases from floor to ceiling and wrapped all around the large space. Two oversized, comfortable-looking chairs sat in the center on a large taupe-colored rug. In the far corner was a cabinet with glass doors. Inside she could see a set of samurai swords covered in an exquisitely designed sheath. A half dozen ninja stars were displayed in there as well.

Leslie took another step into the room and froze when Peter let out a muffled sound and shifted in his chair. Then he started snoring softly, making her smile. Poor guy. The doctors had probably given him some potent painkillers.

Not worried now about startling him, Leslie relaxed and walked into the room, taking it in and narrowly avoided a large bamboo plant. It was so lush and full that it was like a small jungle in a pot. How did he keep it alive? She killed everything with leaves. The one in her office was sort-of-living proof.

Stopping in front of a bookcase, she noticed that although most of the shelves were crammed full of books there were a few decorative objects scattered about as well. Who'd have thought that the guy was into tchotchkes? One in particular caught her attention and she went to it, pulled like a boat to a lighthouse beacon.

How interesting, she thought as she looked at it, her fingers itching to pick it up. At first glance it was a small beautifully carved wooden seal, all glossy gray and plump. But when she leaned closer and squinted she could just see human features morphing its sweet face. What the—?

"It's a selkie."

Startled, Leslie spun around to find Peter looking at her with sleepy, slightly glassy eyes. "I didn't mean to wake you."

"It's all right," he mumbled, his voice gravelly from sleep and the pain meds.

He looked terrible. There were dark circles under his eyes and his skin was pale and drawn. Peter looked like a man in the middle of grieving, not one who'd simply been knocked out of the postseason.

Giving him a thorough once-over, she took in his navy blue basketball shorts and white Jimi Hendrix T-shirt, noting that he wasn't wearing a sling. "How are you feeling?" she asked. Even looking like hell he was still damn sexy. Soulful, edgy athlete. The mix was intoxicating.

Peter, still slouching in the chair, closed his eyes again and yawned. "Like shit."

"Yeah?" Her heart went out to him. Getting injured at this stage in the season just sucked.

He opened his right eye a crack and zeroed in on her. "Yeah."

Though she told herself to drop it, she blurted out anyway, "I tried to call you."

The pitcher just shrugged and then sucked in a breath sharply. Part of her felt bad for him. The other part, the part that was still miffed at her texts being ignored, didn't feel so bad.

"I didn't feel like talking, Leslie. It's been a pretty

crappy day for me if you haven't noticed." He stared at her, his eyes sulky and a little sad.

It made her feel bad. *All* of her. So she dropped it and changed the subject. "The selkie's an Irish creature-thing, right? Where'd you get it?" she inquired, pointing over her shoulder, a little surprised she knew what it was. Sometimes that jumble of random trivia in her brain actually was useful.

He rubbed a hand over his face, yawned again and began massaging the back of his neck. "I made it."

Surprise darted through her. "Really? When?" Since when did he carve wood? God, what else didn't she know about him?

"When I was sixteen. The selkie myth and her singing is all I remember of my mom." His expression clearly stated that he wasn't in the mood for small talk. But she thought it was touching and sweet that he'd carved and painted a seal to remind him of his Irish mother. And now she knew where he got his love of music too. It was probably the only good thing she'd given him, judging by what little of her he'd mentioned.

"Was whittling wood what you gave up bad poetry for?" she joked, hoping to get a smile from him. And it worked. It got a small lopsided one out of him. Good. Peter just wasn't himself without his devil-may-care smile. "I mean, I can see why. It's so much more manly than haiku."

"Yeah, that's when I started to get all the chicks. They couldn't resist my wood." Even though he was trying to make light, she could see the strain it put on him. His normally sparkling eyes were flat and a bit unfocused. Whether it was from the meds or whatever was eating at him she didn't know.

Still, she missed the sparkle. "Well sure. What girl could?"

"You."

Ouch. "Says who?" He was right but she was still trying to make him feel better. But he wasn't nearly as right as he thought he was.

He gestured to his lap, the movement slow and kind of sloppy from the painkillers, and her gaze went straight to his crotch. "It's all yours, princess."

"Tempting as that is, I'm going to have to pass." In the condition he was in right now he wouldn't be able to put it to good use anyway.

His head fell back against the padded chair. "See?" Peter sounded so dejected about it that she was swamped with sympathy. He'd had such a crummy day that she could at least throw him a bone.

The only light on was a floor lamp in the far corner. Leslie was on the other side from it in the shadows and took a step. Moving toward Peter intent on giving him a sound kiss to sooth his battered ego and body, she stepped next to him and stopped short when he jolted. "Damn, Leslie. I didn't see you. Why you gotta sneak up on me?"

His voice was getting all slurry and she could tell that he was getting sleepy again—but sneak? She hadn't done anything of the sort. She was five-ten and a solidly built, for crying out loud. Sneaking about wasn't in her vocabulary.

Brushing it off because his weird behavior was probably just a side effect of whatever the doctors had put him on, Leslie dropped a kiss on his scruffy cheek. "Next time I'll stomp like a herd of elephants. How's that sound?"

"Better," he muttered and she got sidetracked by the heat and masculine scent of him.

Desire began to stir inside her and she pulled back to put distance between them. Jumping him was the last thing he needed right now. What he needed was his bed and a whole lot of rest.

Thinking she should convince him to make his way to his bedroom so that he wouldn't fall asleep sitting up again, Leslie placed a hand gently on his uninjured arm and said, "Why don't you go to bed, darlin'? You look beat."

In the space of a heartbeat Peter rounded on her, reaching out with his good hand and snagging her around her waist. Before the squeal made it all the way out, he had her in his lap, his mouth fused to hers. And he had wood. Boy did he have wood. Her ass landed on it.

And she was right; it was irresistible to the girls.

Because he'd caught her off guard and her defenses were down, Leslie didn't have time to do anything more than react and feel. And good god he felt amazing. All hard, sculpted, lean muscles and hungry, turned-on man.

She couldn't get enough.

Falling into the kiss, she shifted in his lap and wrapped her arms around his neck. Opening to him, she moaned softly when his tongue rubbed against hers impatiently. As much as she knew she'd regret it later, there was no stopping. Something lightning hot and just as dangerous flashed between them.

It was incredible.

"Christ, woman," he growled when he broke the kiss. "Tell me you feel this." He fisted a hand into her straight blonde hair and held her captive. "I need to know you feel it too."

Of course she felt it too. Every single time they touched. It was electric. "I feel it, Peter," she whispered.

He groaned and his mouth was on her throat, devouring her, teeth nipping sharply. The shot of pain was quickly replaced by something a whole lot hotter, his tongue soothing the tender flesh. His agile mouth teased her sensitive skin, the feel of his stubble exquisite torment. She didn't want it to stop.

Running her hands through his thick, wavy hair, Leslie tipped her neck to the side to give him better access. His firm mouth was on her in an instant, his tongue tasting her there. She moaned and found his mouth with hers, opening greedily for him.

He shifted beneath her, his erection pushing into her ass. Groaning, Peter let go of her hair and his hand stroked boldly, possessively down her body until he found her full breasts and squeezed through her sweatshirt. She gasped and tore her mouth from his. "Oh God," she breathed, wanting more, wanting his hands all over her bare naked skin.

"Take it off," he demanded, his voice rough with arousal. "Take off your sweatshirt so I can see them."

Lost in the moment, Leslie ripped off her hoodie and

tossed it on the floor behind her. She shook back her hair and looked down into his face, desire pulsing heavy in her veins. Thick black hair had fallen over one of his brows and when she brushed it to the side his eyes fluttered closed for a second like her touch was something special and almost euphoric.

Then they opened again, crystalline pools of desire. His hand was on her waist and streaking over her back. When he came to her bra strap he grabbed it and flicked it open with one smooth movement, causing her breasts to spill free.

Damn. He had moves.

"Perfect," he whispered and slid a large, calloused hand up her rib cage until he was cupping her breast, his thumb flicking gently across her puckered nipple.

Leslie gasped.

"Yeah, you like that?" he asked and flicked his thumb over her sensitive peak once more.

It set her on fire. And it made her so, so wet. Even now she could feel moisture pooling between her thighs. "Yes," she said in a moan.

"Come here." His eyes were heavy-lidded with passion as he issued the command.

She leaned forward, breathing unevenly as lust permeated her body. There was no way she could have refused even if she wanted to. Her body craved his touch.

Peter's hand on her breast stopped teasing her as he softly kissed her neck. Against her ear he breathed in and whispered, "Your scent drives me crazy."

That was good to know. "Coconut?"

Warm, moist breath caressed her earlobe and a shiver ran down her spine. God, he had a mouth. Sensual and erotic and so very talented.

Peter gave the skin just beneath her ear a gentle open-mouthed kiss, his tongue tasting her, and she began to throb for him. "Yeah, coconut. It's in my dreams." His mouth trailed slowly over her jawbone and his voice became drowsy, "*You're* in my dreams." His hand stilled and his head fell back against the chair, his breathing slow and deep. He whispered roughly, "You haunt me."

Breath caught in her lungs. It couldn't be. "What?"

He started to snore.

Damn him for falling asleep.

Chapter Twelve

THE NEXT MORNING Peter was awake and downstairs before the sun had risen. His shoulder hurt like a son of a bitch and every time he bumped it searing pain dug into his flesh like a fire poker and poured down his arm. He had a massive headache.

And his life as he knew it was officially over. Way preterm. Well not that preterm, but before he made it to the World Series, and most definitely not by his decision.

He'd been forced into retirement early. And it sucked. It sucked because he'd wanted to end this thing on his terms, not have them dictated to him.

Kicking the refrigerator door closed angrily, Peter slapped the milk carton down on the counter and splashed drops all over some half-written sheet music. He swore and scrubbed a hand over his scruffy face. Why did life never go the fucking way he planned?

Everything, every single decision got derailed. It

never failed, which was why he had eventually given up making decisions altogether and learned to just go with the flow. Until his eye problem had gone and screwed it all up, forcing him to think about the future and make long-term plans. Who the hell wanted to do that?

Goddamn *Retinitus Pigmentosa*.

The genetic disease that was ruining his life and the selkie myth were the only things his mother had ever given him. *Thanks, Mom.*

Moody and in a foul disposition, Peter poured a glass of organic whole milk and downed it in one gulp. Then he refilled it and sat down at the kitchen table. The impact jarred his shoulder and he hissed. Great. Just frigging great.

Not only was his life over, but he had a painful reminder about it if he happened to forget. Not that there was much risk of that. No way.

Two more weeks. Why couldn't his shoulder have held out two more weeks? Then he could have taken the World Series by storm, earned his spot in the Hall of Fame, and retired quietly with that notch in his belt.

Peter scrubbed a hand over his face again and dislodged his eyeglasses, almost knocking them off and jamming the nosepiece into the corner of his eye. "Ouch. Shit." Stupid-ass glasses. He was still getting used to wearing them. He'd nearly taken out his eyeball.

Feeling cross, he righted the frames and muttered, "Not like my frigging eye is good for me now anyway."

Knowing that he was sinking deeper into a funk, Peter shoved away from the table, his full glass of milk forgotten. Being Irish and Ukrainian, he could get a damn fine brood on if he wanted to. It was in his genetic makeup to fall into a really dark hole of depression and stay there for a while.

He hated that about himself because it was just like his old man. At least he wasn't drowning his sorrows in Wild Turkey. That was something.

Emotions swirled inside him, growing bigger and more intense by the minute, and he knew that if he didn't find an outlet for it all very soon he would explode. Anger, despair, sadness, grief. All of it swirled in his gut like a hurricane, building momentum.

"Damn it!" Peter slammed his left hand on the table and scowled. He could feel the dark settling over him, into him. Whatever it was—his pop's legacy, his artistic temperament, or just plain emotional problems that caused this side of him to exist—he didn't care. All he knew was that it was like a black hole inside of him.

"I have to get a grip," he mumbled almost desperately. "For fuck's sake, it's just a sport."

Besides, he wasn't completely out, as much as his melodramatic side wanted to wail. There was still a chance of playing if they made it to the World Series and he took care of himself. The fat lady hadn't come out singing just yet. He had to remember that.

Bolstered a tiny bit by the thought, Peter went upstairs and quietly grabbed his guitar, hoping not to wake Leslie. His place was big enough that she wouldn't hear him play from down in the kitchen.

He needed his outlet.

Padding barefoot down the stairs, Peter noted that the sun was just starting to break the horizon, the blackness of night melting into the grays and shadows of pre-dawn.

Once he was back in the kitchen, he could see the few inches of snow on his back patio through the French doors. And it was still coming down. Squinting, Peter could just make out fat snowflakes as they drifted steadily to earth.

Normally the first snow of the season was a happy time for him. He loved it, and the way it made everything look clean and peaceful. Plus the whole world seemed to go quiet. That part he liked a whole lot.

But this morning the new snow didn't help his mood.

Sighing, Peter set his Gibson down next to him and raked a hand through his disheveled hair. Nothing was calming him because he'd never experienced this mixture of feelings before. He was standing on a precipice of a world completely unknown to him, and it was making him panicky.

Turned out that knowing he was going to have to stop playing ball soon and *actually* not playing were completely different things. The former he'd handled with finesse. The latter was making him a fucking mess. He felt ungrounded and directionless.

Grabbing his guitar, Peter went to the table and pulled out a chair. For the next hour or so he lost himself in his music, able to strum the instrument gently enough that his shoulder didn't object too terribly. And it helped. It helped a whole lot to find his center in something that he loved.

But he was still feeling moody when the phone rang at just past eight in the morning. Pinning the Gibson to him with his bum arm, Peter reached across the table and snagged his cell. "Hello?" he asked, wondering who could be calling him so early.

It was the doctor's office needing some more information for his upcoming surgery. Putting on his polite hat, he gave the nurse the requested information and asked a few questions about recovery time. Once he was reassured that it was only a few days and then he would feel back to normal, he was just about to hang up when Leslie came into the room.

She was rubbing her eyes and yawning like a sorority girl after her first frat-house party. Kind of looked like one, too, with her lopsided, messy ponytail and oversized sweatshirt. Except for the bangin' curves. That was all woman.

"Thanks, Joan," he said into the phone. "I'll swing by sometime this morning and get those forms signed." With that he hung up and took another good long look at Leslie.

"What's going on, Peter? I heard you talking about a surgery. Is your shoulder going to need it after all?" She had her head in a cupboard looking for coffee.

He hoped like hell not. The doc hadn't even wanted him to wear a sling. "Nope. Something else entirely. The shoulder's going to be right in no time." Maybe if he said that out loud enough it would come true. "I'll be back in action for the World Series, don't you worry."

She leaned out from behind the cupboard to smile at

him, and surprise overtook her gorgeous face. "You wear glasses."

He scrunched his nose and made a funny face, feeling a little embarrassed. She was the first to see him in them. "You got me."

Her smile cranked up a few degrees and went flirty. "Very nice."

Yeah? Huh. Maybe he'd keep them.

Leslie pulled out a bag of fair trade, whole bean Columbian and went about making her preferred morning drink. "How are you feeling this morning?"

"Fine." Not so much, really.

She slid him a look as she measured out water. "You were pretty loopy last night. Do you remember anything?"

His gaze locked with hers. Yeah, he remembered. He remembered every damn thing. Especially what he'd said to her and, he blamed it all on the Vicodin. It was the only explanation for why he'd say something so stupid.

But he wasn't going to let her know that he knew. Way too embarrassing.

He stared at her levelly. "Nope. Not a thing."

LESLIE HIT THE brew button on the coffee maker and glanced outside at the snow-covered backyard, soaking up the peaceful sight. She wasn't sure if she believed Peter or not. The unflinching way he was staring at her was misleading because she knew that he could play his cards really close to his chest. When he wanted to, he could make his eyes so cool and remote that it was jarring. Like he was this detached observer always watching. Whatever he actually felt was anyone's guess.

Still, she really wanted to know if he remembered what he'd said to her last night. Those words had kept her up tossing and turning far longer than she wanted to admit. "Really? You don't remember the selkie, the kissing?"

Something flickered in his guarded eyes, and she could tell by the way he shifted and began picking at his guitar that he did in fact remember something. "I recall something like that. But I'm lousy on pain meds, girl. My memory is fuzzy."

She cocked her head and studied him, noticing the strain on his lean and rugged face. His complexion was pale, too, and every once in a while he flinched when he moved his bad arm too much picking the strings.

"Are you on any now?" If he wasn't he should be.

"I've taken ibuprofen." His head was down and he was picking out a tune, humming along occasionally.

That's right. She'd forgotten his aversion to prescription meds. He never took more than was absolutely necessary. Which meant that he had been in some serious pain last night. Maybe he really didn't remember much of anything.

Leslie poured a cup of Columbia's fresh-brewed finest and added some organic half-and-half she'd found last week in the fridge. Though she very much appreciated the high-quality food he kept stocked in his kitchen, now she looked at it all a little differently, knowing how he'd grown up. It was no doubt compensation for the time he'd spent as a kid going hungry.

"Do you keep all this fancy food around because you didn't have much when you grew up?"

Peter turned his head slightly to look at her and her tongue stuck to the roof of her mouth at the sight of his amazing eyes framed by those black glasses. The man was so effortlessly sexy. It would be annoying if she didn't enjoy the view so much.

"I guess I never really thought about it, but yeah. You could say that, I suppose. I spent more than a few nights eating only a slice of cheap white bread because Pop had pissed all our money away on booze."

Because her heart was aching for the little boy with a crap-ass upbringing, she made a funny. "I've always thought your growth was stunted."

Humor sparked in his blue eyes and he let out a low laugh. "Not where it counts, princess."

She couldn't resist. "And where is that, Peter?"

He stopped strumming and pinned her with a look that went hot and a little hazy. "If you weren't so hell-bent on winning this bet you could come over here right now and find out." A slow, wicked smile upturned his incredible lips. "In fact, you could just come over here and find out, period."

It was tempting. Really, really tempting after last night. The way he'd made her feel without even trying still had her reeling. And the things he'd said . . . *whoa*.

She replied flippantly, "Or, you could simply agree to play at the club and we could forget this silly bet altogether."

The sun had made its final ascent into the sky, or at least Leslie assumed it had as she admired the view outside. Snow was still coming down steadily and the sky was heavy and overcast. She couldn't actually see the sun.

Turning back to Peter, she caught him staring at her with hard, unreadable eyes. "I don't play in public, Leslie."

"Then why did you even agree to the bet in the first place?" she asked, instantly frustrated and crossed her arms, still holding the coffee mug.

He went back to strumming his guitar, dismissing her, and it got her back up. "I knew I wouldn't lose."

Oh he did, did he? That capped it, now she was officially angry. He thought she was just that easy? "Wrong, Kowalskin. You're going to be performing, guaranteed."

A sound that was suspiciously like a snort of amusement came from him and she bit her tongue to keep from saying something mean that she'd regret later. "I don't think so."

A hard ball of mad formed in the pit of her stomach. She ignored the tiny skittering fear that said he might be right. "What the hell is your problem with playing guitar in public anyway?" she burst out, exasperated. Not liking to play in public was the same bullshit excuse he'd been telling her for two years and she was tired of it.

She wanted the real truth.

He stopped playing abruptly and hissed painfully when he jarred his shoulder. The glare he shot her was withering. "It's none of your goddamn business."

But it was her business if she was going to get her life back. "I deserve to know." Her hand shot to her hip and she took a sip of coffee as a way to direct and diffuse her energy. God, the man had a way of pissing her off like no one else.

"You don't deserve any such thing. But knowing you, you'll keep hounding me until I go insane, so fine, here's the truth: I won't play in public because it's very, very personal to me. It's mine, my heart, and I don't share it with random fucking people."

That shut her up. Briefly. "But you play all the time at barbeques and gatherings with the team."

She watched him grab his guitar and hold it to him like it was a shield for protection. "They're not random."

Leslie puffed out a breath, totally frustrated. The guy had an incredible talent. It deserved to be heard and seen. "This doesn't make any sense to me at all. You're a professional athlete. You play a game that entertains people. How is singing any different?"

He looked her dead in the eye. "It's my soul."

Her mouth opened and nothing came out. Snapping it shut, Leslie tried to think of something to say and came up blank. Mentally scrambling, she finally blurted, "You're willing to play at the club if you lose the bet to me, though. I don't understand. Why then did you agree?"

Peter stopped playing and stared her down with cold, remote eyes. "It's all about my dick, baby."

Chapter Thirteen

HE WAS SUCH an asshole.

Peter shoved his arm through his coat sleeve and swore when his shoulder objected painfully. He deserved it, though, for being such a prick to Leslie. For the rest of the day he'd felt like a douchebag for the crummy things he'd said to her. And all day he'd done his best to avoid his conscience, but to no avail.

Now here it was, pushing two in the morning on a snowy October night, and he was on his way to Hotbox to apologize to her. Apparently his conscience had decided that it couldn't wait one more hour until she was off work and back at his place. Which just figured. His inner good boy always had bad timing.

Hopping in his FJ Cruiser, Peter was one the road and pulling up in front of the nightclub less than twenty minutes later. From the outside the place wasn't much to look at, just a big square industrial brick warehouse. But on the inside was a whole different story. Since Leslie had taken over management it had changed a whole lot, going from a wreck to Denver's hotspot for killer live music. The woman had an ear on her and a way of showcasing unknown bands that went on to do big things eerily fast. It was one of her many gifts.

Peter knew that if she was so determined to put him in the spotlight, it meant he had something special too. And he thought it was great she felt that way about him.

Playing baseball was what he did and he was damn good at it. It was how he defined himself, how he saw himself. And he'd found a home with the Rush and loved being a part of such a close-knit team. They were all more like a big family—the only family he'd ever really known, honestly.

But music, music was *who* he was.

Whether he liked it about her or not, Leslie saw that truth in him. And she pushed. She pushed like a frigging bulldozer to get him to share it with the world at large, believing that it was his duty to share his gift with every-damn-body.

He completely disagreed. Writing songs, singing and playing his guitar—that was for *him*. So why he'd agreed to perform in her club specifically for the bet sure beat the hell out of him. He didn't even understand it, so how could he explain it to her when she'd asked?

He couldn't. But that didn't mean he had to be such an asshole about it. Then again, that was pretty much his M.O. Corner him and push him about his feelings and he lashed out verbally. It wasn't one of his more admirable traits. And given that he wasn't feeling too upbeat about the state of his life at the moment, put together the whole thing was a recipe for disaster.

Peter checked the time on his black leather bracelet, which doubled as a very discreet wristwatch. The bar was just closing. He'd thought he'd get there sooner, give himself a few minutes to prep. Crap.

Mario, the over-muscled bouncer, had just stepped out to lock the front door when Peter hailed him. "Hey, man. Can I get you to hold that for me?"

Catching sight of who was hollering, the enormous ex-bodyguard smiled and pushed the door back open. "For you I will, Pete. How's the shoulder?"

He stepped inside on the landing and replied, "It's been better."

Mario slapped him on the back with a smile and nearly sent him flying over the guardrail. "Recover fast, man. The Rush need you back yesterday."

Didn't have to tell him. "I'm working on it." From his perch on the raised landing, Peter surveyed the now empty place. "Is everyone already gone?"

The bouncer nodded. "Leslie's in her office, but everyone else just left. It went dead the last hour with the weather and she sent us all home. I was just locking up. What can I do for you?"

Peter shook his head, grateful that he'd indulged in an extra dose of ibuprofen earlier. The man was ridiculously large and his backslap had nearly dislocated his shoulder again. He probably thought he was being gentle too. "I'm good. I just came by to have a word with the boss lady."

Mario locked up the front and they climbed the steps down to the main floor of the building before making their way across the hardwood to the hall on the other side. Once there the bouncer continued toward her office. Peter stopped him. "Hey man, why don't you head on out? I'll see to it that Leslie gets to her car safely."

The bouncer cast a quick glance down the hall. "Sounds good." He smiled. "The lady won't be expecting me home early. This will be a nice surprise."

Mario wished him a good night and went out the back door, muttering with a frown, "I thought I'd already locked this." Peter waited until it shut behind him and then secured the latch, not wanting to be disturbed. He had some apologizing to do and didn't really want any witnesses. Or interruptions. But mostly witnesses.

Once that was done he turned toward the hall and was about to walk down it when he heard a shuffle and a noise coming from Leslie's office. What was that girl doing? Rearranging furniture?

Shrugging it off, he had just taken a step when he heard a muffled scream and something crash to the floor. His heart started pounding hard and something like fear lodged in his throat. "Leslie? Leslie, are you okay?"

Another crash came from her office and this time along with her scream he heard, "Stop it!"

He sprinted down the hall and slammed her door open in a heartbeat, his injured shoulder completely forgotten on the rush of fear and adrenaline. Inside he found Leslie sitting on the floor, a table lamp shattered next to her and her potted bamboo plant broken, dirt scattered everywhere.

And stumbling toward her with a crazed look in his eye was Seth.

Rage flooded Peter and he grabbed the bartender by the back of his shirt, bellowing as he yanked, "Don't you dare, motherfucker!"

Seth flew through the air, slammed into the wall, and Peter was on him instantly, ramming his fist into his face. Seth's nose shattered from the force of the blow and began bleeding profusely, but Peter didn't stop. He couldn't see beyond the red haze of fury.

"I just wanted to touch!" the bartender wailed and swiped at the blood pouring down over his lips, cradling his busted nose. "I love her!"

"You crazy bastard!" Leslie cried out as she scrambled to her feet. She was shaking, but he didn't think it was from fear.

Her eyes shot daggers at her employee and she ran toward him, clearly intent on doing bodily harm. Peter grabbed her around the waist and pulled her in tight, effectively stopping her. But she swung out a leg and almost connected with Seth. "How dare you come in drunk and cop a feel on me! You're not even allowed here after hours!"

With blood running between his fingers and down his arm, Seth looked up at them both with unexpected loathing. "You're a bitch."

Peter let go of Leslie and yanked Seth up by his collar, so full of white-hot fury he could barely see, and slammed his fist into his solar plexus. Seth doubled over, gasping for air, and just as Peter was going to punch him again, Leslie made a sound like a choked back sob.

He whipped his head around toward the sound to find her wiping at a cut on her hand, and the sight of her blood pushed him over the edge. He snapped. "How dare you touch my woman!" he shouted and spun back around.

Seth was gone.

His footsteps were fading quickly down the hallway. Then the back door creaked open and slammed shut. Fuck.

Peter was about to go after him when Leslie stopped him with a hand on his arm. Shaking, adrenaline and rage a thundering, furious concoction inside him, he looked up from her slender, bleeding hand. "I'm going to kill that son of a bitch."

"Let him go," she replied. "I'll call the cops and file a report. I've got all his information, Peter. They'll find him."

"Not if I find him first." He couldn't think. Couldn't reason. His blood was pumping and a primitive, primal need to protect her overrode all else.

Panting, Peter raked a hand through his hair, swore, and gave her a very thorough once-over. Other than the wound on her hand and messy hair she looked all right. Definitely less shaken up than him.

But her office was a mess. How much had happened before he'd arrived? "I hope you hit that bastard in the head with your broken lamp," he muttered, grabbing desperately for a measure of control.

Leslie smiled at him in a way that had the anger subsiding a little and said matter-of-factly, "He kept trying to grope me, so I threw it at him."

That's my girl.

"Then I slipped on some potting soil and fell on my ass. That's when you came in."

"Are you okay?" he asked, realizing the question was more than a smidge belated as his brain started functioning again. Not much, but enough to remember to ask.

"I'm okay." But she was looking around at the state of her office, frowning. He raised a hand and grabbed hers, held it still while he assessed the extent of her injury. It wasn't much of one, thank God. Just a small cut at the base of her left thumb. No doubt it'd been from the porcelain lamp shattering.

"I'm going to go double-check the lock on the back door and make that call," Leslie informed him, already striding out the door. And the sight of her ass all smeared with dirt had anger sizzling in his gut like acid.

Stomping after her, Peter was at a slow boil the whole time she made her report. When she refused to have an officer come to the club for her statement he scowled at her. She just held up a finger, giving him the signal to wait, and finished the phone call, providing her statement by phone.

When Leslie hung up, she put the cordless phone back in its cradle behind the bar and said, "An officer will get back to me tomorrow for a follow-up, but they have all they need now to find Seth."

"Good." A tick started in his jaw.

She leaned her elbows on the bar and cocked her head to the side, looking at him with her gorgeous hazel eyes. All he saw was messy hair and her dabbing at the cut on her hand with a bar towel. "Are you all right, Peter? You went after Seth hard and I'm worried about your shoulder."

He didn't feel any pain. "I'm fine."

But he wasn't fine and she knew it. "You're not moving your arm."

Peter glanced at his shoulder, shrugged. "It'll hurt like a bitch tomorrow, but it's fine. Felt good shattering the fucker's nose."

"Thank you for doing that."

For some reason her gratitude pissed him off and he rounded on her. "What the hell was he doing in your office after hours in the first place?" The answer had better be nothing.

Watching him with what looked like caution in her eyes, Leslie answered softly, "Not what you think, Peter. He'd already been sent home for the night, along with the rest of the crew because of the snow. I was shutting down my computer when he came in reeking of whiskey and stumbled into my bamboo plant, knocking it to the floor. Then he tried to get handsy with me."

So the little bastard had needed liquor to bolster his courage to try and grope her? Shit, Peter had to find him now for another sound beating, Philly-style. This was beyond not okay.

Emotions churned in his gut, hot and greasy. The events of the past few days piled up, one on top of the other, and Peter swallowed around the ball of anger that lodged in his throat. Everything was falling apart. His whole goddamn life was upside-down and he didn't know what to do about it. He didn't know what to do with *himself.*

All he knew was that if something didn't change soon he was going to explode.

Leslie rounded the bar and came to stand in front of him, her back to the glossy mahogany counter. "I should have been more careful, I suppose. But I swear to you I didn't see it coming. Not from him. He seemed innocent and sweet. Dumb, but completely harmless."

The fact that she could even say that with sincerity after the asshole had tried to touch her breasts only succeeded in riling him up all over again and he whipped out a hand, grabbing a strand of her disheveled hair. "Right," he scoffed, "he was completely harmless."

She stilled and narrowed her eyes on him. "What's going on with you? Are you okay?"

For whatever reason that question pushed him over the edge. Didn't she understand the gravity of the situation at all?

Dropping the strand of hair like it was scalding hot, Peter took a step away and rounded on her, the dark emotional vortex sucking him in, and he yelled, "No I'm not okay! Christ, Leslie. How could I possibly be okay?"

She crossed her arms over her chest and leaned against the bar. For a woman who'd just been almost assaulted she seemed too damn calm for his liking. "What is it, Peter? Tell me."

He was swallowed by the tide of emotions and couldn't think. It was too much. Everything. Just too fucking much. "I can't tell you!"

Her head tipped to the side and she looked at him with sympathy. "You don't know what's wrong?"

Of course he knew what was wrong, he just wasn't going to tell her. His life as he knew it was over, he was going blind in one eye, and the woman of his dreams was standing before him with a cut hand because somebody had almost hurt her. It brought out every frigging primal instinct in him. All he wanted to do was punch something. Again and again until this claustrophobic, choking feeling left him. "No," was all he said, hoping frantically that she'd drop it.

But she didn't. Of course she didn't. It was Leslie.

She stood her ground, looked at him searchingly, and said quietly, "You called me your woman."

Denial cut through him like a hacksaw. "No I didn't." She wasn't his woman. She didn't want to be.

Peter tried desperately to reel his emotions back in, but when she touched his chin, he teetered on the edge of coming completely unglued. That hadn't happened to him since he'd come to blows with his old man after he'd told him he was going to play ball. Viktor Kowalskin had slapped him in the face for trying to be something special.

Soft, slender fingers of steel gripped his chin and Leslie forced him to look at her. "You did too, Peter, and I think we should talk about it."

"Why?" It wasn't worth the air it'd take. "I was angry. It didn't mean anything."

"Oh really?" she challenged and took another step closer to him. Now her body was brushing against his and he felt the crackle of electricity. "Prove it."

He tried to shove her hand away, but she was strong and held steady. "How?" His gut was still swirling and he didn't trust himself to do whatever she wanted gently. No matter how far he'd come from his days in South Philly, at his core he was still a fighter—a tough-as-nails, rough-around-the-edges, raw, unfiltered son of immigrants who didn't know a fucking thing about tenderness.

"Kiss me."

"No," he said a harshly, about to come unhinged. Christ, he didn't want to hurt her.

Leslie stared him down with challenge in her eyes. "Do it, Peter. Or I will."

Dear God, forgive him for what he was about to do.

Peter grabbed her around the waist and shoved her roughly against the bar, his mouth covering hers possessively.

He came unleashed.

Chapter Fourteen

LESLIE GASPED, COMPLETELY taken by surprise. *Oh my*, she thought with a feminine thrill, *I've never seen that look in his eye*. It was wild and dangerous and hot. So very, very hot.

Her back slammed into the bar and just as pain started to register, Peter's mouth was on hers and she only felt one thing: *need*. Raw, undiluted need. And she went wet and throbbing so fast it made her dizzy.

Ripping her mouth from his on a moan, she gulped for air and tried to grab for some measure of control. But he wasn't having it. His fingers dug into her hips hard and he yanked her to him, thrusting into her at the same time.

"More," Peter growled, and he took her mouth in a punishing kiss.

Lust rushed off him and slammed into her making her knees weak. And when one of his hands streaked up under her shirt to cover her breast, his fingers pinching her nipple sharply, she was so turned on that she groaned into his mouth helplessly. It was exquisite torture and Leslie never wanted it to stop.

Peter ground against her, his erection rubbing her where she ached for him most. And it felt amazing. Like nothing she'd ever experienced before. Every nerve was alive and humming, tuned to only his frequency, eager and hungry for all of him.

Her hands released the bar ledge and stroked boldly over his body, Peter's dark passion pulling her under with every thrust of his powerful hips. She wanted it, could feel the hunger building inside, and she dug her nails into his back.

Peter yanked back and swore, his eyes electric with desire. "Now," he demanded roughly. "I want my mouth on you now."

Leslie dug her hands into the thick wavy mass of his hair, breathing heavily, and felt moisture pool between her legs when he rolled her nipples between his fingers and bit her neck, whispering hotly, "I need to taste your pussy."

Yes, please.

His hand left her breast and stroked down her body until he came to the waistband of her jeans. Then with one hand he worked the button free, lowered the zipper, and shoved his hand inside. He didn't stop until he'd found her curls and slipped a finger between her slick and swollen lips.

They both groaned.

Peter's finger covered her clit expertly, circled for a moment, and then moved lower until he discovered her entrance and filled her. She was on fire. As he stroked her, his thick, long fingers rubbing against her G-spot erotically, she felt the rush of her orgasm begin to build.

"Oh my God, Peter!" she cried and her hands went limp on his shoulders.

Giving her open-mouthed kisses on her neck that were all lust and no tenderness, he nipped the sensitive skin just below her ear and demanded, "Come for me."

Opening her mouth to speak, Leslie couldn't say a word, only moaned in building ecstasy. But she wanted to come for him like she wanted to breathe. It was all instinct.

Peter's mouth covered hers again just as he began rubbing her clit, the movement sure and commanding. And the orgasm tore through her, ripping a groan from her chest.

Panting hard, Leslie pulled back to look at Peter and shivered deliciously. He was unchecked passion. His eyes were glassy with it. And when he focused on her, she felt the intensity of his desire slam into her and her knees buckled beneath her.

Grabbing her, Peter shook his head and growled, "Oh no you don't. I'm not through with you." Then he lifted her up onto to the bar and pushed her onto her back, yanking off her jeans at the same time.

"What are you doing?" Leslie panted, lost in a sea of the most intense arousal she'd ever felt.

Peter shoved her legs apart roughly and made a sound in his chest that was more animal than man.

"I need more of you."

And then his mouth was on her pussy and his tongue was licking her boldly, possessively, pushing her right into another orgasm.

Leslie cried out as she came against his mouth. "Peter!" Her legs trembled and she couldn't think. All she could do was lay there and let the wildest, most intense man alive take her over the edge as many times as he wanted.

"Do you think about this?" he asked roughly, a finger sliding back into her slick folds, making her suck in a breath. "Do you picture me doing this to you?"

"Yes," she replied when she could find her voice.

"What about this?" His tongue stroked over her possessively from his finger to her clit.

Her head fell back on the bar and she raised a leg, put it over his shoulder. "Yes," she nearly whimpered.

God help her, but she loved what he was doing to her.

Peter rose up enough to look into her face, his own face set in hard lines and his eyes darkly erotic. "Good. I do too."

Then he put his mouth on her again, sucking gently while his tongue flicked over her sensitive peak and his finger stroked inside her. And she came so hard it brought tears to her eyes.

"Look at me," he said, his breathing labored and unsteady.

She was floating so high it took an immense amount of energy to lift her head up to look at him. Finally she managed and said breathlessly, "I'm looking."

"Tell me you want me. That you need to feel me inside

you." It was a demand, his eyes blue fire. Energy poured off of him in intense, reckless waves and her lower belly quivered—in both feminine fear and excitement.

She didn't even try to lie. "You know I do." Then she added in a daze, "You're amazing."

Peter froze. "What did you just say?"

Her head lowered back down. "I said you're amazing."

His hands flexed and squeezed her legs briefly, painfully. Then his eyes shuttered. "Right. You've said that before."

He dropped a kiss on her bare thigh and stepped away, the sudden cold air making her miss the heat of him. "Now we're even."

Her brain fuzzy from the onslaught of hormones, Leslie frowned up at him and said, "What?"

"That's four."

And then he stalked away, leaving her sprawled across the bar top half-naked with rug burn on her inner thighs.

"How could you leave me like that?" Leslie demanded the minute she entered Peter's house. To leave her on the bar feeling vulnerable like that. *Ugh!* How dare he do that to her? And *then* he'd had the gall to stand outside, looking all dark and sulky under the streetlight while he'd watched her climb inside her car and lock the door.

That was the second time he'd pulled a stunt like that. It was also the second time he'd left her hanging and she was so beyond pissed about it that she could scream. Really, really loud.

And she almost did when he didn't respond right away.

"Kowalskin!" He'd better be ready to grovel like a beggar. "I know you're here." His annoying yellow Suck-U-V was in the garage.

Nothing.

Not a peep came from anywhere inside the big house. Leslie flipped on a light and scanned the two-story entryway and sunken living room for signs of the jerk. She couldn't believe he was hiding.

Was it possible he'd fallen asleep in the few minutes he'd had before she'd arrived behind him?

"No way," she muttered under her breath. Not unless he was her Grandpa George. That man could fall asleep faster than she could blink. And he did it with his eyes open, which was just way creepy.

As each minute ticked by and she didn't hear anything coming from upstairs, Leslie's temper began to deflate. *Why does he do this to me?* She wondered. *He's so frigging hot and cold.*

It was absolutely infuriating.

If she was also a little mad because of just how quickly her convictions about rebuilding her career had imploded as soon as his hands were all over her, well, she was willing to blame that on him too.

Rational or not, Leslie really didn't care. This was the second time he'd brought her to another world and then left her to come crashing back to earth alone, vulnerable and insecure. The two emotions she hated most. They left her exposed and weak and she just couldn't deal with feeling that way. Especially over a man. So yes, she was willing to suspend fairness and hang it all on him.

"*Peter!*" Something almost like paranoia crept into her stomach and dispersed all through her, sending her nerves pinging. Because of him she had almost thrown her one chance at professional redemption away, and she was terrified. Terrified deep down because she knew what it meant.

It meant one of two things. Either she wasn't nearly as committed to rebuilding her life as she thought she was, or she was willing to throw it all away over Peter because he had a hold on her. The first one she was pretty sure was wrong because every time she thought about giving in to temptation and sleeping with Peter—when she was clear-headed and not strung out on his pheromones—a wall of determination deflected the idea before it could so much as gain a toehold.

The second one was the one that was making her hyperventilate.

How could she possibly have feelings for a man who didn't even really want her? Self-loathing cut into her. God, wouldn't that be just like her though? To go and fall for a man who was wrong for her in every possible way? One who, when it came right down to the bottom line, just plain didn't want her enough? It would be right in line with her history.

At least he couldn't knock her up and then run off to join the military. That was a step up. Maybe there was hope for her after all.

She shook her head, cynicism boring through her like a termite on rotten wood, and snarled, *No, not really.*

A shuffle and a thump sounded from up the stairs, turning her pent-up frustration from herself onto Peter.

There he was. Now they were going to have it out, whether he wanted to or not. There were things she needed to say.

Leslie kicked off her heels and moved to the stairs, her focus solely on getting to the man causing her so much anguish. One of them landed down the stairs on the living room carpet by the gray chenille sectional. The other flew off somewhere down the hall toward the kitchen.

Taking the stairs two at a time, she hit the landing, marched directly down to his bedroom, and flung the door wide open without even knocking. "We're going to get a few things straight right now, Kowalskin—" she started and then her vision was suddenly full of wet, naked Peter.

"Damn it, Leslie." He scowled and reached for the towel he'd tossed on the bed, wrapped it around his waist. "Don't you knock?"

No, obviously. Otherwise she wouldn't have just caught an eyeful of the man's penis. Her inner muscles squeezed with instant and alarmingly potent need. "You bailed on me," she accused, ignoring the sensation. Vulnerability and insecurity rose inside her again and she crossed her arms protectively.

"Yeah, sorry about that, but I needed air." The jerk tucked a corner of the towel in at his waist, securing privacy for his personal bits and tossed her a calculated smile. He was trying hard to act nonchalant, but his eyes were coldly distant and she knew that meant he wasn't really nonchalant at all. Oh no, she knew him well enough by now to know that it actually meant deep down he was boiling.

Fine with her. She was pretty frigging steamed herself. "I want an explanation."

"For what?" He gave that raised eyebrow look of his, and it just wasn't fair at all that she responded to it even though she wanted to kick him in the shins.

Like he didn't know what she was talking about. He was smart as a whip and knew full well what she wanted him to tell her. He just refused to share any tiny little personal feeling he might have. It might make him human like the rest of them if he did. Heaven forbid.

Water dripped from his jet-black hair and fell in droplets down the flat corrugated expanse of his stomach. A black happy trail disappeared beneath the fluffy white cotton and, as she'd just seen, ended in a patch of curly hair that surrounded a very impressive package. She wished it were teeny. Then she wouldn't be so wound up over it.

Probably.

They stood across the room from each other, staring hard and not speaking. Finally Leslie braced her legs apart like she was preparing for battle and tipped her chin. "I need to know why, Peter."

He raked his good hand through his dripping hair and his sculpted bicep flexed, displaying his yin-yang dragon to perfection. And she had a flashback of sinking her teeth into it when he'd wrapped that arm around her neck from behind and made her come so hard she'd forgotten her own name. Damn him.

"I needed space." His profile was to her as he rummaged around in a drawer.

"That's not what I'm talking about and you know it." He was just being his normal stubborn self and it made her jaw clench.

"I don't know what you're talking about."

"You do, too," she said and rocked forward a bit onto the balls of her feet like a boxer preparing for an attack, fisting her hands at her side.

While she stood there he flicked a cold gaze toward her and then dropped his towel, going full nude once again in front of her. This time she kept her eyes up. Right where they wouldn't get her into trouble.

"I'm afraid you'll have to be more specific, princess. It's been a real shitty day. I'm tired and my shoulder's hurting like hell, so I'm not really in the mood to play mind games." The muscles in his back flexed as he bent over to pull on a pair of boxers. As soon as she heard the band on them snap into place her gaze plummeted until she was staring at the front buttons on his blue plaid boxers. And as she stared those buttons started to move, his erection growing with every heartbeat her gaze was locked on it.

Shaking her head none too gently, Leslie forced her gaze back up and replied flatly, "I want an explanation for that night in Miami. It's time you came clean with me about what happened. Because I don't get it and I'm tired of wondering."

Peter shrugged his broad shoulders and sat on the edge of the bed, the front slit of his boxers gaping a little. She pretended not to notice. "What's there to get?"

Oh, like he didn't know. Was he going to make her

spell it out for him? Why? It was already humiliating enough.

"Why you got all heavy with me and then you dropped me dead like a hot potato." She thought about it for a second and then added, getting worked up all over again, "And why in the *hell* you want another go at me when you clearly don't even want to have sex with me!" At this point it wasn't just a matter of pride, her self-confidence was at stake too.

"I *don't* want to have sex with you? Is that what you think?" He gestured to his lap where his hard-on was obvious. "What's this about, then? The breeze?"

Frustration and self-doubt mixed together, making her shaky, and she raked her hands through her hair, fisting them there. "I don't know! You tell me, Peter. What *is* it about?" She dropped her hands and leveled him with a hard stare. "Do you, or don't you want me?"

It was time for an honest answer from the king of bullshitters. Whatever the answer, no matter how much it hurt, Leslie needed the truth. The not knowing had eaten at her for far too long.

Peter let out a long-suffering sigh and stared her down, eyes guarded and sulky. Then something flickered in them and he broke eye contact. He seemed to deflate, the fight going out of him in one breath. "I want you," he finally admitted begrudgingly, his voice hoarse and more than a little tired.

Tears stung the back of her eyes and a sudden lump in her throat made it hard to swallow. "Why?" she whispered raggedly. "Why then didn't you want to have sex with me?" Her hands waffled helplessly. "Why didn't you want *me*?"

He scrubbed both hands over his face, suddenly looking exhausted, and turned to her, his eyes bleak. "Because I choked, Leslie. I fucking choked, okay?"

"No."

Peter frowned hotly. "What do you mean, 'no'?"

Leslie crossed her arms again, scowled right back. "I mean that I don't accept your explanation. Not anymore."

He cocked his head to the side. "And why exactly is that?"

The anger she'd held at bay for three years over his rejection came flooding out. "Because it's all horseshit, Peter!" Her heart began pounding furiously. "You saying that you choked is a complete cop-out."

His black brows slashed dangerously low over his eyes. "It's not a cop-out."

She uncrossed her arms and planted her hands on her hips, her gaze locked on him. "Oh, *really*? Then just what the hell do you call it then?"

He gave her a level look. "The truth."

God he was frustrating! "Stop doing that."

"Doing what?"

He knew damn good and well what. "Stop evading! I deserve your honesty, Peter. Yeah, okay, you choked. Whatever." She waved a hand before pointing her index finger at her chest. "*I* want to know why, and I'm not leaving your bedroom until you tell me."

Abruptly he stood up and paced across the room. Once he reached the door to his bathroom he spun on her, his eyes filled with anguish, and shouted, "Because you acted like I meant something!"

Leslie reeled back. "Excuse me?"

Peter raked his hands through his hair. "You told me I was amazing."

"Yeah, so?" She'd said the same thing to him at the bar an hour ago.

Wait.

"Is that why you left me at the club tonight?" She was trying hard to understand. What was wrong with someone thinking he was wonderful?

"Yeah."

She huffed, confused. "But why?"

Something indefinable flashed in his eyes, but it looked a whole lot like pain and it made her heart squeeze. "Because I'm a lot of things, princess, but amazing isn't one of them. It would be in your best interest to accept that."

Chapter Fifteen

DAYS PASSED BY in a blur while Leslie prepared for the Halloween party, dealt with the police about Seth, and generally did her best to avoid Peter. Her apartment still wasn't ready, so she was spending a lot of quality time in her office making nice with her purple couch. It was better than being at Peter's place.

Now, stepping out into Peter's garage with her hands full, she thought about how they'd barely spoken since the night she'd made him come clean about Miami. Neither of them was in any particular hurry to broach the topic again, and she wasn't willing to risk something physical happening, so they steered clear of each other. It helped a lot that Peter was away with the team while they won the League Championships and moved on to the World Series.

Everyone was super stoked. And she could feel the excitement, shared it even. It would be absolutely wonderful if the Rush took the Fall Classic. They were doing great so it was a real possibility.

Peter's arm was recovering well and with a little luck he might even be able to play in the World Series before it was over after all. Which she thought was great and wanted to tell him, but after the way they'd parted company, she wasn't really sure what to say.

Everything she'd thought about that night in Miami was bogus. Peter hadn't lost interest. Knowing that had all kinds of complicated emotions coursing through her.

It changed everything.

For the past three years she'd felt so much self-doubt around the pitcher. Her confidence had suffered, her belief in her sexual appeal had been bruised and battered. That night had so much more of an impact on how she felt about herself than she wanted to admit.

And now that she knew the truth, she felt free.

Irritated that one man's confession meant so damn much, but still free. Lighter, like a weight had been lifted from her shoulders. Sure there was that whole having-to-deal-with-him-now thing, but she'd get around to it when she was good and ready.

Right now her favorite holiday was just around the corner, and that meant she was only days away from reclaiming her life. There was no way she was going to cave and sleep with Peter with the end of the bet so close. No way, no how. She already had a spreadsheet on her computer full of contacts and ideas on how to promote the crap out of the Rush's all-star pitcher playing at Hotbox.

She could see exactly how to promote it, the angle to use and the people to utilize.

It was going to be spectacular.

If she'd had the idea of jumping him like a trampoline the day after the bet ended, well that was her secret. So was the fact that thoughts of *what if* had drifted across her mind once or twice, or maybe a dozen times.

Her phone rang and she snatched it up, answering as she climbed into her Mini. She set the gift bag she was carrying on the passenger seat and said into the speaker, "Leslie Cutter."

"Hey, sis. Lorelei wanted me to call and double-check that you had the correct directions to our place. She wasn't sure, but she thought that she might have written it down wrong for you." Her brother sounded happy and that made her heart smile. He and Lorelei were having a housewarming party to celebrate their new home.

"I think I remember how to get there on my own, actually. Lorelei took me there a few weeks ago right after y'all had closed on it, remember? But here, hold on a minute and I'll read them off to you." Leslie rifled through her oversized hobo purse and found the scrap of paper the directions were scribbled on.

She relayed the directions quickly and Mark replied, "You got it!"

Well, sure. Women actually knew how to copy down directions. They didn't just set off into the great unknown hell-bent on figuring it out for themselves using the sun and a piece of string as guides.

One time back in high school, she and Mark had

wound up lost and out of gas in Florida's backwoods in their dad's old Buick. All because Mark had insisted that he knew the way to Tammy Lynette's pig farm where there was a kegger waiting and had refused to stop and ask for directions when all the gravel roads had started to look the same.

They slept in the Buick that night and woke the next morning to the greeting of a six-foot snake on the hood of their car and had two very irate parents when they got home.

Leslie shook her head, amused now at the memory. "I'm just leaving Peter's place, so I should be there in forty-five minutes or so."

Mark grunted. It was his non-verbal form of *gotcha*. "See you soon."

She started the car and pulled on her seatbelt. "Yeah."

About to hang up, she stopped when Mark asked, "So how is Peter treating you since you've been staying at his place?"

Um . . . "He's been great."

Mark's voice took on a tone that meant he didn't believe her. "What's going on? Is he giving you a hard time?"

She snorted. She couldn't help it. *Hard time.*

Leslie wished he was giving her a hard time. *After* she won the bet. "No, he's been great."

Her brother seemed to relax and his voice became less sharp. "Okay. Let me know if he steps out of line though, you hear?"

"I'm a grown woman. I can handle my own life." Her conscience nipped at her, pointing out that given her current situation it wasn't so apparent that she could handle it. And *then* it said that she was only in her current situation because her life had been soundly ruined in the first place. She wanted to smack her stupid conscience for reminding her.

He must have heard the mounting tension in her voice because he replied, "I know. It's just that I know Pete too."

"I hear you. Thanks for the concern, but I'll be fine." It felt good to know that somebody cared.

She and Mark talked for another minute as she backed out of the garage and pulled onto the road. Then they hung up and she was left with a quiet, cozy car and the open road. For the next half hour she cruised out of Denver and then hopped on Highway 287, which would take her the rest of the way to Lafayette, where Mark and Lorelei now resided.

Just north of the town, tons of open land sprawled, with the Rockies standing sentry to the West. It was beautiful, all the gently rolling hills. She could see why they'd fallen in love with the location. So much breathing room.

Coming to her turnoff, Leslie slowed her Mini and whipped around the turn, grinning. Her baby cornered like a golf cart. Slinging it around corners was just so much fun.

Slowing as another smaller, tighter turn appeared before her, Leslie scanned the directions again very briefly and took the hard left. Alpine Road. She'd found it. Downshifting, she took that corner at a conservative speed and smiled happily as she passed a pasture full of horses.

Leslie turned down the gravel road to her brother's new place, enjoying the way the house came into view through the trees, their bold autumn colors framing the huge farmhouse beautifully. About twenty or so cars were already parked here and there, most just pulled off into the grass by the side of the drive. Scanning the vehicles, Leslie released a tense breath, unaware that she'd even been holding it.

There was no yellow FJ Cruiser.

Trying to ignore the relief that coursed through her, because if she acknowledged it, it would mean that there was something she had been stressing about, Leslie found a place to park in front of a big, old-fashioned red barn. She grinned and felt warm fuzzies fill her when a small, fluffy, white-and-gray kitten waddled out of the cracked-open door and meowed at her. Instantly in love, she climbed out and grabbed the gift bag, eyes locked on the furry little heart-stealer.

"What's your name, sweetie?" she crooned and crouched down, crooking her finger at the kitten.

The fat little thing let out a tiny cry and hurried over to her, obviously a little lonely and in need of some affection. "You've found the right girl," she said and ran a finger down the kitten's downy-soft head.

She was so completely, hopelessly infatuated with her new acquaintance that she didn't hear the door to the barn creak open. She was lost in the feel of the kitten's soft, round belly as she gave it a good rub, so she jumped when a boy's voice cut through her bubble of love. "Isn't she the most adorable kitten ever in the whole entire world?"

It was Charlie, in a gray hoodie and jeans.

"I saw that somebody had put out a ton of food for them. There's two more inside, but they're still scared and hiding behind the hay bales." Sweet, blue eyes turned to her and Charlie bent his head to the side and asked, "Do you want one of them? Lorelei said that I could have one if Mom agrees, and I bet she'd give you one too if you want."

"No thanks," she said instantly. When would she have time to take care of a kitten? Her life was so busy as it was. "Oh don't you look at me like that, missy," she chided down at the kitten, feeling guilty. What was the use?

She was such a sucker. Little miss was going home with her. The decision made, Leslie gently set the kitten on the ground and stood up. Then she grabbed the gift bag full of baking goodies for Lorelei and said, "Let's leave them for now and we'll come back later. How's that sound, Charlie?"

The boy gave her a sunny smile and nodded, his blue eyes sparkling. "I knew you couldn't resist."

It was the story of her life.

Charlie put his kitten down on the ground next to hers and wiped his hands on the front of his jeans. "Wanna go inside?" he asked, his gaze turning to the big blue-gray two-story house with the wraparound porch.

She tossed her arm over his shoulders and replied, "Sure, kid. Let's go see if there's anything good to eat."

Mark had promised to grill up a couple tri-tips and she had a hankering.

He grinned up at her happily. "My mom made her homemade apple pie. It's world famous."

Leslie felt her stomach growl and said, "Sounds awesome."

They had just stepped across the gravel drive to the huge expanse of front lawn when the sound of a vehicle grabbed their attention. They turned around together to look, her arm still slung over the kids' shoulder and her smile froze on her lips.

Coming down the drive, making its way toward them, was a bright yellow FJ Cruiser. Fantastic. Awesome.

Crap.

Peter had arrived.

Chapter Sixteen

PETER STEERED HIS SUV around the bend, enjoying the view until he spotted Leslie on the front lawn. Then his smile of appreciation turned into a frown and his good mood immediately plummeted. Now that he knew that *she* knew the whole sordid truth, he'd avoided her to the best of his ability, bet be damned.

Humiliation, embarrassment, a slap to his manhood—call it whatever, he didn't care. He felt unmanned. Like he'd plucked off his balls and just handed them to her with a big dumb frigging smile on his face. *Here you go, sweets. Why don't you just keep those for a while? I don't need 'em.*

What kind of dumb-shit guy couldn't do the nasty when he had the hottest woman on the planet naked and begging for it underneath him? It still grated. After all these years it grated every frigging bit as much as it did the night the whole damn thing had happened.

She was his fantasy. He just didn't get it. It should have gone down in the record books as the best night of his life, not the most degrading.

Peter climbed out of his Cruiser just in time to see Leslie turn with Charlie and walk up the front steps into the house. Which was just fine with him. He'd rather not have to talk to her until he'd regained some shred of masculinity back.

Carl Brexler and José Caldera came around the side of the house just then carrying a Wiffle bat and ball. When they spotted Peter, Carl hollered, "Hey, Walskie. You up for a game of Wiffle ball? Mark's got a diamond set up out back and a bunch of us are playing."

Sounded fun, like a great way to keep up this whole *avoiding Leslie* thing he had going.

"I'm in. Just let me take this inside." He held up the bamboo plant he was carrying. He'd brought it for the new homeowners because it was supposed to bring good luck. "Who's manning the grill today?"

Usually get-togethers like this happened at his place, and he got to put on his chef's hat and play grill-master. It was kind of his thing. The last two soirees had been way memorable though, and not in the best way. There'd been more drama than a Greek play. He'd been thinking that he should maybe lay off the party-hosting for a while, so this was great.

But it was a bummer about the steaks. Considering that grilling meat over an open flame while he nursed a brewskie was the only thing he could do in the kitchen realm with any measure of success, he tended to take his duties seriously. He had the apron and everything to prove it. If it happened to have a crude slogan about cooking his meat on it with a highly inappropriate image, so what? He was the master.

Climbing the wraparound porch, Peter opened the door and stepped inside. Players and their families milled about the spacious, traditional farmhouse with moving boxes piled high in the corners. He stopped in the entryway, took off his coat, and hung it on the coat rack.

Mark walked by just then from the half-unpacked living room, carrying a baseball mitt in his hand, and grinned when he spotted Peter. "Welcome to my new pad, man. Give me a few minutes and I'll take you on the official tour. Paulson is whining about his hands like a girl so I'm gonna run this out to him. I'll be right back." He took two steps and stopped, glanced back over his shoulder at Peter. "You brought your Gibson right?"

Peter just raised a brow and gave him a *brother, please* look and the catcher laughed good-naturedly. "Yeah, forgot who I was talking to for a second."

He actually kept a second guitar in his SUV, just in case. He never knew when the mood was going to strike him and he'd want to fiddle. Which was pretty much any time he wasn't playing baseball.

"I want in on the game, so how about we do the tour later and go humiliate Paulson now?" He'd just caught sight of Leslie's straight blonde hair through the doorway, so it seemed like a real good time to go check out the backyard.

Someone hollered for Mark and he recognized JP's voice. "Put a hustle on, Cutter! We're all waiting."

Mark frowned and yelled back, "Tell Paulson to stop being a wussy! I'll be there in a minute."

They made their way through the crowd and Peter tried not to think about just how hard it was and how much effort he was putting into ignoring Leslie. She was everywhere. They went right through the wide archway into the kitchen and she was already in there swapping recipes with Lorelei and Sonny.

And when he and Mark finally made it into the backyard she was already there, too, her hair slicked back in a low ponytail while she took a swing with the Wiffle bat. He couldn't help watching the way her hips spun when she swung the plastic yellow bat, and it made him think of the way her hips had ground and rotated on the bar the other night when he'd had his tongue on her. The memory brought him to full painful attention, and he raked a hand through his hair and blew out a breath.

The woman was going to be the death of him.

"Hey, Walskie. What do you say to a friendly wager?" inquired Drake as he sauntered up with a toddler about three years old, squealing and laughing while he carried him tucked under his arm like a football.

"Again!" the little boy demanded excitedly when the big veteran tried to set him on the ground.

Drake shook his head at their teammate Ken Jenkins's son and said, "Not until I sort out some important business, little man. Go jump on JP and tell him to give you a ride." He pointed across the bare late October lawn to where the shortstop was talking shop with Carl and José. Every few minutes he'd look around the yard, and when he spotted Sonny he'd relax and his smile would go content and easy.

"Okay!" the toddler exclaimed and ran off across the crunchy grass as fast as his chubby legs would take him.

Peter watched him go with amusement. The little kid ran like a windmill, arms churning for momentum. It was actually kind of cute.

Turning his gaze from something cute to something ugly, he looked at Drake and smirked, "What's this friendly wager?"

Out of the corner of his eye he saw Leslie walk past as the backyard ball game was getting ready to resume. She had her nose in the air and was trying real hard to pretend that she wasn't eavesdropping. But he knew her way too well by now. He guaranteed she was listening.

Peter cocked a hip and gave her an once-over from her brown English riding boots and snug jeans that were tucked into them, to her charcoal grey V-neck fitted sweater. The way her clothes showcased her curves had him casually wiping his hands on his jeans. His palms were sweaty.

Paulson caught the direction of his gaze and a chuckle rumbled in his barrel chest. "How's that new deck coming along?"

Part of him wanted to protest, wanted to pretend like he didn't know what the hell the guy was talking about. The other part of him just didn't even have the fight. He was in way over his head with this thing with Leslie.

"Fucking mess," was all he said. Yep, that pretty much summed it up. And wasn't that always the case with his personal life?

Drake laughed again and replied, "Sounds fun." Then he hooked a thumb over his shoulder toward the makeshift diamond and added, "Since you're hurt and I feel bad for you, we'll take it easy, brother. Friendly wager is, you bat as a leftie against me and try to make base. Loser wears their shirt like a girl for the rest of the day." He gestured with his hands to his chest and made a twirling action. "You know, tied in a knot between their tits."

Peter smirked. "You just want an excuse to show yours off."

Paulson grinned, humor twinkling in his brown eyes. "They're beauts, ain't they?" He shoved out his chest, winked like a sailor on shore leave. "You know they make you randy."

Right, that's just how he liked his tits. On a fugly man covered in a brown curly chest rug like Austin Powers. Yeah, baby.

He shook his head, laughing, and replied, "I'll take your bet and win, you sexy bitch."

Paulson tossed back his head and gave a hoot of appreciation for the movie reference, clapping Peter on his good arm. "Let's play ball!" he hollered and walked back over to the diamond.

Pete shook his head, still chuckling softly, and went to join the game. Leslie decided to play, too, of course, and so he got the privilege of pitching to her when she chose the other team. When she stepped up to home plate, Paulson yelled from the side, "Take him down, sweet thing!"

Peter's eyebrow shot up when she looked him dead in the eyes and smiled tightly. "My pleasure."

So it was like that, eh?

Peter rolled his left shoulder and tossed her the ball, still pretty decent as a leftie. But since it was a plastic perforated white ball instead of an actual baseball it waffled through the air and then broke suddenly just before crossing home plate. Leslie swung vigorously and missed it by a mile. Point, Peter.

He waggled his brows at her and grinned smugly. *Woop.*

Leslie, nothing. And she was seriously miffed about it too. Her face stretched tight and her eyes went hard. Then she rolled her head from side-to-side and shrugged her shoulders as she muttered something unintelligible under her breath.

He knew it wasn't flattering.

For some reason that struck him as funny. When he laughed out loud she glared at him and declared, "You pitch like a pansy, Kowalskin!"

A collective gasp came from the crowd of spectators that had gathered outside in the crisp autumn air to watch the backyard game. Somebody, probably Drake, whispered loudly with a finger snap and a barrelful of attitude, "Oh no she *didn't!*"

But she had.

His brows dropped low over his eyes. So she was feeling that way about things. Okay, fine. Two could play that game. "You bat like a girl, sweet cheeks." He put the emphasis on *bat* and *sweet cheeks*, Philly-style.

She tossed her sleek ponytail over her shoulder and raised her elbows into position, looked at him all haughty. "Not the same insult, sorry."

Peter threw the second pitch and she swung and missed again. This time he laughed right at her. "Ouch, that must *sting*."

The last pitch she connected with. It came straight back at Peter and he caught it with his left hand. She was so not happy.

The pretty lady was *out*.

LESLIE WATCHED THE game resume from a chair pulled up along the first base line. She was trying hard to ignore how royally miffed she was that Peter had gotten her out. It was just a stupid game.

She leaned back in her chair and crossed her arms, watching the play continue. Soon Peter was up to bat, and since he was batting left-handed his back was to her. Leslie's gaze raked over him and her pulse kicked up a notch, annoying her.

But he looked good. She had to admit that. The man knew how to wear a fitted thermal Henley. It was open at the buttons and pulled up around his forearms, his black leather bracelet visible. His muscles were showed off to perfection. And his backside? *So. Nice.* As she studied him he flipped his ball cap backward and grinned.

"Bring it," he challenged José.

The young Costa Rican wound up and threw the Wiffle ball. With only his left hand on the bat, Peter pulled it back and released, connecting soundly and sending it flying between first and second base. As soon as he'd hit the ball he started running full-out toward first, holding his right arm steady.

Drake cursed loudly at first base and went running after the ball, the closest player to it. He pointed and waved at Peter as he darted off the base, looking over his shoulder furtively. "Don't you cross that base, Walskie!" With another quick glance over his massive shoulder he bent down to retrieve the round plastic, but it was too late.

With a final long stretch of his powerful legs, Pete crossed first base safely. Running through it, he passed the bases and turned around to the right and jogged back, grinning wickedly. "Show us the goods, Snuffy!"

Paulson tossed his mitt on the grass with an overly dramatic sigh and shrugged out of his thick, padded flannel shirt. "Cover your eyes, ladies," he called out, pretending to be all bent out of shape. She knew he was faking by the sparkle in his eyes. "Don't want all you women gettin' hot and bothered by what you're about to see." He glanced over his shoulder at Peter. "You too, sissy boy. You can't handle this much sexy."

Right. Like that was going to be a problem. As she watched, he took the hem of his T-shirt, pulled it up through the front collar and tied it in a knot, effectively turning the shirt into a bikini top. His thick mat of chest hair sprang out above and below the knot like a Chia Pet.

He spotted one of Carl's older daughters with a head-band and said with his arm out, hand coaxing. "Gimme your hair thing, girlie." She dropped it in his hand with a shy smile and he put the thick pink sequined band on, making his curly afro even bigger. Then he puckered his lips at Peter as he strutted back to first base, saying with a good-natured grin, "How do you like me now, bitch?"

Leslie laughed while the two continued to banter, but pretended that it was Drake—not Peter's wicked sharp sense of humor—that she found so funny. Sonny and Lorelei walked up to her just then and sat in chairs on each side, sandwiching her in.

"So what do you think?" Lorelei asked as she gestured to her new place with an excited smile. "Isn't it great?"

It really was. Big and homey—and it fit the country girl's personality to a T. "It's fabulous, honey."

The game came to a stop then when Mark called it on account of the meat being just about ready. Good, because she was starving. And he'd been tormenting her with the tantalizing aroma of barbequed meat since she'd arrived. So now she was going to elbow her way to a big fat piece.

Darting a glance at Peter, her stomach pitched off-center when she found him staring at her and their eyes locked from across the lawn. His were guarded, but she still saw the sensitivity he was trying to hide, and it made her heart flop over in her chest. Sucking in sharply at the sensation, she quickly looked away. What was she sup-posed to say to him now that everything felt so awkward and tense between them? They weren't even speaking to each other. And not that she'd admit it to him, but she missed the talking.

I want you.

The words echoed in her ear, making her belly quiver. *I choked, Leslie. I fucking choked, okay?* She shook her head and broke eye contact.

What did it all mean?

A tight, breathless feeling came over her and she thought, a little frantically, *what did* she *want it to mean?* She shook her head vehemently. Nothing. She wanted it to mean nothing because then there was nothing to face, nothing to risk—nothing to break her heart and leave her devastated.

Sucking in air, Leslie released a slow breath as she saw Peter stride off toward his Cruiser like a panther, all strength, grace, and prowess. And it gave her butterflies just watching. Turning to Lorelei she said bluntly, trying to take her mind off him, "I want one of your kittens."

Sonny shot her a look of sympathy. "They got to you too, didn't they?"

She crossed her legs and sighed. "You have no idea."

Sonny laughed with appreciation. "Oh, I think I do, since I'm going home with one too."

Leslie replied quickly, sitting up a little with concern, "I get the pretty one. The white, fluffy one with the gray spot on its back." She already had a name. It was Missy. And she was *hers.*

Lorelei piped up, "But what if that's the one I want to keep?"

She brushed her off. "The kitten and I have a connection, lady. We're like this." She held up a hand to show her tightly crossed fingers. "She told me she wants to come live with me, so you've been stripped of any voting right." Leslie was more than a little embarrassed by just how excited and happy she was by the prospect of snuggling up with a warm body in bed at night, of having some company. It was so unlike her.

The brunette's lips twitched and her green eyes glittered with amusement. "Then by all means," she said graciously. "Who am I to stand in the way of true love?"

That made Leslie smile until she heard the sound of a guitar playing through the open back door of the house. And when a cocky, rough male voice started singing along with the melody, in perfect pitch and way, way sexy timbre, she scowled. Without a doubt he was doing it just to tick her off. That was so like Peter.

Standing, Leslie glanced at the women and said with forced casualness, "Deal on the kittens?"

Sonny nodded and tossed her mass of wavy red-gold hair over her shoulders. "Deal. Charlie wants the male tabby anyway."

She looked at Lorelei, who just shrugged her shoulders and replied, "I'm good with whatever."

"Cool." That was all she said, but inside she was giddy. The ten-year-old girl in her who had begged for a kitten mercilessly and never got one because her mom had allergies was jumping up and down squealing, "*Yay, kitty!*"

Together the women walked back inside, the smell of homemade cooking permeating the big country kitchen. Containers and pans crammed the counters full; the ballplayers and their families brought food potluck style. There were baked beans, salads, Sonny's homemade pie that did in fact look legendary, and a ton of other stuff. And it all smelled so good that it made her mouth water.

Logan, Lorelei's bull-rider brother, was in the kitchen with his sweet baby girl Michelle helping her to fill a small plate, his head tucked down next to hers while they shared a bite of melon. He'd taken his cowboy hat off but sported a crease all around his dark head from where it had been, and he smiled at his daughter happily.

Leslie crossed her arms and melted into the wall, taking a moment to appreciate the scene. All these people had come out to her brother's new place to show their support because they loved him like family. They took care of each other.

She was thankful he had that and that she got to be a part of it. Their own family wasn't even a fraction that close, not since her parents had divorced six years ago and were no longer speaking.

Suddenly feeling introspective, Leslie pushed away from the wall and went around the back way to get to the big, cozy living room. When she got there, Peter was sitting on a corner of the raised stone fireplace surrounded by people eating. He had his guitar in hand, picking out the G. Love tune "Rainbow" for their entertainment. Hat still on backward and head down, he was grooving to the music while he sang along with the sloppy blues.

To get to the only open seat, Leslie had to walk in front of him and when she did he changed up chords and slipped into G. Love's "Booty Call," gaining a chuckle from the crowd. Her leg froze mid-stride and she rounded on him slowly, like a player in slo-mo instant replay. *Oh no he isn't.* In front of everyone no less.

"And neither one of us wants to give love a try," he sang around a smartass grin and tossed her a wink, provoking her. "But then we got drunk and fooled around and had a booty call."

Ugh!

Why did he keep referring to that night like that? It was so much more than that. And if he wasn't such a stubborn jerk, he'd be able to admit it.

She took a step and her stride hitched, making her trip on the toe of her boot, almost going down flat on her face. Catching herself, she heard him chuckle under his breath and sing, the dirty rat, "Everybody wants a booty call!"

She shot daggers at him with her eyes and tugged her sweater down with a snap. His blue eyes danced with a naughty humor that ticked her off. Damn the man. Her mouth opened to say something snarky to him just as he changed up chords again and melted back into "Rainbow" like he was innocent as a lamb and had never done such a juvenile thing to begin with.

Whatever.

With a dismissive flip of her ponytail, Leslie was just about to take her seat when a bellow came from the kitchen and Mark came running, carrying Lorelei like she was a bride on her wedding night. Everybody stopped what they were doing to stare at them. His eyes were wide and dazed and he braced his legs apart, tossed his head back and shouted, *"We're having a baby!"*

She *knew* it.

The house erupted in shouts, whistles, and applause, and Leslie's heart tripped in her chest at the ecstatic look on her brother's face. He was cradling his wife to him tightly and gave her a sound, smacking kiss. "I'm going to be a dad! *Whoo!*"

Then he was spinning Lorelei around, and they were both laughing and clinging to each other. Leslie's heart filled up with love and happiness for them both, making her eyes all teary. Movement caught her attention and she saw Peter staring at her.

Riding on the celebratory vibe, she met his gaze and smiled wide. He raised that brow of his and gave her a small boyish smile, tipped his head at the two soon-to-be parents. His guard dropped and his eyes went warm and sensitive and sweet.

And she had no hope of stopping it when her heart took a nosedive and landed her right smack in a big ol' pool of love.

It just *sucked*.

Chapter Seventeen

LESLIE BURIED HERSELF in work as Halloween approached and her boys made it into the World Series. The Denver Rush were hosting the Boston Red Sox at Coors Field, and the nightclub had been absolutely hopping once the Series got under way. It was exhausting.

The past two nights she hadn't even made it back to Peter's place after the place had emptied. Both times she'd crashed out hard on the couch, lured by the promise of a blissful night's sleep cradled in its plush, velvety cushions. Leslie was a victim of the vortex.

If there was added inspiration for the campouts fueled from a very keen desire to avoid the man who'd stolen her heart, well, yeah, okay. So what? The dirty rotten no-good sneaky . . . *thief*.

First chance she had she was going to take it back.

She wasn't going to stay in love. No freaking way. Leslie was going to just sit herself down, have a long conversation, and rationalize her way right back out of the uninvited emotion. It would work—no problem. Or rather, it *should* work. Wait. No, it *would* work. Right?

It had to.

Leslie ran her hands through her hair and tipped back her office chair, blowing out a long, slow breath.

The man was a bad health risk.

"Which of course makes him right up my alley," Leslie muttered dryly.

Dropping her chair down, she slapped her palms on her desk and said to her plant friends in various states of unhappiness scattered about the room, "I declare the rest of today a No Peter day." She opened her mouth to continue, and then what she'd said registered, and she closed it again on a chuckle. Every day was a *No Peter* day. That was the whole point of the bet.

A knock sounded at the door and Leslie sat up in her chair, calling out, "Come in."

She slipped her feet back into her heels and froze when the door opened and John Crispin walked in. "John!" she exclaimed, completely taken by surprise. What in the world was he doing here? She never thought she'd see him again after his trade from Denver to Boston.

Her ex-boyfriend smiled a little bashfully and ducked his head, looking at her through his lashes. "How're you doing, Leslie? Mind if I come in?" He hesitated at the threshold, uncertain.

She waved him in, still jarred by the whole unexpected visit, and forced a smile. "I'm well, thanks. How are *you* doing?" They hadn't seen or spoken to each other since the night he'd asked her to move to Boston with him. Instead of saying yes and making him happy, she'd dumped him and broken his heart.

But she just hadn't been able to uproot and move to another city for a man she didn't love. Especially when she was really just starting to get her feet back under her where she was.

His smile grew and he said, "You're wondering what the hell I'm doing here, aren't you?"

Pretty much exactly, yes.

Leslie took a second to take him in and noted that he looked good. She said as much, "You look great, Johnny." Her nickname for him slipped out before she'd known it had even formed on her lips, and she grimaced slightly. But the truth was he *did* look fantastic. The ballplayer was the big rugged sort. All planes and angles, firm lips and hard man. Except his hair. He had this soft, luxuriously wavy hair that tumbled over his shirt collar, a striking contrast to the rest of him.

His eyes roamed over her and something flickered in them, but before she could really see, he cleared his throat and looked away.

"I'm in town for the Series." His rough, deep voice a shade uncertain. "I was wondering ..." He paused and gave a self-conscious laugh. "Okay, I was wondering if maybe you'd like to go for a drink or coffee or something while I'm in town. You know, catch up, see how each other are doing?"

Leslie smiled softly. "That's sweet, John." She opened her mouth, intent on declining the offer because although he was great she wasn't interested in rekindling anything at all with him, when an image of Peter came to mind and out popped, "Sounds great!"

Damn it.

Mentally kicking herself, Leslie inhaled deeply and jerked when the phone rang. She gave John an apologetic look. "Do you mind? I'm sure it'll be quick." It better be. She had to figure out how to get out of their date. That might take a while.

The brown-eyed player shook his head. "Not at all."

"Thanks."

The phone rang again and she snatched up the receiver. "Leslie Cutter."

He moved to look at the pictures she'd hung on the wall above the couch and she took in his jeans and green fleece, his broad well-muscled shoulders and tight behind. And she felt nothing. Absolutely nothing. All because of one very infuriating Irish-Ukrainian pitcher.

"Ms. Cutter, this is Jerry Patowski."

Finally. She'd been calling his office practically nonstop for days with none of her calls returned. It was so annoying.

"Hi, Jerry." There was some bite in her tone, and she swallowed, forced it down a notch. "I've been trying to call you about my apartment. You said last week that you were waiting on some fittings. What's the current status?" She knew she wasn't being very gracious and didn't really care. It had been weeks. At this point they'd better prorate her rent to the point of free. Maybe pay *her* money. If she was ever in the same room as Kowalskin again she'd mention that very idea.

"Sorry about that, but it's been busy. We got another busted pipe in Apartment 3D." He took a breath like he was pulling on a cigarette and said with a voice like chewed sandpaper, "Your place should be ready on the first."

Her eyes went wide in disbelief. She couldn't have heard that right. "Of *November*?"

"That's right."

No, no. That was wrong. She was supposed to be out of Peter's place and back into hers immediately. Her heart depended upon it. She shook her head. "Wait. Are you telling me that it will have been an entire *month* before I get my place back?" What the hell kind of plumbing problem had they found that took an entire month to fix?

This whole thing was beginning to sound sketchy.

"It's the best I can do," Jerry replied gruffly.

Her sigh was strong enough to cause a tsunami. "Fine."

Leslie hung up, battling the frown she felt forming between her brows, and pasted on a smile for John. "How about you give me a shout when you're free and we'll have that chat?" Hopefully he'd get so caught up in the Series he'd forget about asking her out.

Picking up on his cue to leave, John turned from the pictures and smiled warmly. "Sounds terrific." He glanced around and added, "Well, I should be going. Wouldn't want to be caught in enemy territory, so to speak." He grinned amiably with the joke.

Laughing dutifully, she sent him on his way with a wave and a, "Call me," smiling brightly and not meaning any of it. Public relations schmoozing was a very valuable skill to have, and it came in handy when she wanted to hide her true feelings.

As soon as he left she dropped her forehead to her desk and muttered after a few minutes, "Somebody shoot me."

"That good a day, eh, princess?"

And it just got even better. *Oh, skippy.*

Leslie kept her hands limp at her sides and raised her head slightly, blowing hard at a thick clump of hair that was covering her right eye. "It's super."

"Looks like." Peter crossed his legs and leaned a shoulder into the door frame. "Was that Crispin I spotted leaving just now?" He tipped his head back down the long hallway at the entrance.

Leslie plopped her chin on the desk and muttered again, "In the flesh."

Because Peter looked way better standing there than he had any right to, and because her heart was doing little back handsprings of joy at the sight of him, she closed her eyes and pretended she was in Ft. Lauderdale on the beach. It was working fairly well too, except that her mind had taken a snapshot of him and it was right behind her eyelids like a Polaroid. He was there in all his glory: messy hair, white Eric Clapton T-shirt, faded jeans, leather bracelet, and scuffed-up Vans. And since it was her imagination and not the real thing, imaginary Leslie ran right on up to him like a scene out of *Bridget Jones,* wearing only a long trench coat and killer Ferragamos, and they kissed in grand romantic style.

Ugh! Stupid backstabbing imagination.

Snapping her eyes open, Leslie slapped her palms on the desktop and forced her head up, not waiting for Peter's answer. "Why are you here? Aren't we not on speaking terms, or have you changed your mind and decided to be an adult about things?" *There, go on the offense and get him in retreat so he'll go away before you do something stupid like blurt out your feelings.*

She'd been avoiding looking at him again, but did it now, and it wasn't so bad. He was only marginally amazing. And the fact that his thick, curly lashes and pale blue eyes made her stomach jittery was super aggravating. What had happened to independent didn't-want-a-man Leslie?

At least if she was going to be pathetic-in-love Leslie she could still keep her head about her enough to keep her hands off him until after midnight on the thirty-first. That was only a few days away. It wouldn't be that hard anyway, at the rate they were going. This was the first they'd seen of each other in days.

Peter pushed away from the wall and leaned back into the hallway as she crossed her arms and watched. Then he straightened and held out a plain black duffle bag. "Clothes from your apartment. Jerry called me this morning bitching how you've been phone-stalking him about getting a few items." He dropped it on the floor and gave a low whistle. "Damn, girl. You have some fine looking panties. My personal fave was the black lace thong with the bow from Victoria's Secret. *Nice*." He wiggled his brows suggestively and winked. "They're in the bag."

A laugh bubbled in her chest and she swallowed it

back. The man was incorrigible. "I'm too happy about you bringing me clothes to lecture you about prying through my things." She held out her hands and waggled her fingers excitedly. Things were looking up. "Gimme."

Peter snorted and held the bag down at his side. "How about you come and get it."

Tempting proposition, that.

Leslie decided to play nice since he had been kind enough to go out of his way when he was in the middle of the World Series. She rose from her chair and crossed to him. "Thank you for bringing this to me." She held her hand out for the duffle bag. "Out of curiosity, how'd my apartment look? It should be pretty close to finished."

Peter shrugged his shoulders and made a noncommittal sound. "It looked like your average construction zone."

She took the bag from him and set it on the arm of the couch. With a yank of the zipper she opened it and let out a sigh of relief. Clothes, sweet clothes.

Peter pointed a finger at the bag. "I know how enamored you are with your girl shoes, so I tossed in a pair."

Really?

Rifling through the bag full of clothes, she pushed aside a pair of jeans and stopped when she spotted her favorite pair of heels. They were strappy purple suede Michael Kors that made her legs look amazing. Oh, how she'd missed them.

She could have kissed him.

Oh, what the hell? she thought, caught up in the happy

moment. She spun and planted an enthusiastic kiss full on his lips.

The pitcher rocked back on his heels and let out a sound of surprise. "*Umph!*"

She pulled back smiling. "Thanks, Peter. You made my week."

His gaze was locked on her mouth, suddenly lusty. "For all the effort I put out there getting you clean under-wear, girl, that sure was a lackluster show of appreciation."

Leslie pulled back and arched a brow at him. "Oh really?"

The way his eyes lit with a sudden naughty gleam had her knees turning to jelly. "Yes, really. If you were truly thankful you'd kiss me again. And this time with a whole lot more *oomph*."

A slow smile spread across her face. "I must not be that thankful then, huh?" One big step to the side and she was out of his reach.

Instead of coming after her like she'd half-hoped he would, Peter hooked his thumbs in the front pockets of his jeans and braced his feet apart, relaxed. "What was Crispin after?" The sudden change of topic was sur-prising.

And it was interesting that he was bringing it up. Leslie cocked her head to the side. Why did he care?

She replied breezily with a delicate shrug of her shoul-ders. "Oh nothing really, just a date."

He went very still. "Excuse me?"

Suddenly enjoying herself, she clarified, "He invited me out on a date sometime this week while he's in town."

Peter's eyes went cool. "You said no, right?"

Was that sudden edge she heard in his voice jealousy? Hmm, what if she said . . . "As a matter of fact I told him yes. I'm not dating anyone, so why not?" That last part she'd added just for fun.

A tick started in his jaw and his eyes went from cool to frosty. "Yeah sure, why not?" he ground out tightly.

For a guy who claimed he wasn't interested in anything to do with her beyond clearing his good name—and certainly not any attachments—he sure seemed agitated by her admission. "My thoughts exactly!" Leslie shot him a bright, overblown grin. "*Why not?*"

Peter broke eye contact and looked over her shoulder, rolling his head from side-to-side like a boxer. Then his gaze whipped back to her and he swore, "Shit," and moved with freakish speed, pinning her back against the desk.

His mouth came down hard on hers, his tongue thrusting between her lips in a kiss of straight possession. Leslie couldn't do more than moan and wrap her arms around his neck. Her brain went into overdrive and short-circuited. God the man could kiss.

Immersed in the feel and taste of him, she murmured a protest when he ripped his lips from hers and stepped out of her arms. His eyes were hard and full of warning.

"*That's* why."

Chapter Eighteen

D-Day HAD ARRIVED.

October thirty-first. Halloween. Last game of the World Series between the Denver Rush and the Boston Red Sox. The Rush were tied with the Red Sox 3-3. This last game would determine the Series winner. And most notably, it was also the last day of a *Very Important Bet*.

Peter couldn't believe that he was starting as pitcher. It was like the universe had decided to have mercy on him, and the doctors had cleared his shoulder at the last minute. He was on a pretty heavy dose of ibuprofen, but that was it. There was no way he was going to play the last game of his career doped up on pain meds or a steroid shot. Nope.

This was a day he always wanted to remember.

Scanning the crowd of Coors Field, Peter breathed deep and steady despite the pounding of his heart and the swirling mass of emotions. So many feelings were bubbling around inside him: gratitude, anxiety, fear, exhilaration, nervousness, and anticipation. One minute he was flying high, the next he was swimming in an ocean of insecurity as the realization that when he woke up in the morning he would no longer be a professional ballplayer sprung to mind.

Tomorrow, and for the rest of his life, he was just plain old Peter Brian Kowalskin.

But for now, for this one last game, he was Kowalskin, jersey number fifteen, ace pitcher for the Denver Rush. Winner of the Cy Young Award two years running. And he was there to kick some Red Sox ass.

Cranking his hat down, Peter smiled into the stands. The stadium was bursting at the seams with green and yellow Rush fans, the impressive noise level a tribute to the talent and popularity of his team. A hard knot lodged in his throat and he swallowed around it.

God he was going to miss this.

"You all ready for a show?" he asked the crowd quietly, knowing they couldn't hear him.

"What's that you said, Walskie?" asked Arthur Mc-Murtry, the team manager, as he came over from the dugout to where Peter was standing.

Squinting against the sun, he tucked his ball mitt under his left armpit and rolled a baseball between his hands, cocking a hip. "I was just thinking about the show our crowd is going to get today."

Arthur had a wad of chew in his lip. He spit, saying, "It'll be a good one." Then his coach of fourteen years cuffed him on the shoulder and said, "Give them hell, Kowalskin. One last time."

Yeah. He could do that.

The crowd cheered raucously as someone famous he didn't recognize stepped out to sing the national anthem. After the elaborate rendition was done and the team was back in the dugout, the Denver Broncos' starting quarterback came onto the field to throw out the first pitch to the great delight of the stadium full of fans.

Drake shook his head and grumbled next to him, "Don't see why some football player gets so much love."

Because it was Denver. And it was football. The end.

Peter slapped him on the back. "Don't be a girl, Paulson. You get more love than most entire football teams, and you're only one man. No whining allowed."

"Yeah, yeah," muttered the ballplayer. Then his brown eyes lit triumphantly. "Bet he ain't never had a woman paint her tits in his teams colors though, with the nipples like bulls-eyes and then have him sign 'em with a Sharpie using just his teeth."

Only Drake.

"Probably not, dude." At that moment he spotted Leslie in the crowd down along the first base line and his stomach pitched. She was there with the rest of the posse, preferring to be down near the action instead of clear up high in the skybox where some of the other players' families hung out.

She, Sonny, and Lorelei had gotten way into the team spirit of things and painted signs cheering the Rush to victory. Even Charlie had gotten into it, his face painted part green, part yellow. Leslie even had something painted on her cheeks, but he couldn't tell what it was from the distance. Looked like a heart on one cheek and a big R on the other though.

Seeing her all dolled up for his team made his lungs seize. That woman knew just how to get to him. With a huge release of air, Peter forced his gaze off his favorite cheering section. There would be time with Leslie later.

Now there was the game.

Taking to the mound as Smash Mouth sang "All Star" and the crowd went crazy, adrenaline flooded his body and focused his mind. In an instant he was in the zone, ready to take charge and keep the Red Sox from getting on base. Rolling his shoulder, Peter was relieved at how good it felt.

Mark settled into position, his eyes sharp and intense even from the distance. With a quick glance at his teammates, he saw that they were all the same and grinned to himself. His boys were ready to bring it home.

A flash caught his attention and he looked over to see Charlie holding up a sign, the world's biggest grin on his young face. It said "Kowalskin is a Baseball God" and he recognized Leslie's handwriting. Heat flared in his chest, a hot ball of emotion, and he had to swallow hard against the sudden burn.

Was there no end to the ways the woman believed in him?

Pushing the thought aside, he forced his attention to the Red Sox player getting ready to bat and put everything else out of his mind.

"*Play!*" yelled the umpire with a finger pointed at Peter.

For the next few hours the Rush took on the Red Sox, each team scrapping their hearts out for the pennant. Peter fired red-hot pitch after pitch, his shoulder feeling tender but completely manageable and his left eye holding. Everything else was forgotten, reality and life narrowing down to a tiny pinpoint of focus and concentration.

He forgot about it being his last game and let it all hang out, putting every ounce of effort he had into throwing serious heat.

When one Red Sox player hit a pop-fly high into the air, Peter dashed off the mound and caught it soundly in his mitt. Then he whipped around, arm already cocked and ready, and rocketed the ball off toward second, intent on outing the Red Sox player stupidly trying to steal base. The second baseman tagged the bag with a foot and lunged forward, reaching with his glove.

And the player was out.

By the time the ninth inning rolled around, the game was 5–4 and the Rush were up. Peter's arm was hurting as he started, but he knew that if he could keep Boston from getting on base then the game would be over and the Rush would take the World Series. No big deal. It was just a little pressure.

The late October air was chilly and the sky overcast with the promise of snow. Even so, Peter was sweating, beads of it dripping down his temples. The exertion was immense and he could feel himself beginning to slip, could feel his shoulder starting to go.

But he had to hang in there a few more minutes.

He yanked off his hat and swiped at the sweat just as John Crispin came up to bat. His former teammate's brows were pulled down in a scowl. His eyes were intense as he prepared to take on Peter. He stepped into the box, ground his cleats in the dirt, and swung the bat before pulling it into position.

And all Peter could see was the man who used to date Leslie. The man who had just asked her out on a date. The man trying to move in on his territory.

Not today.

Peter wound up and released the first pitch, a brutal fastball, straight down the pipe. He merely grunted when John swung and missed. Damn right.

Strike one.

He knew John. Knew his weaknesses. Knew how to play him.

So did Cutter.

Mark signaled for a slider and Peter nodded, more than happy to oblige. Pulling his arm back, he ignored the sting and released the ball. John took a step forward and swung high, cursing profusely and earning another strike.

Strike two.

Panting with the effort, Peter wound up one more time and went with another slider, knowing it was Crispin's Achilles' heel. The big, gruff player took a huge forward step and swung with everything he had. And he connected.

The ball ricocheted right back at Peter, coming hard and fast at his head. He didn't have time to move. All he had time to do was react. In a flash he raised his mitt to his face.

And caught the ball, the velocity of it slamming the leather glove back into his collarbone, narrowly missing his chin.

The force of it stung like a bitch until he heard, "*Out!*" That one call changed everything, made all the pain disappear in a blink.

The Rush won the World Series.

Fans screamed, his team came running, everybody was yelling in celebration. Drake loped over to him and scooped Peter up, spinning him around, hollering, "Yeah, Walskie!" Exhilaration flooded him, took him on a high so glorious that he never wanted to come down.

He did it. He fucking did it. He won the goddamn World frigging Series.

He couldn't believe it.

Riding the wave, Peter was laughing and smiling when he looked into the stands and saw Leslie. She had her hands to her mouth When she spotted him looking at her she dropped her hands from her mouth and waved, her smile absolutely beaming. And he felt the echo of it inside him wrap warm around his heart.

It was the greatest moment of his life.

Chapter Nineteen

HOTBOX WAS HOPPING. The kind of hopping that made it hard to breathe from all the bodies smooshed together in a confined space. And Leslie couldn't have been happier.

A blast of music hit her ears like a hammer, the beat thumping and pulsing heavily as her favorite local reggae band Gyration burned up the stage in their Rastafarian zombie costumes. Colored bulbs had been installed, and red beams of light rained down over the throng from the ceiling. Spider webs were strewn all about, from the liquor display behind the bar to the upstairs railing with arachnids of varying shapes and sizes perched and hunting for prey.

She'd hired some fifth-year theatre majors from the nearby university to dress up as witches and spend the night stirring a big steamy cauldron of dry ice by the front entrance. From where she was standing she could see white smoke crawling along the floor in thin, curling fingers. Every so often one of the drama students would cackle or lunge, teeth snapping at those who entered. They were having a blast, really getting into character. It was pretty creepy.

And way freaking awesome.

Even Mario had gotten into the spirit of things and was dressed like a jailbird who'd been dead and decomposing for a few decades. Already imposing in his natural state, there were more than a few faint-of-heart partygoers who had taken one look at him and slipped to the back of the line. They were probably hoping that another stint in the falling snow would get them pumped up for when he scared the shit out of them the second time. It was really quite amusing.

To top it all off, every once in a while the lights would flicker and stall out and there would be a thundering boom—with just enough time lapsing to get a nice roll of murmurs going. Then they flashed back on again like nothing had happened and it was business as usual, confusing them further. It made her smile every single time.

The on-air radio deejays set up near the stage were having a really good time. In front of them and to the left was the Rush's unofficial table. She'd dubbed it that since they always gravitated there.

The club looked awesome, if she did say so herself.

Speaking of other stuff that was pretty killer, Leslie thought as she brushed her palms down the front of her costume, she was doing all right herself. Oh, okay. She looked frigging fantastic.

Tonight she was a princess; an exposed-shouldered,

bosom-enhanced, deep amethyst, embroidered-velvet medieval princess who was ready to take back her crown. And she would, too, in about two hours.

A shrill scream came from the entrance, drawing Leslie's attention. A group of college-aged girls dressed like characters from *Twilight* were huddled together, clinging because Mario had scared the daylights out of them. The looks on their faces had her giggling.

That giggle turned into a howl of laughter when Drake Paulson stepped through the door. He was in full costume, from the top of his newly green afro head to his grass green feet. Even his lips were green.

It was the Jolly Green Giant.

Leslie laughed so hard it brought tears to her eyes. That had to be one of the best costumes she'd ever seen. It put all the Storm Troopers and naughty nurses out on the floor to shame.

She was dabbing at the corner of her eye with a section of her huge bell sleeve when Peter stepped inside and she nearly jammed her finger into her eye socket. Damn the man. Why did just seeing him have her mouth turning to sawdust?

He wasn't even dressed up. Oh no, Peter Kowalskin was too cool for a costume. He dressed like his normal self in a white Pearl Jam T-shirt, faded jeans, leather jacket, and Vans. Just like any other day.

But it wasn't just any other day and they both knew it when he stopped in front of her, his incredible blue eyes glinting with a whole lot of naughty. "Happy Halloween, *princess*. Nice costume."

Leslie slid him a look through her lashes, enjoying the banked heat she could see simmering in his. "Sonny and I found it at a consignment store in Boulder. You like it?" She knew he did. It was written all over his rugged face.

His gaze flicked over her, from the golden crown woven into her hair to her purple suede Michael Kors heels on her feet. Those weren't so historically accurate, but they were her magic-makers. Every time she wore them something fabulous happened. And, well, they just so happened to match her dress. How about that?

And if he didn't stop staring at her she was going to start squirming. Not the fun kind, either. "Congratulations on your win today," she said, hoping to diffuse the tension between them.

Peter hooked his thumbs in the front pocket of his jeans and tipped his chin, smiling when Carl Brexler hollered to him before he turned his attention back to her and answered, "Thanks. It felt good. *Still* feels good," he finished with a laugh and a satisfied smile.

"How's the shoulder?" she inquired as they made their way toward the table with the rest of the Rush players. There was a thick crowd when they neared the table, and Peter slid his hand to rest on her lower back, guiding her through the crush. The heat of his large palm bore into her and had a different kind of heat flaring in her belly. He had no idea how capable and strong his hands were, how completely they possessed when they touched.

It was intoxicating.

They reached the long table just as one of the waitresses, Megan, set down a tray full of shot glasses and a bottle of their finest whiskey. "Congrats on your win, guys," she said with a wide smile and melted back into the crowd. It looked like the boys were having a good time toasting their success. That was the second bottle already.

Leslie opened her mouth to say something when Peter's hand slipped from her lower back down to her ass and between her legs. Through the sumptuous fabric his fingers caressed her intimately, his body blocking anyone from seeing.

Her panties were damp in a heartbeat.

Lust slammed into her hard, scrambling her brain and blurring her vision. Suddenly she was feeling nervous, a lot less certain. And suddenly she had a very real concern about making it until midnight.

She threw a slightly panicked look at the wall clock. Ten forty-five. After all, it was still so very far, far away.

Applause erupted suddenly in the large nightclub and echoed off the brick walls, putting a halt to their little intrigue. She felt Peter melt away with relief. A reprieve, thank God. It gave her a few minutes to get her hormones in order.

The radio deejays were holding court near the stage, perfectly distracting her as they announced the night's costume contest winner. It was Lorelei, the rodeo queen.

Mark burst out laughing and pushed her toward the deejay table. "Way to go, Fonda Peters!" He was laughing so hard Leslie was afraid he might strain something.

His wife tried to scowl but couldn't hold it together. She started laughing, too, as she sashayed like a model to retrieve her Blues Traveler tickets. Once she took them she spun around and gave a playful curtsy.

"Thank you!" Then she scrambled back over to the Rush's table, giggling, and shared a secret smile with Mark. Which made it official—Leslie *really* didn't want to know what that was all about.

When the brunette stopped next to her, Leslie suggested, "You know, Mark's not much of a John Popper fan, but I know someone who is. You should think about taking her instead because she'd properly appreciate the event."

Lorelei arched a brow, green eyes dancing. "Really now? And just who might that be?"

"Hey! Nuh-uh, Leslie. Don't you go trying to muscle your way in on my date." Mark draped a muscular arm over his wife's shoulder and pulled her into his side. "Go get your own."

Leslie shot him a look, brow raised, and attempted to distract herself by teasing him. "That's what I was trying to do before you butted your big crooked nose into things, *Scooter.*" She used his childhood nickname, amused when his nostrils flared.

Lorelei's head whipped around to her husband. "Scooter?"

Mark leveled a warning glare at Leslie over Lorelei's head. "It's nothing."

He didn't scare her. It was the opposite, actually. Mark was bigger, but she fought mean. "He earned that prestigious nickname when he was fourteen and we were on a family camping trip. He used some plants to wipe with—"

"Shut it, Leslie," Mark interjected, voice ripe with embarrassment.

And she just continued, ignoring his threats, "—and found out the hard way what poison ivy looked like. I caught him scooting across the tent trying to scratch his itchy butt at one in the morning like a dog. It was super funny." She gestured dramatically. "Hence, Scooter."

The way her brother cringed was priceless. Lorelei started laughing, and he shook his head, muttering, "Calamine lotion is a joke."

A heavy green arm settled over Leslie's shoulder and she glanced at the enormous hand holding a beer. Paulson was one large man. "What's so funny over here?" he said around a slight belch.

Apparently the Jolly Green Giant was inebriated.

"Reminiscing about Mark's brilliant youth." Her brother narrowed his gray eyes and she smiled innocently.

"We telling stories?" the gruff player inquired and leaned into Leslie. The weight of him almost took her down.

Before she could launch into any more, Mark diverted the veteran's attention and together they went over to the college students in costume so that Drake could have a turn stirring the bubbling cauldron. The guy was happy like a three-year-old with a sucker.

Lorelei cleared her throat loudly. "So, you going to confess?"

"About what?" Of course she knew what, but denial had a way of making liars and avoiders of everyone.

The mom-to-be took a sip of her cranberry juice and ice and said casually, "Oh, nothing much. Just about how you're totally crazy for Peter."

Her mouth dropped open and she was about to speak when Lorelei cut her off. "Don't even pretend, hon."

Leslie's stomach flopped. Awesome. "Who else knows?"

"If you're referring to Mark, he doesn't know anything."

Thank God. She really wasn't up for dealing with an angry overprotective brother at the moment. Stealing a glance around the busy nightclub, she let out a breath. "Good. There's nothing for him to know anyway."

Her companion snorted. "You're such a bad liar."

No she wasn't. She was great. In fact, she lied convincingly to herself all the time. "Look, there's not much to tell. Peter and I just have a stupid bet going."

Lorelei put a hand on her arm and gave it a reassuring squeeze. "It looks like a whole lot more than that, honey. I've never seen Kowalskin so amped up."

A part of her thrilled at that, the part that was stupid in love with him. And that was all of her. "It's nothing. Really. No need to tell anybody." And by anybody she meant Mark.

"How can I not say anything, Leslie?" The brunette looked torn. "You're his sister. The only family he's close with. And Peter's his best friend. If you two are sniffing around each other then he's going to want to know."

"Uh-uh. You can't say anything. Sister-in-law confidentiality."

Big sigh. "Leslie."

A hard brick wall rose up inside her, closing her off. She wasn't ready to admit to anything. "It's just a bet, Lorelei. Just a stupid bet."

The brunette eyed her skeptically. "You swear?"

Leslie looked her dead in the eye. "Yes. It doesn't mean anything."

See? *She was too a good liar.*

PETER LET OUT a low laugh when he stepped close behind Leslie sometime later and placed his palm against her hip. Then he slid his hand over her ass and watched her shiver. He was still riding high from the Rush's win and feeling good. Really good. Not that he'd ever wanted his career to end, but since it had to, going out this way had been just about everything he could ask for. Yeah, things were great. Everything was working out exactly as it should. And, by the way, the princess in front of him was shaking in those ridiculously sexy shoes, he knew that there was something else that was going to work itself out very soon too.

He wanted Leslie. Christ, he wanted that woman like he wanted oxygen. It was fundamental and basic, at the core of who he was. There would be no performance anxiety tonight. No choking. Peter was determined to win the bet and make this a perfect night. One for the record books.

To win the World Series and Leslie in one swoop was pretty much every dream he'd had for the last four years rolled up into one. And he was feeling lucky. He was feeling a lot like it was past time to have it out with Leslie. The sexual tension they'd built between them was more dangerous than a landmine.

He was ready for the explosion.

Peter leaned forward and whispered into Leslie's ear, "Tonight."

He felt her back snap straight as a helpless little whimper escaped her lips, betraying her. "I don't know what you mean."

The hell she didn't. Her breathing had gone shallow. Peter could feel her core get hotter and pushed his middle finger into her gently, teasing her through the fabric. It killed him, what she was wearing.

Princess.

Knowing that she had picked it just to torment him made it so fucking sexy. Almost as hot as the way her breasts were displayed, all pushed up together with the best cleavage he'd ever seen. It had nearly dropped him to his knees when he'd first laid eyes on it.

Glancing down the table to see if Mark was watching, Peter nipped the back of her neck and said roughly, "Don't play coy."

He was going to say more when Mark glanced over at them, frowning slightly. So instead of keeping his hand on her like he wanted to, he stepped back and said, "It's still on."

She tossed him a look meant to be dismissive, but the hint of uncertainty he saw in her eye ruined the effect and had his gut squeezing. So she knew it too. Tonight was their night.

"Hey, Kowalskin! Come join the celebration!" shouted Drake. "You're missing all the fun." The jolly green ballplayer waved down the table to the stacks of empty shot glasses.

"I'll be there in a second," he replied, his attention on Leslie as she sashayed away with her nose in the air, looking every bit the regal, royal princess she was pretending to be.

She was headed straight toward Paulson. Once she reached him, she poured a shot glass full of whiskey and raised it up, shouting to be heard over the music. "To the Rush!" And then she downed the drink, not waiting for anyone to join the toast.

"Hey!" protested the veteran. "Sharing is caring, sweet thing."

Leslie smiled tightly, and Peter couldn't help admiring the way her hair looked all bundled up like that with little strands dangling against her neck. It was different than what she normally did. It was softer. He liked it.

"Sorry about that, y'all," she said with an apologetic smile. "Crazy night."

Right then the lights flickered and went out, making somebody scream, and she added dryly above the noise, "Case in point."

He was just starting to become uncomfortable in the dark when the lights came back on. The first thing he saw when his eyes readjusted to the brightness was a giant ugly green man with an afro like a head of broccoli. The second was the most beautiful woman he'd ever seen wearing a purple dress potent enough to drop a man at twenty paces. He might not have gone down, but that didn't mean the impact of her hadn't hit him like a wrecking ball.

She was a fantasy.

His fantasy. Peter's very own princess.

"What's on your mind there, Walskie?" How had Paulson snuck up on him? The guy moved like a lumberjack.

"Visions in purple," he replied, not even trying to pretend.

The veteran scratched his chest and muttered gruffly, "Damn stuff itches something fierce." His green shirt was open in a deep V like a seventies porn star—he was making the Green Giant into a perv, apparently—and he'd used one of those green spray cans of hair paint on his chest, turning his thick patch the color of summer leaves.

"I have to give you props. When you go at something, you really commit," he said, gesturing to the getup.

"It's all about the love." Drake held out a shot glass full of fine malt whiskey. "Hey, your vision is about to hit the floor with the Lone Ranger. Unless you want to see her ride off into the sunset on Silver, you better intercede, man."

Peter's gaze whipped to where Drake had indicated, and sure enough his princess was taking to the dance floor with some poser in a cheap costume. His jaw clenched and his gut turned sour.

It shouldn't matter. He shouldn't care. This whole bet thing with her was just physical anyway. All he wanted was to replace the memory of their shitty night with a new, improved one. Why it mattered so much, he didn't know. Didn't really want to know. He just knew that he was tired of carrying the memories with him like a frigging ball and chain. He wanted them gone. As long as he got what he wanted then it shouldn't matter at all what the hell she did.

It shouldn't.

But it did.

Chapter Twenty

LESLIE SAW HIM coming for her. Like a panther stalking his prey, Peter was stealth and grace, cutting through the crowd like a big cat in the tall grass, his eyes locked on her. Her pulse skittered and her breath caught in her throat. God help her, but it was exciting.

"Come closer, fair maiden," said her dance partner with a suggestive wiggle of eyebrows almost hidden by his mask.

Oh God, *really*?

She should have known that any guy who'd be the Lone Ranger for Halloween wouldn't know how to pick up a woman successfully if directions had been written on the inside of his ten-gallon hat. But, whatever. He had just been a handy excuse to get away from Peter anyway.

Or so she'd thought.

Now she had a way nerdy and slightly creepy dance

partner and a dangerous man stalking toward her. With nowhere to run. Or hide.

As the ballplayer bore down on her from across the dance floor, she cozied up to the Lone Ranger, completely unashamed of the fact that she was doing it just to see what kind of reaction she could get out of Peter. Until she figured out how to not be in love with him anymore she was stuck with it—stuck with feeling vulnerable.

And if she had to feel that way, then it was time to poke at the pitcher and see what was hidden behind that cool, detached exterior of his. See if he really was jealous. Because if he was, then it meant that she had a hold on him too. And that would be okay because then she wouldn't feel so alone.

"Here, like this," she shouted as "Thrift Shop" by Macklemore and Ryan Lewis came on, the rap music filling in for the reggae band while they took a much deserved break. Leslie spun around, hiked up her full skirt, held fistfuls of it on her knees, and rocked against the Lone Ranger.

He put his hands on her hips and moved with her, calling out, "What's your name?"

Never going to happen, was all she could think to reply, but then she saw Peter scowling and shoving his wave through the crush of hot bodies toward her. Oh my. The look on his face was one she'd never seen before. It was hard with warning, and when she did a booty shake and backed up to the Ranger, Peter's eyes flashed like diamonds in the sun and her instincts went on high alert.

Leslie's feet wanted to bolt from her spot, but her heart

needed her to stay right where she was and look for proof that she hadn't made another ginormous mistake. That she hadn't just tossed her heart away for a man. She needed desperately to feel that Peter was deep in this thing too.

He was moving to her, getting closer and closer with every bass beat as Macklemore went on about popping tags and only having twenty dollars in his pocket. Excitement had her breath coming in hard, fast bursts. Her heart raced from exertion and from having a very tough, very sexy man barreling down on her with a look in his eye that promised trouble once he got his hands on her.

Part of her was scared. Any sane woman would be. Peter Kowalskin on a mission was a sight to see, all pale lethal eyes and hard athlete's body. Her stomach pitched and her nerves were singing. He had that effect on her.

Suddenly a full-figured Hispanic woman dressed up like Fergie during her Black Eyed Pea days spun around and discovered Kowalskin right behind her. With an, "*Hola chico guapo!*" she grabbed him up by the waist and wrapped herself around him like a vice, hooking one heavy thigh around his hip and her hands around his neck, stopping him dead in his tracks. The look of utter astonishment on his face was absolutely priceless.

Leslie started laughing and couldn't stop. Peter glared at her, tried to unwind himself and failed, glared again. In return she just shrugged delicately and rotated her hips. Her dance partner hollered into her ear, "Can I buy you a drink after?"

That was sweet, really, but, "Thanks for the offer, but no."

The Lone Ranger stopped moving, clearly disappointed in her response. "I'm done here then," he practically spat and left her standing alone in the middle of the dance floor with her purple dress around her knees.

Suddenly self-conscious, Leslie reached out and snagged a shot glass full of something from a passing server's tray and tossed it back. She needed fortification. When she glanced back at Kowalskin, she found him giving her a smile that wasn't really a smile at all. It was the self-satisfied smirk of a predator who had a clear line on his prey and was just about to pounce.

And she ran.

She couldn't help it. Every instinct in her told her to tuck tail and run for dear life. The panther had been bated long enough and now he was after her.

It was terrifying. Exhilarating. *Erotic.*

Leslie took off through the crowd, blind to anything but putting distance between her and Peter so that she could breathe. She'd made a mistake, teasing him. She took it back.

With a quick glance over her left shoulder, she swallowed a cry when she saw he was right behind her, successfully untangled from the big-chested Latina. And he was still grinning.

Leslie broke free on the far side of the dance floor, "Thrift Shop" still slamming through the speakers to the delight of the party crowd. A laugh bubbled up in her chest and let loose as she took off running down the hall that led to her office. Was he still coming after her?

She glanced back again and there he was, pushing out

of the crowd after her. *Oh God, here he comes.* Nerves, anticipation, fear, arousal. All of it pooled in the pit of her stomach and began swirling, mixing in an intoxicating concoction that made her light-headed.

Leslie reached the door to her office, yanked out the keys she'd shoved between her breasts, and stepped hastily inside. And that's when it happened.

The lights went out.

A scream rose in her throat. Rationally she knew she was okay. It was her club, her office, and it was Peter stalking down the hall toward her, not some random guy.

But it was *Peter.*

"Come on, lights." She muttered under her breath and fumbled for the door knob in the pitch dark, trying to close it before he reached her. Because she wasn't sure what was happening. She'd baited him and now he was coming after her. There would be no turning back if he got his hands on any part of her. The look in his eye had said as much.

And she didn't know what time it was, didn't know if she had the willpower to hold him off. Didn't know if she even *cared.*

Now anger took a stand and joined her, and she welcomed it. It helped reel her back in. How could she even think of caving now when she was mere minutes away from winning her career back?

Relief flooded her when her hand finally gripped the cool round doorknob and started to pull it shut. It was replaced by a skitter of fear when it was yanked out of her hand and her back was pushed up against a wall, a hard body pressing flush against hers.

He'd found her.

"Now you're mine," he growled against her ear, and in the dark with her senses heightened his Yankee-tough voice was just about the most erotic thing she'd ever heard.

She was wet and needy for him in an instant.

"No," Leslie whispered raggedly, not really meaning it. His mouth was on her neck, kissing her in that sweet spot just below her ear that was so sensitive. She grabbed at her control and fought against the intense arousal coursing through her.

Peter thrust a heavy thigh between her legs and pushed them apart, one hand pinning both of hers above her head, the other streaking boldly, possessively over her hips. "No more games, princess. You want this. You know you do."

So help her, she did.

His lips scalded her neck and Leslie let her head fall back, moaned when his tongue slowly tasted her, teased her sensitive flesh. Through the door she could see the lights were back on down the hall, but her office was still dark. It only served to excite her more, being in the semi-dark with Peter. The feel of his hard, unforgiving body pressed against hers made her knees weak.

"We can't do this." The words sounded hollow even to her ears. One of his hands stroked down her leg until it reached her knee and gathered the fabric of her skirt, pushing it aside. Then his jean-clad thigh was rubbing against her crotch and he was taking her mouth in a hungry kiss. Tongue and teeth and primal, aroused male. Never had she been kissed like this, not with this much unbridled passion.

It pushed the last of her resistance right out of her mind.

On a moan of surrender, Leslie opened to him and began kissing him back with matching heat. She tugged her captive hands, but he held her steady, ground out, "Not yet," his voice rough with need.

His hand skimmed up her bare thigh and when Peter reached her panties he yanked them to the side and slid a finger in between her slick lips. "Fuck, Leslie," he growled. "You're so wet for me."

Always. She was always wet for him. "Yes," was all she could say because his thumb had found her clit and was rubbing it, driving her closer and closer to orgasm.

"Come," he demanded. "Come *now.*"

Like she was a puppet and he was her master, Leslie came. The orgasm tore through her with almost violent force and she cried out, "Peter!"

"Again," was all he demanded, his fingers taking no mercy on her as he drove her straight into another orgasm, blowing her mind.

"Why?" Leslie whispered raggedly when the second orgasm began to subside.

Peter trailed kisses over her jaw, searching for her mouth and when he found it he kissed her slowly. "Because you coming is the most beautiful sound in the world," he breathed against her lips, devastating her.

Her heart flung wide open and tears stung the back of her eyes as love and arousal coursed through her. The rush of emotion that overcame her had her gasping and clinging to him.

"Touch me," she breathed. His hands on her were what she needed, what she craved most. Every stroke was charged with emotion; so much of what he couldn't say was communicated through his fingertips.

Needing to feel him, needing to know his heart, Leslie captured his lips with hers in a lingering kiss and moaned when she felt his sexual energy change from aggressive to fluid and erotic. She was suddenly swimming in an ocean of sensuality that verged on dark and decadent. If she'd let him, he would pull her under. And it was so, so tempting.

But she needed to know his feelings first. "Put your hands on me." Leslie couldn't tell if it was a command or if he was begging, and she didn't care. All that mattered was getting his hands on her *now*.

And she got them. Peter released her captive wrists and ran his hand down the length of her arm, across her breast and over her rib cage, with a touch that was confident and possessive and oh-so-hungry. "I want more," he said against her mouth. "More of you coming for me, panting my name."

She wanted that too. But because she wanted to hear him say it, Leslie ran a freed hand down his flat, chiseled stomach and didn't stop until she was holding his straining erection in her palm.

"Why so needy?" she whispered as she stroked him

through his jeans, loving the feel of him, hard and thick with desire for her. He sucked in a sharp breath and moaned softly.

Then he reached out with a hand and flung the door shut, flicked on a nearby lamp, and looked at her with eyes that melted into her soul. His voice was rough and gravelly against her neck when he growled, his hands stroking boldly up her bare thighs. "Because princess, I've come so many times for you, you don't even know. Now it's your turn."

A mental image of Peter touching himself over her, stroking himself off, had her going so achy with sexual hunger that it overrode all her senses, and all she could do was moan helplessly, overwhelmed with the knowledge that he'd wanted her like this all along.

Then her hands were all over him, ripping at his shirt, tugging at his jeans. Peter naked was all she wanted—everything she could need. When his shirt got caught at his chin, he laughed and yanked it the rest of the way off.

"Better?" he said, eyes hot and hazy with passion. She was about to respond when he snagged two fingers into the front of her bodice and tugged hard. Her breasts sprang free and he grinned wickedly. "No, *this* is better."

A laugh bubbled loose and she tossed back her head just as his mouth captured one of her nipples and sucked gently. Then she groaned and grabbed for his zipper, yanking it down. As soon as he was free, she wrapped her hand around him and smiled victoriously when his hands dug into her hips hard and he hissed between his teeth. His forehead fell to hers and he closed his eyes, panting. "Jesus."

Her thumb slipped over the head of his penis, traced the plump ridge and he shuddered, swore. It drove her crazy. Stealing a peek down her body, Leslie moaned softly at the sight of her hand wrapped around his thick shaft, stroking. Her fingers circled the base, and when she moved them down the impressive length of him she noticed it.

Peter's tattoo.

And she suddenly burst out laughing. "Oh God, you really do have one! I was so drunk that night I thought I'd imagined that!"

But she hadn't. There, right where the base of his cock met his groin in stylized black script was his THANK YOU FOR RIDING tattoo.

Still laughing, Peter nipped her skin playfully and growled against her neck as he spun her around and moved her to the desk, "What's so funny?"

Her ass was on the flat surface and his large hands were moving up her thighs under her skirt again, making her breathless. "What your tattoo says."

He pulled back and grinned devilishly. "Well it's true, princess. I'm thankful every damn time."

The way he said it had her head falling back as she laughed. He really did make giving thanks dirty. Bless his heart.

When she lifted her head again and saw his eyes intense with emotion, her heart rolled slowly, helplessly. She was so in love with him it was scary. Completely terrifying.

It must have shown in her eyes because Peter took one look at her and took her mouth in a brutal, passionate kiss. "Fuck, Leslie." Then he was pushing at her skirts, hiking them up around her waist. He covered himself with a condom in record time and gripped her hips. "Look at me," he commanded, his voice harsh with sexual desire and something more. Something unfiltered from somewhere deep inside him.

It made her wild.

The plump head of his penis pushed into her as she looked into his blue eyes totally glazed with passion, and he growled possessively. "*Mine.*"

Yes, his.

"Say it." He panted and pushed into her a little more, making her moan with need.

Because she knew in her heart he was right, Leslie wrapped her legs around his waist and dove her hands into his hair, fisting there. "Yours, Peter."

His whole body shuddered and he thrust into her deep on a ragged groan. "Mine," he said again, this time softly. "Always mine."

Always.

Peter pulled her tight into his embrace, his powerful arms wrapping around her, holding her close as he thrust into her slowly, deeply. Leslie clung to him, her nails digging into his back as the hot circumference of him filled her up and took her right to the edge. The orgasm tore through her with such force that she cried out, tears stinging her eyes, her brain fried.

"I love you, Peter!" she said on a gasp, unaware of

what she was saying as she began to float back down, heart pounding and body tingling.

He went still.

"Christ." He breathed the word like it was a prayer. Then his arms tightened around her almost painfully and he was driving into her, over and over, his breath coming heavy until he thrust into her so deep she could feel him against her womb, and he came forcefully, explosively, calling her name, "Leslie!"

They clung to each other, panting and unmoving, riding on the wave of afterglow and endorphins until they heard a voice from outside the door say loudly, "Shit, where's the bathroom, man? I don't wanna miss the apple-bobbing contest that's about to start. There's some hot chicks out there who are gonna get nice and wet."

The bet.

Reality came crashing back with zero mercy. Suddenly apprehensive, Leslie stole a peek around Peter's shoulder to the clock on the wall, blew a frizzy strand of hair out of her face, and saw the truth.

11:52 P.M.

Her rosy afterglow went *poof!* and her stomach plummeted. God. Typical frigging Leslie.

So much for getting her life back.

Chapter Twenty-One

PETER FELT LESLIE tense around him and was hit with disappointment. He wasn't ready to let her go yet. The way her lush body was wrapped all around him felt so good. So very, very good.

In fact, there wasn't a part of the woman that didn't feel absolutely amazing. And after all these years, all the regret and humiliation, he had finally sorted it out with Leslie. Now he knew what he had missed out on. Every fantasy, every daydream he'd had of her hadn't come close to comparing with the reality.

The reality of Leslie was fucking amazing.

"Well played, Kowalskin."

He thought so too. He'd always been good at catch. But it sounded suspiciously like Leslie wasn't as thrilled about his skills as he was. Peter pulled back some to get a good look at her, and what he saw had his insides going cold.

Her face was pale and her eyes were bitter. Gone was the passionate woman from a few minutes ago. Now he was looking at a whole lot of angry. Though his brain was in a temporary state of hormone-induced euphoria, he could still tell that something was very wrong with Leslie.

Shit. After all the build-up and anticipation, was she disappointed in his performance?

"I need some air." Her hands were flat against his chest and she gave a sound push. Letting her go, he skimmed his fingertips down her thigh as she disengaged, needing the feel of her silky skin one more time.

"What's the deal, princess?" She'd just said she loved him. He was still reeling from it. And now she wanted space. What the hell? She couldn't just turn off like that. It wasn't fair.

She practically jumped off the desk and went about straightening her clothing, yanking at the fabric, the whole time scowling and not looking at him. Considering he'd just had the best sex of his entire life with the woman of his dreams, it was a bit deflating to see her in this state. Made him want to have a go at her again and not stop until all she was able to do was lie there and smile.

Because she sure wasn't smiling now. "Don't play dumb, Kowalskin. It isn't becoming."

Suddenly frustrated, Peter raked his hands through his hair and began redressing. "I don't know what the hell you're so upset about."

She stopped what she was doing and leveled him with a hard stare. "You really don't know?" The way she said it made it sound like an accusation, not a question.

It was damn irritating. "No, Leslie," he drawled. "I really don't know." How could he? From where he was standing things were way good.

Her face contorted in anger and she flung her arm out toward the wall, pointing. "You won. Are you happy?"

Peter saw the wall clock, noted the time. It wasn't quite midnight. Well, damn, it looked like he actually had won the bet after all.

Amused, Peter zipped his fly and laughed softly. "Of course. It's been a damn good day."

His T-shirt suddenly hit him in the chest and he looked up quizzically just in time to see tears fill Leslie's eyes. "For *you*. It's been a good day for *you*, Peter." She fisted a hand in front of her mouth, sucked in air. "*I* lost."

She was upset about the bet? "It was just a bet, princess. No big thing."

Her eyes went huge and she huffed, clearly offended, "*No big thing*?"

The sudden glint in her eye had him reassessing, backtracking. "Well, that's not maybe the right wording." Then he shrugged it off, because yeah it was. "We both know it was nothing more than an extended game of foreplay, an excuse for this." He gestured between them in their respective states of undress. "Why so upset?"

Leslie exploded. "Because it was my life! It was my chance to reclaim what's mine—my career, my self-respect. It was my new start." Her eyes were dark as forests and full of bitter heartache. "The bet was everything, and I went and fucked it up just like usual."

Peter could see she was working herself into a big

tizzy and was about to respond when his cell phone went off in his pocket. What the hell? Nobody called him this late at night.

Reaching into his jeans for it, he glanced at Leslie, who was busy crossing her arms and muttering to herself, and spared his caller ID a quick look. His blood went cold. Shit.

"I have to take this." He didn't even wait for her acknowledgment.

His cell continued to ring and he hit the talk button. "This is Peter," he said tightly in Ukrainian.

The voice on the other side was gruff and spoke only in the Slavic language. Peter listened to the message and responded in his father's native tongue, his good mood morphing into something else entirely in an instant. By the time the call disconnected his mind was a million miles away and his gut felt hollow.

It must have shown on his face because when he shoved his phone back in his pocket Leslie reached a hand out and placed it on his arm. "What's wrong, Peter?"

His gaze slid from her hand to her face, and he took in her big, concerned eyes. And he felt nothing. Nothing at all, only numb. "I have to go."

The moment was gone, his perfect day completely ruined with one phone call. He didn't see Leslie standing there with her heart on her sleeve. Didn't see beyond the sudden whiteout in his mind.

"What? Why? What happened, Peter?"

He looked at Leslie without really seeing and said flatly, "My father is dead."

Then he walked out on his dream to go deal with his nightmare.

"AND THEN HE just left, y'all."

Drake rubbed his chin, confused. "You're saying he told you his dad died and now he's gone? Where?"

Leslie shrugged her bare shoulders, worry for Peter tying her stomach in knots. "Not sure, but I'm assuming Philadelphia. Isn't that where his dad lived?"

Everybody shrugged back.

"Doesn't anybody know anything about his family?" she asked with mounting frustration. Her heart ached for Peter and she wanted to help. It was damn aggravating that nobody seemed to have any useful information. How could she go after him if nobody knew where he was?

"Not to complain, sweet thing," started Paulson, "but maybe we could remember things better if we weren't all stuffed into your office and could breathe."

There was a murmur of agreement.

Leslie huffed, crammed in between Mark and Lorelei. "Nobody could hear me out on the floor when I first tried to explain, y'all. It was necessary."

"Squished in like a can of sardines," came a disgruntled voice. That was Mark, standing next to her.

Leslie elbowed him in the ribs and said to everyone huddled in the space. "Look. I need to know he's okay. Somebody has to call him. I've been trying since he left, but he's not picking up. Who's going to volunteer?" Maybe he was on a plane and that's why he hadn't picked

up. But given the way he'd ignored her attempts at contact the last time he'd been upset, she wasn't willing to
put money on it. And right now his heart must be broken.
It was killing her, not being able to comfort him.

JP spoke up from behind Paulson. All she could see
was the top of his hair behind a massive green shoulder.
"I'll call. It's time Sonny and I got home anyway and relieved the babysitter."

She called out a "thank you" to the couple holding
hands as they waved goodnight.

Turning back to find three people staring at her expectantly, Leslie said, "What are y'all looking at me for?"

Everybody shrugged.

Deciding that the night shouldn't be ruined for everyone, she pasted a smile on her face and said, even though
her heart was hurting, "Let's head back out, shall we?"

The relief was palpable as two very large professional
ballplayers vied for prime position, trying to be the first
to exit. Drake and Mark reminded her of cattle being
shoved down a chute. If she wasn't so worried about Peter
she'd laugh over all the jostling.

Lorelei hung back and leaned into her side then,
saying quietly, "Don't worry, hon. I'm sure he'll be just
fine."

Yeah, maybe. "I want to go after him so bad." She
sighed and hugged her sister-in-law briefly with one arm.

"I know, sweetie. But nobody knows where he is. It's
best to stay put—for now," she ended hastily when Leslie
frowned.

Lorelei was probably right, but she hadn't seen the

look on his face when he'd been talking in Ukrainian. Peter had gone so cold and detached that he'd looked like a marble statue.

Which meant he was really hurting.

Knowing that pushed the disappointment over losing the bet right out of her mind. There were more important things to worry about now. Things like Peter handling his dad's death alone.

And things like how she'd told him that she loved him.

She hadn't missed that fact. As much as she might like to lie and pretend that she didn't remember declaring her love for him, it just wasn't true. Leslie remembered all right. It had come back to her when she'd thrown his T-shirt at him. She just wasn't going to remind him.

When he returned she was just going to hug him hard and pretend like she'd never uttered such nonsense. Maybe he hadn't even heard her. There was always that possibility. If he never heard her then it wouldn't even be an issue. They could just go on.

Yeah, that would be great.

Wasn't going to happen, though. She knew Peter and he was going to pick at her, poking and prodding until she lost her shit and told him everything he wanted to know—and a whole lot of what he didn't.

Chapter Twenty-Two

PETER STEPPED OUT from the shabby corner Dunkin'
Donuts into the freezing Philadelphia air and huddled
into his leather coat, one hand cradling his coffee. The
heavy gray sky that was just starting to snow perfectly
matched his mood.

He'd been in the city for almost a week handling the
details of his father's death. Not that there was much to
handle, truthfully. Mostly he was there out of a sense of
obligation and to see that he was buried properly. It was
the first time since he'd turned eighteen that he'd been
back to the city for anything other than a ball game.

It was hard.

Flipping up the collar of his coat, Peter shoved his free
hand in a front pocket and glanced around at the urban
decay of South Philly. He had decided to park his rental
car in a more stable neighborhood and walk the rest of
the way to the house where he'd grown up; a long stroll

was preferable to a car-jacking and he wasn't concerned about being mugged. He knew how to handle himself. Along the way he passed crumbling structures covered in colorful graffiti. One of the dilapidated brick buildings had a two-story mural of a smiling Jamaican woman at home in her native land, lush palms behind her and a basket full of plump sweet potatoes.

The juxtaposition of such hope, pride, and beauty amidst such poverty and despair was beyond jarring. But it spoke to the heart of the people that made their home there. In a land that was supposed to take care of its own, they were living in a third-world country. It wasn't right. It wasn't even close to right. Still, they kept the hope. They saw beauty.

They were his people.

He hadn't helped his father.

The thought came at him from left field, catching him unaware. It wasn't for a lack of trying. Considering his pop was the only family he'd had, Peter had gone to the mat for him and tried to get him clean, tried to get him help. But Viktor Kowalskin had wanted nothing more than to kill himself with drink.

At some point in the last two years, Peter had just quit trying. And now his pop was dead from liver failure and he felt guilty. Like he should have tried harder. Like he shouldn't have given up on his old man. But what was he supposed to do? The man was an abusive drunk, unwilling to change. And now he was gone.

There was a part of him, although tiny, that felt relieved. It was over. Now he could move forward without this always around his neck, weighing him down. It was a crappy, selfish feeling and he knew it. But he was just so tired of fighting against everything. It had made him weary.

He'd fought against the inevitable and lost. His pop, his eye disease, Leslie. In the end, no matter how much of a fight he'd put up, it hadn't been enough.

His life felt a lot like the wreckage and rubble that he was strolling through.

He crossed the street as a low-rider Buick painted in gray primer cruised down the street past him very slowly. A group of young thugs were huddled inside the car, giving him a very thorough shakedown. Any other person would be perturbed by the territorial display.

But they weren't Peter.

His body posture changed and he morphed into the kid who'd known these streets, who'd known how to act. He wasn't worried. Hunching his shoulders, he continued walking, sipping casually from his to-go cup of coffee.

The car sped up suddenly, the juveniles shouting obscenities at him as they whipped past and threw a beer can. But then they rounded a corner and headed out of sight, the sound of the souped-up Buick fading in the distance.

Peter took a left as he got closer to his old neighborhood and felt anxiety twist painfully in his gut. A pit bull on a chain rushed him from the right, barking hard and slobbering. The clearly underfed dog was crazy-eyed. Reaching into his pocket, he pulled out the last of his breakfast burrito and unwrapped it. Then he tossed it to the foamy-mouthed canine. "Here, dog. Eat." He knew all too well what it was like to starve in this place.

The busted sign declaring that he'd arrived at his designated street came into view as a damp, frigid wind blew a gust hard enough to have him sucking in a breath. Damn, that was cold. He'd forgotten how different Philly winters were from Denver. The cold here was wet and heavy and had a way of seeping right into the bones, chilling a person to the core.

Turning off the main road into a small, sad-looking ethnic neighborhood, Peter scanned the barely-habitable shacks, noticing a curtain flutter in one of them as he went by. It wasn't every day that these people had a random guy walking in their hood. And if they did it was normally a cause for concern. If it was him, he'd be peeking out his window wanting to know who the hell was out there too. It was a matter of safety.

He didn't have to be there. Didn't have to go back to his roots. But after avoiding it for almost a week by busying himself with all the legal hoopla and logistics of burying his old man, he'd finally accepted that he couldn't stay away. Who he was now stemmed from growing up in this place.

The shacks he walked past were really worn-down, buckling old bungalows. Nothing more than rectangles with front steps, the tiny houses butted right up to the street. There was no grass, no green. Lawns were for rich people.

His old place came into view down the road as the memory of Leslie asking him about food came to mind.

That woman saw everything—things about himself that he didn't even recognize. It was more than a little scary. And now she said she was in love with him.

It ruined everything.

Peter didn't want to be loved, or so he told himself as he strolled down his old street. The heavy sky kicked into gear and snow started to fall steadily now, covering the ground in minutes. He just kept on walking, taking reassuring sips of steaming coffee.

What the hell was he supposed to do with love?

Sex, he understood. Passion, desire, lust—those emotions he got. But love? About that, he didn't know a fucking thing. All he knew was that it always screwed everything up. His mother leaving his pop for another man under the premise of "love" was his only point of reference, and it was a pretty shitty one.

Nobody loved him.

And that was okay. It was a flawed concept anyway. So why did Leslie have to go and mess it all up by claiming to be in love with him? They were good the way they were. Two independent people with a ton of sexual chemistry. That he understood. It made sense. Besides, even if she was in love with him now, it would only be a matter of time before she realized he wasn't worth it.

She was a princess. He was this.

Peter shook his head, lips pressed together tightly as snowflakes clung to his dark hair and he approached his childhood home. He could see it up ahead and his gut went greasy, unsettled. The squat shack was literally falling down. Its roof was bowed and one of the back corners drooped, leaning listlessly to the side like the foundation had washed out from under it. The gray paint was mostly peeled and some of the windows were boarded up with a combination of cardboard and duct tape.

Pretty much looked the same as it always had.

Still two houses away, Peter whipped his head around when a front door nearby creaked open. Bracing himself, his body instantly relaxed when he saw who stepped out.

"Hey, Mrs. Petrov," he greeted in Ukrainian, his breath releasing white puffs into the air. He couldn't believe the old lady was still alive. She'd been ancient when he was eighteen. It was her grandson Ivan who'd called him Halloween night. Peter had assumed she'd died ages ago. Tough old Slavic bird.

"Is that you, Peter Kowalskin?" Her voice was paper thin and raspy with age. He could still remember the way it used to get all shrill when she yelled at him and some of the other neighbor kids, including Ivan, for stealing fireworks and setting them off in the middle of the street.

Peter smiled at the memory and strolled over to give her a kiss on each of her frail cheeks. Her faded blue eyes crinkled and she swatted a hand at him, chiding, "You stay away too long, boy. But look at you all grown and strong and handsome. Doing well for yourself. You came back for him," she ended, not asking but rather making a statement.

He nodded. "I did."

"Sad sight he was, at the end." She made a *tsking* sound and pulled her head scarf tighter around her chin, shaking her head.

"So I heard." He hadn't, really.

"Shame what happens to a soul when it gets lost like that." She made a sign of the cross with three fingers over her thin chest. "May he rest in peace."

"You have a good heart, Mrs. P." In a lot of ways she'd been his surrogate mother, taking care of him and her grandson when her daughter had taken off in the middle of the night with a local kingpin on a drug run. Far as he knew she'd never returned.

"*Pssh*, boy." She batted at him again, but her cheeks were pink. "You're one to talk, the way you spoil Ivan and me every Christmas with your basket of goodies."

He'd thought he'd been sending it only to Ivan as thanks for keeping a watchful eye out, and now he felt bad. This year's basket was going to be even bigger now that he knew she was still around. His conscience was making him feel guilty for not keeping in better touch with Ivan. Mostly their interactions had consisted of him giving the guy his number to call in case of emergency and the gift basket every year at Christmas.

The old Slav must have read his mind because she patted his arm reassuringly. "You did what was right for you, boy. You got out of here. He was proud of you for that, you know."

Peter made a face, unbelieving. "Could have fooled me."

She cuffed his ear unexpectedly, reminding him just how much respect a tiny Slavic woman could command. "Hush. He loved you, Peter. It was himself he couldn't stand."

"I hear you, Mrs. P." So she wouldn't get worked up,

he dropped another kiss on her cheek, diffusing her. It might have been a long time ago, but he still knew how to soften her up.

Just then a car turned onto the street and both Peter and Mrs. Petrov craned their necks to see who was coming. Most of the cars in this neighborhood didn't run. And they certainly weren't fancy.

This one was both.

Suddenly apprehensive, Peter wrapped an arm around the old lady and smiled charmingly. "Why don't you get yourself inside where it's warm. It's freezing out. All this snow will make you catch cold."

She patted his hand with one of hers and let him help her up her front two steps. "Come by and have something to eat before you leave." It wasn't really an invitation. He knew it too. It was a command, and he wouldn't miss it. The woman made a mean potato stew.

Peter kept up the smile until she was safely inside where it was at least dry and warmer. Then he rolled his shoulders like a boxer and turned his attention to the sleek black sedan that was crawling down the street toward him. Coming from the opposite direction, the car stopped directly in front of his old house, confusing him.

As he watched, a man climbed out from the driver's side, bundled up in a wool coat, hat, and gloves. Peter's apprehension kicked up another notch. He couldn't put his finger on it, but there was something familiar about the guy.

Peter took another sip of the rapidly cooling coffee and

strolled over, taking his time scrutinizing the stranger. About his age, the guy had a lean and rugged build and a face to match. Though his clothes were tailored and obviously high quality, there was a toughness about the guy, an earthiness that no amount of designer clothing could completely hide.

"Nice day," Peter broke the silent stare-down, keeping it casual as he strode over and stopped directly in front of his pop's home.

The stranger rounded the hood of his car and gave a guarded smile. "Reminds me of home. Sean Muldoon," he finished with an outstretched hand.

Peter's eyebrows shot up in surprise. Was that an Irish brogue he heard? This neighborhood was Ukrainian. Who was this guy? "I'm Peter." He held out his hand and was impressed when it was met with a solid handshake. "Where's home, Sean?"

"Little town outside Dublin, Ireland." Pale green eyes assessed him openly. "You're not from here, either." It was another statement. He was getting a lot of those today.

"I used to be."

Sean visibly relaxed and tipped his head toward Peter's childhood home, thick black eyebrows arched in question. "Then you know the man who used to live there?"

Oh hell. His pop hadn't left a debt with the Irish mob, had he? "I do," he replied neutrally, eyes quickly scanning the Irishman's body for concealed weapons, a little trick he'd picked up during his youth, and found none. He relaxed some then too.

"Place is a shithole." The guy's gaze was locked on the crumbling structure that held all of Peter's childhood memories.

He crossed his arms. "Yes, it is that." Not that he hadn't tried to change that. But his father had refused every attempt he'd ever made to help.

They both stood staring at the tiny bungalow, arms crossed, feet braced apart. It occurred to Peter that he still couldn't place why the guy seemed so familiar. He should probably just ask. Yeah, he should do that.

"My father used to live there," Sean said.

Peter's gaze whipped to his right, locked on the Irishman. "Excuse me?"

Sean motioned to the house in front of them that looked sad and pathetic in the falling snow, all boarded up and crumbling down. "My father, Viktor Kowalskin, lived there. He just passed away. Did you know him?"

Shock slapped him upside the face and Peter swore, rejecting it. "What the fuck? He isn't your father." He couldn't be.

Sean's blue eyes went hard. "The hell he isn't."

Peter was reeling. "But he can't be your father."

"Why is that?" demanded the black-haired Irishman.

"Because he's *my* father."

Both men stared hard at each other in awkward silence as the truth of their relationship hit them. Then Sean swore something decidedly Gaelic and threw back his head, laughing. Peter scowled. Frigging Irish, always thinking every damn thing was a joke. How could he laugh at a time like this?

Could his life get any more fucked up?

"Well that was unexpected. Should we properly toast the old man's passing with a stiff drink and get to know each other, *brother*?"

Yeah. Apparently it could.

Chapter Twenty-Three

"HEY Y'ALL, THANKS for coming tonight," Leslie said as she opened the door to her guests. There were only two of them, Sonny and Lorelei, but it was all the girls she needed to help celebrate the return to her abode.

Lorelei was the first inside and was unzipping her coat when she asked, "Are you loving being back home?"

"*So* much." Although she had gotten used to all the space in Peter's house scarily fast. Made her apartment feel teeny.

Even so, it felt great to finally be home, even though she was still worried crazy over Peter and bummed over losing the bet. For the past week Leslie had been back in her apartment, thoroughly enjoying having her old bed back.

Missy hadn't been as enthused. The kitten had kept yowling until, fed up, Leslie had driven to Peter's place in the middle of the night and snatched one of his dirty

T-shirts. As soon as the baby had gotten a good whiff of his scent she'd stopped crying and fallen asleep on it in a little ball of fluff.

If Leslie had held it briefly to her nose, inhaling his scent too, well, there was no proof.

God she missed him. So much so that she'd put the damn shirt on and slept in it, Missy curled up into her side, purring contentedly. It had been a darn good night's sleep.

Sonny hung her coat and scarf in the entryway closet and looked around. "Your place is great, Leslie. I really love the bold colors. Mind if I snoop around?" Her gaze was already down the hallway.

Coming from the woman who had such a funky, easy style, Leslie took that compliment seriously. "Thanks, darlin'." She gestured behind her to the open living room. "Snoop."

The natural beauty grinned. "Awesome. I'll be back in a few."

"I've never been to a stitch'n'bitch before." Lorelei held up a bag full of yarn and two large knitting needles. "In fact, I've never really even knitted."

"I'm still pretty new at it myself, so it should be fun. Mostly it's an excuse to sit around and bitch to your girlfriends about life." There were one or two things she could get off her chest.

"You mean like about how I now vomit more times a day than a regular person eats meals?"

Leslie patted her shoulder. "Exactly, love."

"Fabulous!" Lorelei's smile was bright and full of humor.

Just then Sonny strode back into the room looking gorgeous and bohemian in black leggings and an over-sized off-the-shoulder knitted sweater the color of plums in spring. "You have great decorating taste, Leslie."

"Thanks." She motioned to the empty chair next to her. "Have a seat."

"I just need to grab my bag quickly." She was back in no time with a picnic basket full of yarn and needles. "I'm so glad we're doing this. Life has been so crazy that I've stalled out on this sweater I was making. This gives me the motivation to start again."

Lorelei inquired, "Where's the boy tonight?"

"On a date with JP. They went out to see the new big sci-fi flick at the theater." Sonny tucked her feet under her and settled a ball of yarn on her lap.

Leslie did the same, tucking her bare feet under her and snuggling down inside her own baggy sweater. She was wearing her oldest, most favorite worn-in pair of jeans. The knees were about to blow, but that was okay. She was a loyal girl. She'd wear them until the ass ripped out.

She gestured to the tea tray in front of her. "In honor of the pregnant lady we're doing decaf tea. There's a variety of flavors to choose from, so help yourself."

Lorelei was already pouring a cup. "So, have you heard anything from Peter?"

She shook her head and pulled out her knitting basket from its cubby tucked under the end table. "I haven't, actually. And it's been a week since he left." One very long, very worrisome week.

"No doubt he's fine, sweetie. He's probably just taking

some time for himself." Sonny added a slice of fresh lemon to her tea.

"I'm sure he'll get a hold of Mark when he's back." Leslie said casually, like it didn't matter to her at all that she'd had mind-shattering sex with the man and then he'd taken off before she'd even gotten fully dressed. Or that it didn't matter that she'd wasted so much time and energy planning for an event that was never going to happen in any reality because she didn't know how to keep her hands to herself. Peter had come along wanting up in her skirt and she'd tossed every functioning brain cell out her ears, only keeping the warped ones to make decisions for her.

And now she was back to square one. Back to being lonely, independent Leslie who worked at her brother's nightclub and didn't have anything of her own. Sounded terrific, didn't it?

A slap on her knee jolted her. "Hey, so you need to fill us in on this bet that you had going with Peter. Give us the details." Lorelei leaned back in her chair and sipped at her peach tea.

Her first instinct was to keep her mouth shut. It was probably the right one. So of course she chose the opposite. "Y'all know how I've been trying to get him to play at the club, right?" They nodded. "Well, he bet that he could get me in the sack by the end of the World Series, or he'd play at Hotbox and let me promote the hell out of it to help the business—which I'd be buying with the down payment he'd also give me."

Sonny's eyes went round and she stopped knitting.

"So he's playing at the club, *and* you're buying it? That's great! I'll definitely come see him."

Ugh. This was the awkward part. She should have kept her mouth shut. "Um, well, not exactly."

Lorelei gasped and slapped her knee again. "Is *that* what you two were doing on Halloween when you both disappeared?"

Sonny dropped her knitting needles. "Wait. You slept with Peter?"

Damn it. Stupid mouth. Leslie cringed. "Sort of, yes."

Both women just stared at her, their mouths open. Neither spoke for a good minute. It was making her self-conscious.

Finally Lorelei blurted, "Was it good?"

Leslie's gaze flew to her. When she saw the mischievous glint in her eyes she relaxed, smiling playfully. "Everything you think it would be, plus some."

Sonny murmured, "He does have big hands."

It was Leslie's turn to gasp. "Sonny!"

The woman shrugged delicately, her eyes sparkling. "Just sayin'."

"Seriously," said Lorelei. "How do you feel about him?"

Did she have to answer that? It was all so confusing.

Just then her sister-in-law shot out of her chair. "Be right back." Then she bolted across the great room and down the hall to the bathroom.

"Poor thing." Sonny's voice was full of sympathy.

"Yeah. It's a shame men can't be the pregnant ones."

She snorted. "Good thing. It'd be the end of our species if they were."

Leslie laughed. So true. Women were the real warriors. Every single one who gave birth to another human being. "Yeah. Take Mark, for instance. He can't even handle a hangnail."

Lorelei came back into the room several minutes later looking pale and picked up the conversation thread. "Hey now. He can too. It's paper cuts that make him whine like a sissy."

Her brother, the hero.

Sonny spoke up then. "What are you holding, Lorelei?"

The brunette glanced down. "Oh. Here, Leslie. I found this behind the toilet." She pulled a face. "Don't ask what I was doing when I found it."

Holding out a hand, Leslie took the piece of paper and frowned. It looked like a shipping confirmation tag. Quickly scanning it, she saw that it was indeed a receipt. For a plumbing fixture. From overseas.

Dated three weeks ago.

Her blood ran cold as all the possible ramifications hit her. Jerry had told her they were still waiting on the overseas part and she was positive it was the only one. She remembered him saying so. But if that was true then it could only mean one thing: She had been played by a pitcher. For weeks.

And that made her very, very angry.

"THANKS FOR THE wonderful night, John. It was great to catch up." Leslie rummaged around in her clutch for her keys, eager to get inside and kick off her shoes. It had been a long evening.

Perfectly pleasant, John Crispin had been a fine date. Intelligent, well read, courteous. He was everything that she normally went for in a man. But for some reason her appreciation for Armani just wasn't the same lately.

That reason was Peter.

She was still fuming over his little stunt. After Lorelei and Sonny had left she'd marched down to the superintendent's office and pounded on the door until he'd opened up. Then she'd waved the incriminating evidence and rained all kinds of hellfire down on him until he'd come clean and admitted the truth.

Her apartment had been finished two weeks ago, but Peter had *inspired* him to hold her off until the first of November.

Ugh! It still galled her because she knew he'd set her up hard. By keeping her at his place it had given him the opportunity and time to seduce her into bed, to stack the deck against her.

It was signature Kowalskin. Dirty pool all the way. And because she was just so mad at him, she'd decided that she wasn't in love with him anymore. Done. The end. Completely over it.

Over *him*.

As proof of her new liberating decision she'd called John up and asked him for that date after she'd found out he was still in town visiting friends. Seemed appropriate and like a fine way to forget about her brief foray into emotional stupidity. "Well, thanks again." She put her key in the lock and felt the tumblers click.

"Do you mind if I come inside for a minute? There's something I've been wanting to ask you," the big, masculine ballplayer said softly from right behind her. She could feel his broad chest brushing her back slightly as he reached around her and pushed the door open.

Actually she did mind—she was exhausted and wanted nothing more than to change into her pajamas and flop onto the couch for an hour with Missy and a book. But that wasn't the polite thing to do. Her Southern manners chose the oddest times to kick in and start dictating.

Leslie stepped through the door and forced a smile. "Not at all. Come on inside."

Dropping the keys on her kitchen counter, she spotted her kitten waddling toward her, meowing with her tiny voice, and Leslie set her purse down and scooped her up. "Hi, sweetheart. Did you miss me?"

A deep male voice said behind her quietly, "I did, Leslie."

Uh-oh.

Turning with the kitten in her arms, she took in John's serious expression and heard warning bells go off in her head, spiking her anxiety. She played it cool. "That's a sweet thing to say." Hopefully if she didn't encourage him he'd ask his question and leave.

Maybe going on a date with him hadn't been the best idea.

"Leslie," the ballplayer started, "I know that we went our separate ways when I got traded to Boston, and I get it. I don't blame you for breaking it off."

Crap. She could tell where this was heading, and her stomach sank. "John—"

He held up a hand and cut her off. "Let me finish." She clamped her mouth shut and he continued, "It was a lot for me to ask you to uproot and move with me when there was no firm commitment between us—no future plans."

Oh no.

Leslie's heart began pounding and she looked over her shoulder, held the kitten to her and began petting her furiously. "It's okay, John. Really. We just weren't meant to be." She flashed him a wide smile, hoping that he'd just shut up and stop talking. *No, no, no. Don't do this.*

He took a step toward her and she took one in retreat. "I can see that you're nervous. And I think I know why." He took another step toward her and she stepped back, coming flat up against the refrigerator. *Damn it.*

Another step and he was directly in front of her, taking Missy out of her clenched, clinging fingers and setting her on the floor. Her breath went shallow and her brain scrambled for a way out of this. But she was so frazzled that she couldn't think of anything.

Large, hard hands cupped hers and brought them to his chest; his brown eyes went warm with invitation. "You're nervous because of the chemistry. It's still there, Les."

That wasn't why she was practically shaking.

"John," she said a little helplessly. It had definitely been a bad decision to call him up for that date.

A thick finger covered her lips and she gave a tiny

squeak. "Shh, let me speak. I've been thinking on this ever since my trade and there's something I need to ask you."

Please don't!

The ballplayer dropped to his knee. "You're an incredible woman. Strong, feisty, intelligent."

"John—" she croaked weakly. *God, don't do this to me.*

Brown eyes filled with hopeful expectation looked up at her as he shifted both her hands to one of his and reached into the front pocket of his slacks. "I love you, Leslie Ann Cutter."

"Great!" she squeaked, not thinking.

John opened the box in his hand and right there in the middle of it was a huge diamond ring. "Will you marry me?"

Her mouth dropped open and she blanked, couldn't say anything. Went numb with shock.

The front door slapped against the wall, making a loud thump. Leslie jerked, and her eyes went round and panicked when Peter sauntered in.

He took one look at the scene and stopped dead, scowling hotly. "Are you *fucking* kidding me?"

Chapter Twenty-Four

PETER COULDN'T BELIEVE his eyes.

John Crispin on his knees proposing to Leslie. It was wrong. Just all around *wrong.* "What the hell do you think you two are doing?"

The ballplayer looked from Leslie to Peter, clearly confused. "I was trying to ask her to marry me before you busted in without knocking." He frowned. "*Why* didn't you knock?"

Peter clamped his mouth shut and stared at Leslie. She had a whole lot of explaining to do, and she'd better start quick. Because it looked a whole lot like she'd screwed him senseless last week and declared her love, only to turn right back around a minute later and give her heart to someone else. Christ. He'd known it—known it the moment he'd spotted Crispin at the club during the Series that it was only going to bring trouble.

Damn her hot, fickle ass.

A growl started to rumble low in his chest as she stared at him blankly while another man crouched on his knee before her with a giant goddamn ring.

It looked like he wasn't immune to the good ol' Kowalskin family curse. He couldn't keep his woman either. Terrific.

"Now, Peter," Crispin started, putting the ring back in the box. "If I'm in your territory, brother, I didn't know it. But I'm not sorry. I care for Leslie."

"I can't. John, I'm sorry. I just can't." Her voice was soft and resigned.

So the mouse finally found her voice, did she? "You can't what? Marry another man after you've been screwing me?" His anger had gained momentum and was currently churning in his gut like a storm. He didn't know why it hit him so suddenly, so violently. All he knew was that the minute he'd spotted Leslie all dolled up in a slinky dress with another man, he'd wanted to hit something.

He couldn't stand the thought of her being with anyone else.

"It's not like that." Her eyes were round with sincerity.

But he didn't buy it. Why wouldn't she want a guy like Crispin rather than him? The guy came from healthy stock, a solid upbringing. He wasn't damaged goods like Peter.

"Oh really? Then why don't you tell me what it's like, *Leslie*." He spat. Under the anger was a whole lot of hurt, a lot of stinging betrayal. And he didn't understand it. Didn't want to understand it.

She was supposed to love *him*.

John hastened to his feet and held out his hands to Peter in a show of peace. "I can see that I made a mistake here, so I'm just going to leave."

Peter barely flicked him a glance. "Yeah, I think you better." His attention was only on the heartache in the black dress in front of him.

The big ballplayer left as the tension stretched almost to the breaking point. Then the two of them were left alone, staring at each other, chests heaving. Silence stretched and Peter's nerves frayed.

He couldn't stand it. "What were you doing on a date with John? God, you didn't even wait, did you? You just went right to him the minute my back was turned." He knew he was being an asshole, but he couldn't help it. He *hurt*. In a way like he'd never experienced before. It was tearing him up inside. And he didn't know what to do with it, didn't know where to put it.

"Now you hold on there," said his unfaithful princess, fire lighting in the dark-forest depths of her eyes and her back snapping straight. "You don't get to accuse me, Peter Kowalskin. Not after what you've done."

What *he'd* done? "I've done nothing, you pretty little liar."

She reared back, her hand flying to her barely contained tits in her low cut dress. "Excuse me?" she gasped incredulously. "*You're* the lair."

He raked both hands through his hair. "What the hell are you talking about? You lied to *me*." Pain lashed him and he couldn't quite hide it when he looked at her and said, "You told me you loved me."

Leslie crossed her arms. "I changed my mind." Her voice dripped with challenge as she stared him down, practically begging him to call her out.

"You did, did you?" His voice was deadly soft.

"Absolutely." She snapped her fingers. "Just that easy."

Peter opened his mouth, but she cut him off. "Like you should really give a shit anyway, you lying jerk."

His chest burned in response to her words. Wasn't love supposed to be more loyal than that? How could she just up and change her mind? "Fine. What did I lie to you about?"

Her cheeks were flushed, her voice glacial. "My apartment."

That stopped him. "What?"

"I know about my apartment. I know you lied to me and you made Jerry lie too. Lorelei found a package tracking receipt."

He snorted. "Is that what you're all bent about?"

"Yes." She ground out.

"Fine. You got me. I'm guilty." He threw up his hands. But he didn't feel bad. His lie didn't even come close to comparing to the whopper she'd told him. And here he'd been starting to think that Leslie being in love with him might not be such a bad thing. In fact, he was sort of starting to depend on it.

Her lips pressed into a tight line. Seeing the strain on her face took some of the fury out of him. He couldn't stand to see her cry.

"How could you do that to me?" Her eyes were bright with unshed tears.

"You know why, Leslie."

She shook her head vigorously. "I don't. I don't know why."

He could tell she was being sincere. His hands dropped from his hair and fell to his sides, his heart squeezing painfully. What was the use in evading?

He didn't. "Because I was desperate to have you."

A smile he'd never seen before twisted her beautiful lips. It was more like a snarl and filled with self-loathing. "It wasn't that hard. You got me. Congratulations."

It broke his heart.

LESLIE PUSHED AWAY from the refrigerator, her heart pounding and bitterness making her eyes tear. She was so mad at Peter for manipulating her. And she was so fucking mad at herself for sleeping with him, for throwing away her convictions so easily.

She rounded on him, shouting, "You set me up to fail!" There was so much anger, so much bitterness. All she wanted was someone to blame.

"How's that?" He crossed his arms and leaned back into the counter, looking at her with one brow arched.

"You knew I couldn't resist you." There, she'd admitted the truth.

"How is that my fault?" He replied flatly.

It was a knife in the heart. She sucked in air, stunned. "How could you say that to me?"

"How can you take back loving me?" He crossed his

ankles, too, looking oh-so-cool-and-casual. It was so misleading.

The question fell, raw and unfiltered—just like the man who'd spoken it. And it took her knees out from under her. Her shoulders slumped from the weight of her lie. "Because."

He uncrossed his ankles. "That's it? Just because?" His lips twitched.

"Yes."

Slowly he untangled himself and walked toward her. The expression is his eyes began to change, began to heat. "Then how about you fall back in love with me—just because?"

About halfway across the kitchen he stopped and muttered, "What the hell?" looking down, confused.

Leslie leaned around him to see Missy attached to the back of his pant leg, chewing at the frayed strings. "Your fan girl missed you."

Peter reached down and scooped the kitten up with one hand. She was so small and his hand was so large that he cradled her like a baseball. His eyes softened. "Hey, furball." She was on her back purring like her life depended on it, boneless in complete bliss. Her guy was back.

It was adorable. Without thinking Leslie said, smiling. "She loves you, too."

Like she'd thrown a bucket of ice on him, Peter went rigid and cold in one breath. He stared at her, his gaze suddenly watchful as he stroked Missy. "That seems to be a theme lately. Is she going to change her mind about it, too?"

The way he said it had irritation welling up in her. "Is that such a terrible thing? I thought you didn't want to be loved?"

He smiled slightly, cradling the kitten to his chest. She wondered if he even realized what he was doing. "It can be damn inconvenient," he agreed. The way he looked at her through his lashes made it clear he was baiting her.

It worked, because she didn't like the thought of her love being an inconvenience to him, regardless of whether she actually did or not.

Her irritation grew teeth. Leslie smacked her forehead, suddenly fuming. "Oh that's right!" Her voice dripped molasses and sarcasm. "I forgot about Mr. Commitment-Phobe. Can't handle anything that might require something of you in return."

Feelings she didn't even know she had started spewing from somewhere deep inside. "But that's the funny thing about love. It doesn't require anything in return. So what's the deal?"

"Why do you care?" The look he gave her was chilling. She snapped. "I don't!"

He didn't want her love. The truth of it made her a little crazy. She yelled, "*I'm not in love with you!*"

Pain flashed briefly in Peter's eyes before he could hide it. But she still saw it and her heart squeezed. "Good. Because I'm not in love with you either."

The words fell heavy on her ears and she pushed past him hard on her way out of the kitchen. "Get away from me." Her voice was flat. Whether he'd just said it in retribution or not, it didn't matter. The words hurt bad.

He let her go. As she walked away he said, "So it's okay for you to say it, but not me? Why is that, Leslie?"

She spun around, heart weeping, and shouted, "*Just leave!*" She didn't wait to see if he listened.

But he damn well better leave Missy.

Chapter Twenty-Five

PETER HAD A pre-op appointment the next day for his
eye surgery. Though he didn't want to see or speak to
anybody and was in a foul disposition, he crawled out of
bed and took himself to the early morning meeting. The
whole time he was there, while he was supposed to be
listening to them go over the steps of the procedure, all
he could think about was Leslie. The way she'd looked at
him when she'd screamed at him to leave. Never before
had he seen such emotion come from one single person.

Because of her, he hadn't slept a wink.

All night he'd tossed and turned, replaying their fight
in his mind, wondering if or where he'd gone wrong. And
he couldn't figure it out. She was the one who'd decided
to end things.

Christ, love was messy.

It grabbed a hold of a person. Maybe it was better that
they'd split. He and Leslie were too independent, too au-

tonomous to let love happen to them. It would kill their sparks. What would the two of them do with something like love?

Parking his FJ Cruiser, he climbed out and went through the garage door into the house. Peter kicked the door closed forcefully behind him. Who the hell was he trying to kid?

The whole ugly frigging truth was that he didn't want Leslie to be in love with him because he wasn't worth it. If she loved him he wouldn't be able to hide his bad side forever and eventually the truth of who he was would eat away at their relationship until nothing remained of something that used to be good.

Until one day she woke up and realized she'd picked the wrong guy.

The house was quiet as a tomb when he entered the kitchen. Leslie wasn't there anymore. But he could feel her. The woman was everywhere. Wherever he looked, he saw her. She was curled up on the sofa, her tiny fur-ball nestled in her lap. She was standing in his kitchen in a tank top and skimpy panties eating cold leftovers. She was even in his bedroom, staring him down with miserable, wet eyes demanding to know why he hadn't been able to make love to her.

Leslie had gone from haunting his dreams to haunting his reality. If given a choice, he'd rather it be his dreams. Because in his reality everything in his house smelled like a damn piña colada. Even his stupid towels smelled like coconut.

And it all made him think of her. Made him *miss* her.

He didn't want to miss her.

If he missed her then it meant that he cared about her. And caring brought entanglements. Commitments. It meant sticking around somebody for a long, long time— somebody who was going to have expectations, who was going to require things of him. Somebody who was going to see the worst in him.

He didn't want that somebody to be Leslie.

No, he wanted her to always see the best of him. Peter scrubbed a hand over his scruffy face, suddenly bone tired. What did it matter if she saw his bad side? The life he'd lived had shaped and molded him in a lot of ways. Some good, some not. He damn sure wasn't perfect. Someday somebody was going to get close enough to see that. Why was he always struggling against the inevitable?

"Probably because you've been fighting your whole life and you just don't fucking know when to stop, idiot." Sounded about right.

With a sigh, Peter glanced out the French doors to the back patio. It was a gorgeous November day. The sky was clear and the sun was out. Deciding to take in some fresh air, he grabbed a clean gray Rush hoodie from the dryer, put it on, and poured a glass of orange juice.

Peter picked up the glass and as he crossed the kitchen he had a memory flash of Leslie in her flannel pants and sloppy ponytail sitting on the floor while she dangled a string for her kitten, a smile of absolute delight on her gorgeous face. His chest went tight like it was caught in a vice grip. Damn it.

The woman was going to give him a heart attack.

Muttering to himself, Peter pushed through the French doors and stepped out onto the patio. Taking a minute, he surveyed his property—his home. And it struck him that for a guy who claimed to be scared of commitment and responsibility, he sure hadn't had a problem with either when he'd bought his house.

In fact, it was one of the very few things he relied on as a constant in his life.

A gaggle of geese flew overhead squawking and Peter squinted against the sun, following them across the sky. When they were gone he lowered his gaze and scanned his huge backyard. Clarity started to settle over him.

His house was built for a family. It wasn't meant for someone alone. That's probably why he threw so many frigging parties. Because his home was meant to be full.

And he'd bought the large five-bedroom house with its private one-acre lot without hesitation. So what did that tell him about his fear of commitment?

It told him that it was bullshit.

His real fear was letting someone in. Letting someone truly get close to him. For so many years he'd hidden behind his smile—the cocky ballplayer with the fast arm. He'd laughed and joked and pulled one outrageous stunt after another. And the whole time no one saw the real Peter—even himself.

He'd made being a professional pitcher his whole identity. He'd let it become his life, while only his music spoke the truth of who he really was. It had worked. It had contented him. But now that the pillar of his self-identity had been stripped away, he didn't know what to do.

Maybe it was time to find something new to throw his all into.

Yeah, maybe.

Maybe that something new should be Leslie.

Peter drained his glass of orange juice and set it on the patio table next to him. Then he put his hands in the front pouch of his hoodie and stepped onto the grass, enjoying the sunshine on his shoulders. The rays were warm and gentle when he closed his eyes and turned his face toward the sun.

The sound of a door opening behind him had his eyes popping open. He swung his head around to see who it was and came face-to-face with an extremely pissed-off Mark Cutter. "You son of a bitch!"

Uh oh.

The catcher swung a fist and connected hard with Peter's left eye, dropping him like a stone. Stars exploded behind his eyes as pain radiated from his cheekbone and he landed on his ass in the grass. He shook his head, clearing the daze, and looked up to find Mark standing over him with fisted hands and heaving chest.

"You know." It wasn't a question.

The catcher offered him a hand. As soon as Peter was on his feet, Mark clocked him hard again, his fist like granite. "Fuck!" That one connected with his lip, soundly splitting it and whipping his head back.

"That's for sleeping with my sister, asshole."

Peter swiped a hand across his split lip as emotions welled up inside him. "She slept with me too, man."

Mark cocked his arm again, eyes hard like diamonds, and let it fly. Peter was ready this time and dodged the swing. Unwilling to let it go, the catcher dropped low and slammed a shoulder into his solar plexus, taking Peter down hard. For the next few minutes they scrapped, threw elbows, and clipped chins. The only sounds were of them grunting and swearing.

One of Mark's elbows connected with his jaw, snapping his teeth together and making him wince. "All right, jackass. Enough." Peter had let the catcher have at him, considering it his brotherly right, but he'd had enough now and rolled away.

He sat up just as the blond-haired ballplayer did too. They were both out of breath and just sat on the grass in silence while they tried to slow their racing hearts. Mark sat staring straight ahead at the giant oak tree by the back fence, a tick working his jaw.

Finally he said very quietly, "My sister acts tough, but she's not. If you hurt her I'll bust your jaw."

Fair enough. "Deal. Although I don't think you have anything to worry about. She threw me out the last time I was around."

The catcher slid him a look. "Yeah?"

Peter nodded. "Yep."

His lips twitched. "Good."

It hadn't felt good when she'd done it. "How'd you find out?"

Mark squinted into the sun and pulled at a few blades of grass. "Lorelei told me."

Figured.

The two of them sat there in silence for another minute. Then Mark exhaled loudly. "Why did you do it, Pete? Couldn't you have done your sniffing around someone else?"

That was a good question. "No, man. I couldn't."

Mark shot him a lethal glare. "Why the fuck not?"

Another good question. "She gets to me, dude."

The catcher tossed the shredded blades of grass back down and bent his knee, resting his forearm on it. "Are you saying that you have feelings for her?"

There it was, the moment of truth. Did he have feelings for Leslie? "Yeah." Deep, profound feelings that more than bordered on scary.

"She deserves someone who'll take good care of her and treat her right."

Peter swallowed around the sudden lump in his throat. "Yeah."

Mark stared at him with hard gray eyes. "Is that you?"

He heard what her brother was really asking and it made his stomach squeeze. There was no turning back. Was he ready for this?

Peter met his gaze, took a deep fortifying breath. "Yeah, it is."

"Yeah? Shit." The catcher swore. "Then you gotta prove it, pal."

Chapter Twenty-Six

─────────────────────────

Leslie took a break from balancing the club's financial accounts and smothered a yawn. It was ten at night on a Tuesday, but she felt tired like it was already Friday. Leaning back in her padded leather chair, she took a good hard look around her office. From her framed pictures over the couch to her bookcases and unhappy foliage. She studied the exposed red bricks, the hardwood floor, and the piles of mail on her sleek wood desk.

This was her life.

"Oh for crissake," she muttered and snatched up the cup of coffee in front of her. It's not like what she had was bad. Most people would consider it a pretty sweet life. She really needed to stop feeling sorry for herself and just get over it. Get over *him* and move on.

It'd be a whole lot easier though if she wasn't still in love with the jerk.

As much as she'd tried to lie to herself, her heart had

known better. It had seen the truth that she was trying to hide from. Peter Kowalskin had a hold on her good, and it wasn't going to let go any time soon. Like, never.

She was stuck with love.

Frowning, Leslie took a sip of the strong brew cut with half-and-half and considered the state of her life, trying to look on the positive side of things. So okay, she'd lost the bet and Peter wasn't going to play in the club. That wasn't so bad. And she didn't get the down payment she needed to buy Mark out. Okay, fine. It just meant that it was going to take her longer to save up like she'd origi-nally planned. It did not mean that it was over. She wasn't a quitter.

In the meantime, she had the club to manage. And it was great, really it was, building her brother's busi-ness. She had sunk a lot of effort into it and turned it into something good. Mark was proud of her. *She* was proud of her. And someday in the far-off future it would be hers to own, so none of her effort was going to waste.

Leslie had her work and her apartment and her kitten. Soon there would be a new niece or nephew to spoil too. Everything was wonderful really. Maybe not perfect, maybe things hadn't worked out like she'd wanted, but that was okay.

She could deal with it.

And late last night she'd made a decision to stop beat-ing herself up for her mistakes. Because the reality was that Leslie Cutter wasn't perfect, not by a long shot. She made stupid mistakes and bad judgment calls. The bet was just one of them.

Same with falling in love with Peter. It was a dumb thing to do given who he was and she'd known it. Known it and didn't stop it. So she had nobody to blame but herself for her current situation. But she'd learned another hard lesson and she just wanted to let it go, to chalk one up for life and just be done. It was all so wearisome, always judging herself so harshly.

And she was done being angry at Peter for lying about her apartment, for playing her. It was just who he was and she couldn't blame him for it. All along she'd known he was a scrapper, an opportunist. Given how he'd grown up there wasn't much chance of him being any other way. He'd learned how to work angles, how to exploit others for his own self-interest.

It had been a matter of survival.

Her heart couldn't hold a grudge against him for that. Just like she couldn't hold a grudge against him for not loving her back. Oh, she'd wanted to all right. At first. Man, when he'd stood in her apartment and stated that he didn't love her with such cool, detached eyes it had taken all of her willpower not to clobber him upside the head with a frying pan. That kind of rejection stung, *bad*. And it had succinctly destroyed the idea she'd been growing about having her business back *and* Peter.

Truth was, she had neither. Just herself and the determination to forge ahead alone. Maybe Peter would always have her heart, but she could go on. *Would* go on. Even if there was always a part of her that was missing.

The sudden sting of tears surprised her. So did the pain in her chest that flared up at the thought of never being able to love him out loud and in the open. Because he didn't want it, her love was going to get shoved down deep somewhere inside her where it would huddle, wasted and unused.

Maybe given enough time it would just disappear into dust. Then they would both be free. Yeah, there was always that hope.

"Ugh!" But that's not what she wanted *at all*. Not really. "God he's such a stupid man!" Her heart swelled with sudden sorrow.

All she wanted to do was love him.

And she would have, if he would've let her. But that damn infuriating man wanted nothing to do with it. Too frigging chicken was what he was. Scared of a little thing like love.

Commotion outside her office door turned her attention and Leslie slipped back into her heels before going to see what the fuss was all about. And yes, they were her purple suede Michael Kors. She was feeling sentimental.

Sucking in a breath to steady herself, she stepped out into the hall and quickly made her way to the main floor. She was shocked when she got there and saw a dozen Rush players huddled around the bar talking over each other, the expressions on their faces ranging from disbelief to confusion. Her instincts went on high alert.

The season was over. Why were they all here?

"Hey, y'all," she said casually as she stepped behind the bar. The new bartender, a woman in her forties named Marie, was busy mixing a cocktail. She looked up from the tumbler and gave Leslie a friendly smile.

She'd just smiled back when Drake Paulson elbowed his way up to the bar. His afro was back to its normal color. And she had to laugh because even though it was thirty degrees outside he was wearing a bright red Hawaiian shirt opened almost halfway. It was enough to see just how much chest hair the giant man really had. *Eeesh*.

"Did you hear the news, sweet thing?" the gruff ballplayer asked and then popped a handful of peanuts into his mouth. His brown eyes were watching her expectantly.

Leslie shook her head and reached for a bottle of tequila when a customer hollered an order. Mixing drinks kept her hands busy and helped distract her from the dull ache that had taken up residence around her heart. She wondered if it was permanent.

Probably.

"I've been in the back, big guy, and haven't heard a thing. What's the breaking news?" It must be pretty good if it had a bunch of pro ballplayers in a tizzy.

More than a dozen of them were deep in conversation, their voices blending into a constant drone of white noise under the heavy thump of bass coming through the sound system.

Carl Brexler raked a hand through his hair and she just made out, "Huge-ass shocker."

What was a huge-ass shocker?

Glancing up from the margarita she was blending, she hollered over the grating sound of the blender chopping ice. "I'm waiting, Drake. What's up?"

He set his beer down and opened his mouth to speak.

Then he closed it again on a grunt. "What the—?" He spun around, ready for a fight. "Who was dumb enough to sock me in the back?"

Her brother stood behind Drake, grinning evilly. "What are you whining about, Paulson?"

"Hey!" Leslie rapped her knuckles sharply on the bar top. "Focus, Paulson."

He looked at her with big sad eyes. "Aww, but—"

"Get revenge on Mark later. You were about to tell me what all the hoopla is about." She waved her hand at the group of animated ballplayers. Then she slid the marg down the counter to the waiting customer with a smile. "There you go, darlin'. Enjoy."

Drake reluctantly turned his back on her brother, who shot her a grateful look. "You ain't off the hook, brother," he said to Mark, his voice full of warning. Then he looked back at Leslie waiting impatiently, and let out a long sigh. She could tell he was just dragging out the moment for dramatic effect.

Leslie rolled her eyes and bit her tongue to keep from saying something snarky. She wasn't in the best mood and it wasn't fair to take it out on him. Her brother, on the other hand, was used to her mean streak.

"Why are you here?" she demanded. By the way Drake was taking his sweet time getting to the news blast, she figured she could be standing there waiting for the rest of the night.

Mark raised a brow, gave her a look. "What? I can't be at my own club?"

"Not when you have a pregnant wife at home you

can't." She tossed her hair over her shoulder and met his look with one of her own.

"Who says she's home?" He tipped his head toward the Rush's table. Sure enough Lorelei was there sitting next to Sonny, heads together while they chatted. When had they gotten there?

The question must have been written all over her face because Mark said, "You were in the back."

Ah. That explained it. But it didn't explain what everybody was doing there tonight in the first place. Usually as soon as the season ended the guys disappeared for a few months. Well, except Drake and Mark and Peter. JP, too, although Leslie fully expected not to see him again since this was his first off-season with Sonny and Charlie. But for now he was there, too, huddled together with the rest of the crew, talking about whatever this "big news" was.

Speaking of . . . she looked back at Drake. The way he was procrastinating was driving her bat-shit. "Any day now, Paulson."

He glanced down at her, eyes twinkling, and suddenly she became very aware of just how much fun he was having at her expense. She shook her head. Jerk.

She smacked him. "Just say it already!"

He relented. "Kowalskin just announced his retirement."

What?!

Everything inside her went still. It couldn't be. Peter wasn't retiring. He loved playing baseball. It was his life. No, Drake had to be wrong.

Leslie set down the drink she was currently working on. Her hands started to shake and her heart began to race. She took a breath and scanned the ballplayers. They were all talking animatedly about something, and now she knew what. It was true. Peter was out of baseball.

Holy shit.

Mark cut into her shock. "I just heard, man. I can't believe he's out, either. It's nuts. Nobody saw it coming. He's got some eye thing apparently. Says he's going blind in one eye and can't pitch anymore."

Leslie's stomach plummeted. Poor Peter. A flash of memory came back to her of the morning they'd fought about why he didn't perform publically. She'd overheard the tail end of a conversation about some kind of surgery. It had confused her then when she'd thought it was about his shoulder because it hadn't seemed that bad.

Now it made sense. The surgery wasn't for his shoulder. It was for his eye.

And it hit her then, the stuff Peter must have been dealing with by himself. The fear and stress and worry. Terrible feelings that he'd borne alone. It made her sad and angry all at once.

He didn't have to be alone.

Just like she didn't have to let her life drift on by because she'd made a mistake. They both had choices.

JP shoved his way in between the two ballplayers and said, "The guy was throwing heat like a true hall of famer. Whatever was going on with his vision, he did a damn good job hiding it."

"I know it, brother. Walskie was the best pitcher the

Rush has ever seen. We're going to miss him something fierce." Drake shook his frizzy head sadly.

"Now I understand why everyone here is all up in arms." She said to no one in particular.

"It's a big deal, sis. Kowalskin stepping down really shakes things up."

"You think José is going to step up and become our new ace?" JP asked.

Mark shook his head. "I don't know, man."

Something occurred to her. "Okay. I get why y'all are upset. What I don't get is why y'all are here?"

Just then the music went dead and a *thump thump thump* sounded from the stage. A murmur rose from the crowded nightclub as everyone turned their attention to the unexpected interruption.

"Excuse me, everyone," came a tough, sexy male voice with a Philly accent.

She knew that voice.

"Some of you may know me, but for those of you who don't I'll introduce myself. My name is Peter Kowalskin."

The crowd erupted into applause. The noise level was deafening. Someone let out an ear-piercing whistle that had her cringing, and Drake shouted something highly inappropriate.

Her heart squeezed painfully and her stomach went wild with nerves as she stepped out from behind the bar, looking for a clear line of sight to the stage. She found it next to her brother, and when she looked up and saw what was happening, her heart rolled right on over in her chest.

It was impossible to breathe.

There, up on stage under the glaring lights, was Peter in his signature white T-shirt, leather bracelet, and jeans. Looking sexy and tough and so, so wonderful.

And he was sitting on a stool. In front of a mic.

With his Gibson guitar.

Chapter Twenty-Seven

PETER SPOTTED LESLIE through the crowd and felt his palms go sweaty. What he was about to do was the hardest thing he'd ever done.

He needed Leslie to know how he felt.

She might slap him in the face and tell him off for the way he'd treated her, but he had to take that chance. For the first time in his life he was willing to risk it all for someone else.

For her.

It had taken Mark's fist upside his head to get him to see the truth. To have the balls to admit it to himself. And it was hella scary. But it was there and it was real and he damn well had to get used to it. He had to face the fact.

He was in love with Leslie.

And he was going to show her in the best way he knew how, by doing the one thing he'd sworn he never would, the one thing he knew she really wanted. Peter was going to perform live. In front of a hell of a lot of random fucking people. He was going to sit there and pour out his feelings to her through song. Exposed and vulnerable and wide open to rejection. All because his worthless heart was hers, if she still wanted it.

The lights glared down on him and sweat trickled down his temple. He stared out over a large, cheering crowd and looked for the reason he was there. When he found her staring at him, hand in a fist at her mouth, eyes huge, his lungs locked up and he couldn't breathe, couldn't sing. But he had to push through it for her.

Leslie deserved this.

Suddenly the lights above him changed. The stage went dark, except for the blinding spotlight now on him. He lifted a hand to block the glare, cradled his guitar on his raised knee. Who the hell had decided he needed a spotlight?

The answer came quickly. "For dramatic effect, brother!" It was Paulson. Figured.

Peter adjusted the mic in front of him and wiped his palms against the thighs of his jeans, smiling self-consciously. "Thanks for letting me crash the stage everyone. I've got a tune I wrote that I'd like to perform, if that's all right."

Cheers. Whistles. Catcalls.

Finding Leslie in the crowd, Peter waited until she was looking at him and said, "Somebody once told me that I had something worth sharing." He laughed softly. "I sure hope she was right. Here goes."

Peter took a deep breath and shut down. He shut out

the lights and noise and nerves. Closing his eyes he went to that place inside him that had only ever been touched by one person. By Leslie. She believed in him.

It gave him strength.

For a moment he sat there and waited until the club went quiet. Then his fingers started to move on the strings, the sound of his guitar bringing him to his center. God, he hoped she understood what he was trying to do, what he was trying to say.

"For my princess," he said. Then he plunged deep and forgot about the strangers staring at him. Peter lost himself in the music, in his message to Leslie.

And he sang.

LESLIE DIDN'T RECOGNIZE the song. After a few bars she realized the reason she couldn't place it was because it was new. Peter had written a song for her. The truth choked her up.

The stripped-down acoustics made the lyrics sound so beautiful. They touched her and now that they were being sung by the man she was hopelessly in love with and she knew that it had been written for her, well, it was amazing.

The nightclub was silent as Peter strummed his guitar and sang about her being too beautiful to turn away from even though he was unworthy. He looked incredible up there, so rugged and tough and soulful. Just like she knew he would.

And he was there for her, singing for her. He'd called

her his princess. Her lips trembled and she swallowed hard, her heart pounding frantically in her chest.

Pushing through the crowd blindly, Leslie didn't stop until she was standing at the front of the crush, just steps away from the stage. She didn't care who saw, she just stood there as the tears formed and fell, one by one, down her cheeks. Because she knew, knew what Peter being there meant, and it was everything.

"I don't deserve it, but give me a chance," he sang in his amazing voice.

And it felt like he was saying it directly to her. That they weren't just lyrics to a song. They were words from his heart. And knowing him, knowing what music was to him, and how he kept everything locked up tight, Leslie knew he was saying what was inside him in the best way he knew how.

Peter continued playing, his nimble fingers working the guitars strings expertly. His voice built along with the song, and before long he was pouring his heart out, singing, "I'm not perfect, just imperfectly yours. I'll love you like you've never known before."

His voice broke and he looked directly at her. He let his guard down and let everything he felt show in his eyes as he finished the song. "Imperfectly yours for the rest of my life."

Oh God.

Leslie started sobbing. And she couldn't stop. Because she was so in love with him it was ridiculous. It made her a blubbering fool.

All for Peter.

He stopped strumming his guitar and the club slowly went quiet as the crowd held a collective breath. For a long moment he just sat there and looked at her, his pale blue eyes shining bright. Then he raised that brow of his and gave her a small half smile. "I love you," he said, completely unaware or uncaring that the microphone had picked it up and broadcast it throughout the entire club.

Peter sat his Gibson down and jumped off the stage. As soon as his feet hit the ground he swooped her up and covered her mouth in a searing, heartfelt kiss. All she could do was cling to him as everything inside her rejoiced, and the crowd around them erupted, went wild.

He pulled back and rested his forehead against hers. "I love you," he said again. Now that he'd said them once they were the only words he wanted to speak. "And I'm sorry. So, so sorry for being such a coward, Leslie."

She placed a hand on his cheek and looked into his eyes. They were filled with love and fear and uncertainty. "Why are you a coward?"

"For not having the balls to tell you that when I fell for you four years ago. I took one look at you—the first one—and it was over for me. A part of me knew it then, but I was just so scared." He smiled slightly. "Shit. I'm still scared."

She opened her mouth to speak, but he shook his head. "I need to finish this. Talking about what's in here"—he pointed to his chest—"is fucking hard for me."

With trembling fingers, she caressed his chest and smiled gently. "Go on."

"That night we were together in Miami I tanked because I felt it. I felt what you meant to me deep down in my gut and I freaked. And the stupid bet was just a way to have you without being honest with myself or you about the reasons why."

He scanned the crowd of avid onlookers. "I hate performing in public. I really do. But I'll play here every single night for the rest of my life if it's what you want. If it will help you achieve your dream. Because all I care about, all I want is you. I'm not good enough and I don't deserve you, but I love you." He tucked a strand of hair behind her ear. "My baseball career is over. I'm having eye surgery next week, but my vision will never be completely normal. I don't know where my life is going. And I don't care, as long as it's with you."

Her heart flung wide open and filled up with love, so very much love, for the man standing before her. She loved him so much it was pathetic. "We're a pair, aren't we?"

Both of them. Complete messes.

Peter leaned in and whispered into her ear. "That's why we're good together, princess."

She could see it, all the ways that they were good for each other. They were both strong-willed, independent people who were afraid to trust. But they were also good-hearted people, who went to bat for the ones they loved. "Would you really play at the club every single night?" she asked, her heart soaring.

He nodded. "I would. I mean, I will if that's what you want. If you still want me." His eyes stared into hers, searching. "If you still love me."

For so long she'd kept herself at arm's reach, never

getting too close to anyone. And for what? It had earned her nothing.

It really was time to turn over a new leaf. For both of them. She didn't know where it was going to lead, but she wanted to be right there with him every step of the way. "I love you, Peter."

"Are you sure?"

Suddenly she felt like laughing. The worried look on his face was priceless. "Yes, I'm sure. Even though you're nothing but trouble, I love you. I always will."

Peter wrapped his arms around her and pulled her close. "Girl, 'trouble' is your middle name."

Leslie slid her arms around the back of his neck, enjoying the way his eyes went warm and sweet. It was a new look for him. She very definitely approved. "That's why we're perfect for each other."

Peter grinned. "That's the truth, princess." Then he kissed her, softly, sweetly.

And they turned over that new leaf.

'"HURRY UP, PETER. I don't want to be late." Leslie pushed through the hospital doors that led to the maternity wing and took a sharp left.

"What's there to be late about?" he drawled right behind her. "Half the damn team is already there waiting."

As soon as they entered the waiting room area she saw he was right. "Hey, y'all. Sorry we're late." She cast a quick glance over at Peter and smoothed her hair. "*Mad* traffic."

Drake snorted and cuffed Peter on the shoulder. "Bad traffic always gives me bedhead too."

Just then a pretty, young nurse came through carrying a clipboard. She wasn't looking where she was going, she was so busy reading the chart, and she ran smack into Paulson. "*Oomph!*" The petite woman would have gone down hard—she'd ricocheted of his barrel chest like a ping pong ball—but Drake reached out with surprising speed and caught her.

"Whoa there, teeny thing. You okay?" He looked down at the petite redhead in his arms.

The nurse blushed so hard her face matched her hair. "I'm fine, thanks. Excuse me." She stepped out of his embrace and glanced around the room quickly and left. Paulson's gaze lingered on her retreating form.

Peter slapped him on the back. "Happens to us all, man."

Drake muttered distractedly, "Yeah, what's that, Walskie?"

"The fall."

His eyes lit up. "You know, I've been thinking about taking a break from my breather. You know, get back in the swing of things." He slapped Peter's shoulder. "I'll be back." Then he stepped through the archway and disappeared out of sight.

"Hey, coach."

Peter turned to JP and smiled, shaking his hand. "What's up, my man?"

"Can you believe Cutter's about to become a dad?"

He shook his head and grinned. "It's crazy, isn't it?"

JP nodded. "Yeah. Hey, what'd you bet on—boy or girl?"

"Boy. Eight pounds even." He had a lucky feeling about it too.

"How are you liking the new position?" The shortstop asked.

The Rush management had offered him a permanent

position as their pitching coach after he'd healed from his eye surgery. It was his first season with the team on this side of things and he'd been surprised at just how much he enjoyed it. It was great, actually.

"I'm liking it a lot. Keeps me around you knuckle-heads. You know somebody's got to keep an eye on you."

Leslie sidled up behind him and wrapped her arms around his waist. His stomach flopped and his palms went damp. The woman still did that to him. You'd think he'd be used to it by now, but no. It was still damn disconcerting.

"I love you." She whispered against his ear.

Though she said it daily, it gave him a thrill every single time. He didn't think he'd ever get used to it. "You too, princess."

Life was a funny thing. Just when a person thought it was only going to go from bad to worse, it went and threw a curveball. It became amazing.

Mark burst through the door to the waiting room, turning everyone's attention. "It's a boy! A perfect, incredible boy!" The look of wonder on his face had Peter smiling.

Before anyone could congratulate the catcher he disappeared again, leaving Peter to say to Leslie over his shoulder, "You know I want like, eight, right? Enough for a whole team."

She pinched his butt. "Not going to happen, Kowalskin."

He spun around and wiggled his brows, giving her a naughty grin. "That's okay. The fun is in the trying."

She tossed back her head and laughed. "In your dreams."

Yeah, it had been in his dreams. But then he'd grown some balls. And now, now his reality was amazing.

Because it included Leslie.

An Excerpt from

STEALING HOME

> When Lorelei Littleton steals Mark Cutter's good
> luck charm, all the pro ballplayer can think is
> how good she looked . . . and how bad she'll pay.
> Thrust into a test of wills, they'll both discover
> that while revenge may be a dish best served cold,
> when it comes to passion, the hotter the better!

RAISING HIS GLASS, he smiled and said, "To the rodeo.
May you ride your bronc well."

Color singed Lorelei's cheeks as they tapped their
glasses. But her eyes remained on his while he took a long
pull of smooth, aged whiskey.

Then she spoke, her voice low. "I'll make your head
spin, cowboy. That I promise."

That surprised a laugh out of him, even as heat began
to pool heavy in his groin. "I'll drink to that." And he

did. He lifted the glass and drained it, suddenly anxious to get on to the next stage. A drop of liquid shimmered on her full bottom lip and it beckoned him. Reaching an arm out, Mark pulled her close and leaned down. With his eyes on hers, he slowly licked the drop off, his tongue teasing her pouty mouth until she released a soft moan.

Arousal coursed through him at the provocative sound. Pulling her more fully against him, Mark deepened the kiss. Her lush little body fit perfectly against him and her lips melted under the heat of his. He slid a hand up her back and fisted the dark, thick mass of her long hair. He loved the feel of the cool, silky strands against his skin.

He wanted more.

Tugging gently, Mark encouraged her mouth to open for him. When she did, his tongue slid inside and tasted, explored the exotic flavor of her. Hunger spiked inside him and he took the kiss deeper. Hotter. She whimpered into his mouth and dug her fingers into his hair, pulled. Her body began pushing against his, restless and searching.

Mark felt like he'd been tossed into an incinerator when he pushed a thigh between her long, shapely legs and discovered the heat there. He groaned and rubbed his thigh against her, feeling her tremble in response.

Suddenly she broke the kiss and pushed out of his arms. Her breathing was ragged, her lips red and swollen from his kiss. Confusion and desire mixed like a heady concoction in his blood, but before he could say anything she turned and began walking toward the hallway to his bedroom.

At the entrance she stopped and beckoned to him. "Come and get me, catcher."

So she wanted to play did she? Hell yeah. Games were his life.

Mark toed off his shoes as he yanked his sweater over his head and tossed it on the floor. He began working the button of his fly and strode after her. He was a little unsteady on his feet, but he didn't care. He just wanted to catch her. When he entered his room he found her by the bed. She'd turned on the bedside lamp, and the light illuminated every gorgeous inch of her curvaceous body.

He started toward her, but she shook her head. "I want you to sit on the bed."

Mark walked to her anyway and gave her a deep, hungry kiss before he sat on the edge of the bed. He wondered what she had in store for him and felt his gut tighten in anticipation. "Are you going to put on a show for me?" God, that'd be so hot if she did.

All she said was "Mmm hmm," and turned her back to him. Mark let his eyes wander over her body and decided her tight round ass in denim was just about the sexiest thing he'd ever seen.

When his gaze rose back up he found her smiling over her shoulder at him. "Are you ready for the ride of your life, cowboy?"

Hell yes he was. "Bring it, baby. Show me what you've got."

Her smile grew sultry with unspoken promise as she

reached for the hem of her T-shirt. She pulled it up leisurely while she kept eye contact with him. All he could hear was the soft sound of fabric rustling, but it fueled him—this seductively slow striptease she was giving him.

He wanted to see her. "Turn around."

As she turned she continued to pull it up until she was facing him with the yellow cotton dangling loosely from her fingertips. A black, lacy bra barely covered the most voluptuous, gorgeous pair of breasts he'd ever laid eyes on. He couldn't stop staring.

"Do you like what you see?"

Good God, yes. The woman was a goddess. He nodded, a little harder than he meant because he almost fell forward. He started to tell her how sexy she was when suddenly a full-blown wave of dizziness hit him and he shook his head to clear it. What the hell?

"Is everything all right, Mark?"

The room started spinning and he tried to stand, but couldn't. It felt like the world had been tipped sideways and his body was sliding onto the floor. He tried to stand again, but fell backward onto the bed instead. He stared up at her as he tried to right himself and couldn't.

Fonda stood there like a siren, dark hair tousled around her head, breasts barely contained—guilt plastered across her stunning face.

Before he fell unconscious on the bed, he knew. Knew it with gut certainty. He tried to tell her, but his mouth wouldn't move. Son of a bitch.

Fonda Peters had drugged him.

An Excerpt from

PLAYING THE FIELD

Single mother Sonny Miller has spent years avoiding love. So when hotshot ballplayer JP Trudeau swaggers into her carefully constructed life, even as every fiber of her being tells her to keep running the bases! Sonny may be hell-bent on keeping JP at arm's length, but this rookie has a plan. To get the girl, he must step up to the plate and convince her to take another chance on love . . . before this game gets rained out.

JP REACHED OUT an arm to snag her, but she slipped just out of reach—for the moment. Did she really think she could get away from him?

There was a reason he played shortstop in the Major Leagues. He was damn fast. And now that he'd decided to make Sonny his woman she was about to find out just how quick he could be. All night he'd tossed and turned for her, his curiosity rampant. When he'd finally rolled out of bed, he'd had one clear goal: to see Sonny. Nothing else had existed outside that.

Her leaving her cell phone at the restaurant last night had been the perfect excuse. All he'd had to do was an Internet search for her business to get her address. And now here he was, unexpectedly very up close and personal with her. So close he could smell the scent of her shampoo, and it was doing funny things to him. Things like making him want to bury his nose in her hair and inhale.

No way was he going to miss this golden opportunity.

With a devil's grin, he moved and had her back against the aging barn wall before she'd finished gasping. "Look me in the eyes right now and tell me I don't affect you, that you're not interested." He traced a lazy path down the side of her neck with his fingertips and felt her shiver. "Because I don't believe that line for an instant, sunshine."

Close enough to feel the heat she was throwing from her deliciously curved body, JP laughed softly when she tried to sidestep and squeeze free. Her shyness was so damn cute. He raised an arm and blocked her in, his palm flush against the rough, splintering wood. Leaning in close, he grinned when she blushed and her gaze flickered to his lips. Her mouth opened on a soft rush of breath and for a suspended moment something sparked and held between them.

But then Sonny shook back her rose-gold curls and

tipped her chin with defiance. "Believe what you want, JP. I don't have to prove anything to you." Her denim-blue eyes flashed with emotion. "This might come as a surprise, but I'm not interested in playing with a celebrity like you. I have a business to run and a son to raise. I don't need the headache."

There was an underlying nervousness to her tone that didn't quite jive with the tough-as-nails attitude she was trying to project. Either she was scared or he affected her more than she wanted to admit. She didn't look scared.

JP dropped his gaze to her mouth, wanting to kiss those juicy lips bad, and felt her body brush against his. He could feel her pulse, fast and frantic, under his fingertips.

It made his pulse kick up a notch in anticipation. "There's a surefire way to end this little disagreement right now, because I say you're lying. I say you *are* interested in a celebrity like me." He cupped her chin with his hand and watched her thick lashes flutter as she broke eye contact. But she didn't pull away. "In fact, I say you're interested in *me*."

JP knew he had her.

Her voice came soft and a little shaky. "How do I prove I'm not?" The way she was staring at his mouth contradicted her words. So did the way her body was leaning into him.

Lowering his head until he was a whisper away, he issued the challenge. "Kiss me."

About the Author

JENNIFER SEASONS is a Colorado transplant. She lives with her husband and four children along the Front Range, where she enjoys breathtaking views of the mighty Rocky Mountains every day. A dog and two cats keep them company. When she's not writing, she loves spending time with her family outdoors, exploring her beautiful adopted home state.

Visit www.AuthorTracker.com for exclusive information on your favorite HarperCollins authors.

Give in to your impulses . . .
Read on for a sneak peek at three brand-new
e-book original tales of romance
from Avon Books.
Available now wherever e-books are sold.

THE GOVERNESS CLUB: CLAIRE
By Ellie Macdonald

ASHES, ASHES, THEY
ALL FALL DEAD
By Lena Diaz

THE GOVERNESS CLUB: BONNIE
By Ellie Macdonald

An Excerpt from

THE GOVERNESS CLUB: CLAIRE

by Ellie Macdonald

Claire Bannister just wants to be a good
teacher so that she and the other ladies of the
Governess Club can make enough money to
leave their jobs and start their own school in the
country. But when the new sinfully handsome
and utterly distracting tutor arrives, Claire
finds herself caught up in a whirlwind romance
that could change the course of her future.

What would a "London gent" want with her, Claire wondered as she quickened her pace. The only man she knew in the capital was Mr. Baxter, her late father's solicitor. Why would he come all the way here instead of corresponding through a letter as usual? Unless it was something more urgent than could be committed to paper. Perhaps it had something to do with Ridgestone—

At that thought, Claire lifted her skirts and raced to the parlor. Five years had passed since her father's death, since she'd had to leave her childhood home, but she had not given up her goal to one day return to Ridgestone.

The formal gardens of Aldgate Hall vanished, replaced by the memory of her own garden; the terrace doors no longer opened to the ballroom, but to a small, intimate library; the bright corridor darkened to a comforting glow; Claire could even smell her old home as she rushed to the door of the housekeeper's parlor. Pausing briefly to catch her breath and smooth her hair, she knocked and pushed the door open, head held high, barely able to contain her excitement.

Cup and saucer met with a loud rattle as a young man hurried to his feet. Mrs. Morrison's disapproving frown could not stop several large drops of tea from contaminating her white linen, nor could Mr. Fosters's harrumph. Claire's heart sank as she took in the man's youth, disheveled hair, and rumpled clothes; he was decidedly *not* Mr. Baxter. Perhaps a new associate? Her heart picked up slightly at that thought.

Claire dropped a shallow curtsey. "You wished to see me, Mrs. Morrison?"

The thin woman rose and drew in a breath that seemed to tighten her face even more with disapproval. She gestured to the stranger. "Yes. This is Mr. Jacob Knightly. Lord and Lady Aldgate have retained him as a tutor for the young masters."

Claire blinked. "A tutor? I was not informed they were seeking—"

"It is not your place to be informed," the butler, Mr. Fosters, cut in.

Claire immediately bowed her head and clasped her hands in front of her submissively. "My apologies. I overstepped." Her eyes slid shut, and she took a deep breath to dispel the disappointment. Ridgestone faded into the back of her mind once more.

Mrs. Morrison continued with the introduction. "Mr. Knightly, this is Miss Bannister, the governess."

Mr. Knightly bowed. "Miss Bannister, it is a pleasure to make your acquaintance."

Claire automatically curtseyed. "The feeling is mutual,

sir." As she straightened, she lifted her eyes to properly survey the new man. Likely not yet in his third decade, Mr. Knightly wore his brown hair long enough not to be following the current fashion. Scattered locks fell across his forehead, and the darkening of a beard softened an otherwise square-jawed face. He stood nearly a head taller than she did, and his loosely fitted jacket and modest cravat did nothing to conceal broad shoulders. Skimming her gaze down his body, she noticed a shirt starting to yellow with age and a plain brown waistcoat struggling to hide the fact that its owner was less than financially secure. Even his trousers were slightly too short, revealing too much of his worn leather boots. All in all, Mr. Jacob Knightly appeared to be the epitome of a young scholar reduced to becoming a tutor.

Except for his mouth. And his eyes. Not that Claire had much experience meeting with tutors, but even she could tell that the spectacles enhanced rather than detracted from the pale blueness of his eyes. The lenses seemed to emphasize their round shape, emphasize the appreciative gleam in them before Mr. Knightly had a chance to hide it. Even when he did, the corners of his full mouth remained turned up in a funny half-smile, all but oozing confidence and assurance— bordering on an arrogance one would not expect to find in a tutor.

Oh dear.

An Excerpt from

ASHES, ASHES, THEY ALL FALL DEAD

by Lena Diaz

Special Agent Tessa James is obsessed with finding the killer whose signature singsong line—"Ashes, ashes, they all fall dead"—feels all too familiar. When sexy, brilliant consultant Matt Buchanan is paired with Tessa to solve the mystery, they discover, inexplicably, that the clues point to Tessa herself. If she can't remember the forgotten years of her past, will she become the murderer's next target?

She raised a shaking hand to her brow and tried to focus on what he'd told her. "You've found a pattern where he kills a victim in a particular place but mails the letter for a different victim while he's there."

"That's what I'm telling you, yes. It's early yet, and we have a lot more to research—and other victims to find—but this is one hell of a coincidence, and I'm not much of a believer in coincidences. I think we're on to something."

Tears started in Tessa's eyes. She'd been convinced since last night that she'd most likely ruined her one chance to find the killer, and at the same time ruined her career. And suddenly everything had changed. In the span of a few minutes, Matt had given her back everything he'd taken from her when he'd destroyed the letter at the lab. Laughter bubbled up in her throat, and she knew she must be smiling like a fool, but she couldn't help it.

"You did it, Matt." Her voice came out as a choked whisper. She cleared her throat. "You did it. In little more than a day, you've done what we couldn't do in months, years. You've found the thread to unravel the killer's game. This is the breakthrough we've been looking for."

She didn't remember throwing herself at him, but suddenly she was in his arms, laughing and crying at the same time. She looped her arms around his neck and looked up into his wide-eyed gaze, then planted a kiss right on his lips.

She drew back and framed his face with her hands, giddy with happiness. "Thank you, Matt. Thank you, thank you, thank you. You've saved my career. And you've saved lives! Casey can't deny this is a real case anymore. He'll have to get involved, throw some resources at finding the killer. And we'll stop this bastard before he hurts anyone else. How does that feel? How does it feel to know you just saved someone?"

His arms tightened around her waist, and he pulled her against his chest. "It feels pretty damn good," he whispered. And then he kissed her.

Not the quick peck she'd just given him. A real kiss. A hot, wet, knock-every-rational- thought-out-of-her-mind kind of kiss. His mouth moved against hers in a sensual onslaught— nipping, tasting, teasing—before his tongue swept inside and consumed her with his heat.

Desire flooded through her, and she whimpered against him. She stroked his tongue with hers, and he groaned deep in his throat. He slid his hand down over the curve of her bottom and lifted her until she cradled his growing hardness against her belly. He held her so tightly she felt every beat of his heart against her breast. His breath was her breath, drawing her in, stoking the fire inside her into a growing inferno.

He gyrated his hips against hers in a sinful movement that spiked across her nerve endings, tightening her into an almost painful tangle of tension. Every movement of his hips, every slant of his lips, every thrust of his tongue stoked her higher and higher, coiling her nerves into one tight knot of desire, ready to explode.

Nothing had ever felt this good.

Nothing.

Ever.

The tiny voice inside her, the one she'd ruthlessly quashed as soon as his lips claimed hers, suddenly yelled a loud warning. *Stop this madness!*

Her eyes flew open. This was *Matt* making her feel this way, on the brink of a climax when all he'd done was kiss her. *Matt.* Good grief, what was she thinking? He swiveled his hips again, and she nearly died of pleasure.

No, no! This had to stop.

Convincing her traitorous body to respond to her mind's commands was the hardest thing she'd ever tried to do, because every cell, every nerve ending wanted to stay exactly where she was: pressed up against Matt's delicious, hard, warm body.

His twenty-four-year-old body to her thirty-year-old one.

This was insane, a recipe for disaster. She had to stop, now, before she pulled him down to the ground and demanded that he make love to her right this very minute.

She broke the kiss and shoved out of his arms.

An Excerpt from

THE GOVERNESS CLUB: BONNIE

by Ellie Macdonald

The Governess Club series continues with
Miss Bonnie Hodges. She is desperately trying
to hold it together. Tragedy has struck, and she
is the sole person left to be strong for the two
little boys in her care. When the new guardian,
Sir Stephen Montgomery, arrives, she hopes that
things will get better. She wasn't expecting her new
employer to be the most frustrating, overbearing,
and . . . handsome man she's ever seen.

When he reached the water's edge, Stephen stopped. Staring at the wreckage that used to be the wooden bridge, he was acutely aware that he was looking at the site of his friends' death.

Images from the story Miss Hodges had told him flashed through his mind—the waving parents, the bridge shuddering before it collapsed, the falling planks and horses, the coach splintering, George's neck snapping, and Roslyn—God, Roslyn lying in that mangled coach, her blood pouring out of her body. How had she survived long enough for anyone to come and see her still breathing?

Nausea roiled in his stomach, and bile forced its way up his throat. Heaving, Stephen bent over a nearby bush and lost the contents of his stomach. Minutes later, he crouched down at the river's edge and splashed the cold water on his face.

From where he crouched, Stephen turned his gaze down

the river, away from the ruined bridge. He could make out an area ideal for swimming: a small stretch of sandy bank surrounded by a few large, flat rocks. Indeed, an excellent place for a governess to take her charges for a cooling swim on a hot summer day.

Stephen straightened and made his way along the bank to the swimming area. A well-worn path weaved through the bush, connecting the small beach to the hill beyond and Darrowgate. The bridge was seventy meters upstream; not only would the governess and the boys have had a good view of the collapse, the blood from the incident would have flowed right by them.

No wonder they barely spoke.

Tearing his gaze from the bridge, he focused on the water, trying to imagine the trio enjoying their swim, with no inkling or threat of danger. The boys in the water, laughing and splashing each other, showing off their swimming skills to their laughing governess.

Stephen looked at the closest flat rock, the thought of the laughing governess in his mind. She had said she preferred dangling her feet instead of swimming.

His mind's eye put Miss Hodges on the rock, much as she had been the previous night. The look on her face after seeing his own flour-covered face. Her smile had been so wide it had been difficult to see anything else about her. He knew her eyes and hair were certain colors, but he was damned if he could name them—the eyes were some light shade and the hair was brown, that he knew for certain.

And her laugh—it was the last thing he had expected from her. He was in a difficult situation—not quite master but regarded as such until Henry's majority. For a servant, even a governess, to laugh as she had was entirely unpredictable.

He shouldn't think too much about how that unexpected laughter had settled in his gut.

The image of Miss Hodges sitting on the rock rose again in his mind. The sun would have warmed the rock beneath her hands, and she would have looked down at the clear water. She would laugh at the boys' antics, he had no doubt, perhaps even kick water in their direction if they ventured too close. Her stockings would be folded into her shoes to keep them from blowing away in the breeze.

Good Lord, he could almost see it. The stockings protected in the nearby shoes, her naked feet dangling in the water, her skirts raised to keep them from getting wet, exposing her trim ankles. The clear water would do nothing to hide either her feet or her ankles, and Stephen found himself staring unabashedly at something that wasn't even there. He gazed at the empty water, imagining exactly what Miss Hodges's ankles would look like. They would be slim, they would be bonny, they would—

Thankfully, a passing cart made enough noise to break him out of this ridiculously schoolboy moment. Inhaling deeply through his nose, Stephen left the swimming area and made his way back for a closer look at the ruins.